Close of Play

Robert C Linsdell

Acknowledgements

I would like to thank Tom Wylie for both his cover design and constant support. I'd also like to thank everyone that took the time to read through my various versions and provide their feedback. Particular thanks must go to Richard Hoare for being my first editor (of sorts) and Darren and Sally Coxon for their time and thought.

I should also acknowledge the authors of all the books I have read about World War I – from life on the home front through to the staggering realities of trench life. I have tried to do some small justice to their efforts in some of the descriptions that follow. Deviations from fact may be present for reasons of poetic licence but any genuine errors are innocent and mine alone.

It would also be wrong not to acknowledge the real-life Harrys, Walters and Lilys that became the unwitting and gracious heroes of their time. We all have a debt of thanks to them, and those like them, that no words can capture or represent.

Finally I'd like to thank my wife, children and family for being the happy normality in my little life and the threads that keep me sane.

"In some ways, what happens in the gap between asking the question and finding out the answer is everything. Indeed, it is your life."

For all those that strive to live well in the gap.

And for Team Linsdell, always x

RCL – March 2014

I just sat in the bath and wept.

I lay my head on my bent knees and wept until my forehead hurt and my nose drained salty rivers onto my top lip. Such was the depth of my sadness. Such was the breadth of my fatigue.

I didn't hear her open the door but she revealed herself to me the way special people do, through the way she changed the air in the room. I didn't move to acknowledge her, nor did I flinch when her hands dropped into the lukewarm water, picked up the cloth and wrung it softly into the bath.

She placed the balled cloth onto the back of my neck. I welcomed the coolness of it and felt tiny lines of water cut down my chest. She held it there for a while before moving it across my back with great tenderness and understanding. Slowly, I raised my head and straightened my legs as best I could. I caught sight of her for a moment but couldn't bear to look at the raw expression on her face. I closed my eyes and leaned my head back against the rim of the bath. I heard her stifle a gasp, or it may have been a sob. Even with my eyes firmly shut, I felt the need to turn my head away. After only a small pause, she laid the cloth on my chest and drew it earnestly from side to side. I imagined the few hairs there being pulled first one way and then the other, fighting for breath above the months of grime. She treated my scars so carefully that I felt sure they were fresh again and rich blood was flowing. I opened my eyes just enough to see the creamy water and heard her offer quiet comfort.

The cloth was drawn up and down my thighs, running liquid into the small pool at my groin. My scuffed right knee was given particular attention, as though mere affection could replace the layers of lost skin. Next she addressed my gnarled and broken feet. Feet that were many marches beyond tired, many damp mornings beyond sore. The toes were a rotten patchwork of death and the soles of my feet felt numb to almost an inch. She spent many minutes soaping each in turn, before rinsing them with soft handfuls of water. And when each foot was rinsed she would start again, the endless process of trying to clean and soothe.

She finished with my hands, lifting them from the water and running her fingers over mine, drawing shapes on my palms as though I were an infant.

Then she rubbed soap into each finger, each nail, each crease, fold and tear. She was breathing new life and vitality into ageing skin, new feeling into parts that had long since become disconnected from the whole. When each hand was done she eased it back into the water, out of sight, with the lingering touch of someone burying a much-loved pet. She was silent for a while and then I heard her tired knees click and creak as she stood, the neckline of her dress falling onto my chin. She planted a long and measured kiss on my forehead and then wiped it away as though it were a secret. I listened as she slid out of the room on stocking-less feet, closing the door behind her with a little weight, so I would know she was gone.

I raised my head and squinted into the bright and empty room. I drew my legs up again, buried my head against my sweet-smelling knees, and wept.

Chapter One

Cromer, England, April 1920.

This was Lily's favourite time of the day.

The large bedroom window afforded her a modest view of the sea; a small grey chip in an otherwise green world and each morning she could watch the embarrassed spring sunshine sneak through the surf and onto England's bewildered sands.

Laced between the roses on a delicate china cup, her small fingers were scalding somewhat, but she liked the way her body adjusted to and overcame the stinging sensation. There was comfort in coping.

The thin window pane bowed towards her slightly under a chuckling breeze and reflected back soft, pale and childlike features. She was pretty in a very fine sort of way, like her beauty was balanced on the head of a pin. A thin spray of fog curled from the cup and licked itself gently onto her image, obscuring all but her tired eyes.

Lily stared into the mid-distance for a few minutes, allowing herself to take respite in a moment of exquisite nothingness. Such opportunities of release were fleeting and so her mind took flight, dipping and dancing in the air like a smitten bird. How she used to love the magic and mystery of her own thoughts, the boundless images of immortal youth endlessly fighting with the wilting innocence of her adolescence. But now the simple things in life had been stripped away leaving just an aching loss in her heart and the greying, apologetic creases of a once proud uniform.

Lily was stroked back to life by a long, sharp finger of milky sunshine climbing up her chest and across her face. She raised her hand to shield her eyes and, for a moment, a saluting silhouette of a petite young nurse was burned onto the biscuit wall behind, in a warped and leaning scar.

Beneath her feet, Lily could hear the regimented protests of the old wooden stairs as Florence made her way heavily to bed. Her colleague tapped on the door as she passed. Lily opened it, fastening her bonnet as she did so.

"I'm up to my bed now," Florence whispered badly. "Not much to report although Private Lambert had a bad night. Hopefully he'll sleep it off during the day."

"Ok, thanks," Lily replied through a mouthful of hair pins. "Sleep tight."

Florence smiled wetly and made a token gesture of closing the door. Draining her cup and placing it back on an ill-matching saucer, Lily stepped quietly out of her room, down the stairs and into the vast open expanses of Perryman Hall.

Silence governed the main hall, but not all the patients were asleep. One or two of them found a smile as Lily passed but most of them failed to notice her small frame break their eye line. The room was wide, grand even, and Lily walked directly down the middle, keeping an even gap between the beds.

Beyond the small desk and overcrowded office were four side rooms where, typically, men would be taken for short periods of private rest. This morning three rooms were occupied. Private Lambert was sleeping, jerking intermittently and fighting something as terrible as it was invisible. Next door to him Gunner Wilson was visible only as a foetal echo beneath his blanket.

Harry Parker's room was a few yards beyond the others. A small porthole in the door offered a view of the bed and Lily could see Harry sitting up, a book balanced on his knees. He was a tall man, once, with an earnest and serious face, pointed features and a hungry expression. He was beyond thin.

Lily caught his eye and he smiled honestly, beckoning her in.

"Morning Nurse Lily," he said brightly, "another lovely spring morning…"

"I'll be round with the breakfast soon Harry," Lily spoke softly, with an informality that would have irked Matron. "I just need to see to the other men first though."

"Of course," replied Harry cheerfully. "I'm okay here."

Harry dropped his eyes to the book once more. Nurse Lily edged out of the room and closed the door softly behind her.

Lily's day unfurled like any other – skittish, uncomfortable and occasionally haunting. The men were excited and demanding, like dogs in the snow, and by the time the shadows began to cut chocolate triangles along the polished floor, most of the inhabitants of Perryman Hall were wearied into stillness.

Florence re-appeared at dusk, a little late, looking like a woman drunk on sleep. She leant herself heavily on the table in the office whilst her younger colleague rattled sharply through the drug lists. They both knew it was just another day.

In the cool darkness of the office Lily slid the shards of metal from her chestnut hair and felt it fall to her shoulders with surprising weight. Immediately, the strap of pain she wore along her forehead slipped away, bringing new air to her lungs and with it, the exhaustion of the deserving. Kicking her feet from her thin shoes she padded barefooted into the shadows, stepped through a familiar door and fell into an old armchair in the corner of the room. Here she curled herself into a small handful of human being, grabbed the blanket from the back of the chair and tied it into a reassuring fist between her breasts. For a few moments she watched the outline in the bed in front of her rise and fall until, imperceptible at first, her thoughts lost shape and everything about her drifted into sleep.

As was so often the case now, Lily dreamed of her brother. Sometimes these dreams were like burying her head in an old box of photographs, where she would be softly suffocated by the sounds and smells of a happy childhood. Other times nightmares would unfurl themselves in a chorus of hideous nonsense, always ending in the same way, with a frightened teenage girl chasing round and round the backdrop of her life trying to find her brother.

The chair was uncomfortable and Lily shifted restlessly, freeing herself from the grip of worn fabric and exposed springs. Less than a dozen feet above her head her own bed was waiting – cool, crisp and empty – but it would be past midnight before she would straighten herself, climb the stairs and fall upon both the mattress and the mercy of her dreams. Since Christmas so many of her evenings had been spent here, in a forgotten chair, alongside what remained of one of Cromer's golden generation. Her colleagues, who once questioned and discouraged this habit, now chose not to notice and let them be; a pretty young girl called Lily and a reputable young man called Harry. It could perhaps have been a love story, but there weren't many of those left any more.

Some nights sleep would reject her and, with glazed eyes, she would sit thinking of home and the great shell of sadness it had become. It had been so different just a few summers ago, when the blazing heat of 1914 had cracked itself open along the coastline, bringing thousands of people to their town like ants to the sweetest of jams. Lily and her brother had treated the sunshine like their own personal achievement, lauding and displaying it at every turn. Cousins, so many cousins, had appeared from nowhere to feel the fresh warmth of another world. It had been glorious and so had they.

When there was first talk of war, Lily didn't hear it. Her head spun with ice-cream, dried blossom and the vague, happy mysteries of her brother's many friends. For him though it was different, and the chiming bells of war talked a language he'd been learning all his life. For a long time after he joined up it seemed that nothing was going to happen. Then they went, all of them, and everything changed.

In the many bleak hours since, Lily had wondered what it was about him that she now missed so much. His company, of course, but there was something more. She missed being near him, close to him. She missed the weight and smell of his body and how it would surround her, soak her. She missed how they would hug and wrestle, hold hands on long summer walks and lounge across each other in front of a winter fire. It took her more than a year to realise that no one touched her anymore.

As children, they were hugged and held. They would dance with their mother and even their reserved father would plant long, hard kisses upon their brows in the soft contentment of bedtime. Their home was warm, in every sense of the word, and even the sharp wind tearing off the North Sea would whimper and die in the great, thick blankets of their affection. But then a smart, sombre man had marched to that brightly coloured front door, tapped apologetically on it with a shining glove, and handed her father a small card from a sad, copious pack. Lily had watched from the top of the stairs as he had thanked the man politely, closed the door and folded to his knees in defeat, making a noise that Lily could neither describe nor forget.

Over the weeks that followed, Lily watched her handsome parents fade and weaken like stars in the fog. In time, the acute agony of failing to fill the mighty crater that had been blown in their lives became too much for her and so she chose nursing as her imperfect release. Lily had been home just a handful of times since the end of the war and each time she would find fewer reasons to return and more reasons to regret. And now, as the hardship of peace replaced the horror of war, so she began to realise that her life and her sadness were one, like brother and sister.

Harry made a short, snorting noise in his sleep and Lily's eyes burst open. Her ankles cursed her as she unfurled from the chair. The air was cool so she kept the blanket tight across her shoulders all the way back to her bedroom before climbing into bed, pressing her pillow tightly between her legs and rocking herself absently into a thick, foggy doze.

*

Summer arrived suddenly one afternoon after what seemed like weeks in the grip of heavy clouds and wild, cantankerous showers. The darkness that had stained the edges of Perryman Hall evaporated in a haze of clean, sweet smells and the temperature swelled. For Lily, the summer months brought a blessed relief from the nagging chill that otherwise stung the tips of her fingers and toes. She also knew that the change in light and temperature would soothe most of the patients, lifting the prevailing mood.

For one patient though, the arrival of summer was deeply unsettling. For most of the year, Harry Parker tolerated his incarceration with reasonable humour. Though he would spend many hours sat by his window, he seemed to view the outside world with disapproving frustration and never strained like some of the men for an opportunity to feel the scraping power of a winter wind. But as soon as the sunshine began to stretch the necks of flowers, so Harry would begin to mentally pace around his room.

Lily could see him, feel him, growing into something more challenging, demanding and expectant. Like a mother herding her children through the last hours of Christmas Eve, she would have to distract him as best she could with menial tasks and small, empty rewards. She would be endlessly patient and tolerant, stroking his disappointed brow with rosy and magical views of the future and, unlike the other nurses, Lily would allow his precious faith in his friends to breathe and have life.

In the carefree summers before the war Harry and his friends had established themselves among the beautiful people of Cromer. They wore their youth like medals and knitted themselves comfortable and happy tales with the seemingly endless ribbons of sunshine. Many of their weekends were spent on the cricket field, flexing athletic aspirations in front of a small but effervescent collection of young women. Now, in this very different world, Harry's summer dreams were still dominated by these boys, these men, and visions of playing cricket alongside them once again. After all this time, Lily now shared this dream with every wisp of her soul and each summer's day, like Harry, she would search the horizon for their bright shadows.

"I rather suspect they will be here this afternoon," Harry said to Lily one morning at the start of June. "The weather is clearing every day." Lily went on working the pillows in silence, leaving his words to fold in on themselves. Impatiently, Harry filled the gap.

"Do you think Lily? Do you? I'll need my shirt of course and my tie, I know it's here somewhere."

"Harry…" Lily whispered in the gentlest voice she could muster.

Harry's face hung like a child searching for a dropped toffee in the sand. Lily squatted at his bedside and found his eyes.

"We talked of this last week, didn't we?" Lily said, feeling a familiar sadness loop through her chest. "You're not well enough to go outside yet." Lily felt the body in front of her gain weight and bend in on itself. "I promised you that as soon as the doctor says you are better, we will go to the sea."

"But I feel better now," Harry replied pathetically, sounding out each word so she would understand. Lily unrolled a thin but affectionate smile and moved for the door.

“When they come,” Harry began, breaking her stride, “you will send them in won’t you?” Something approaching a smile appeared again beneath Lily’s eyes.

“I promise,” she replied, and closed the door tight.

*

Midsummer’s day was hot and foreboding with a storm that refused to break. Lily had carried a sharp headache with her for three long days and it was starting to make her unravel. Her stomach was swilling crudely, and even amidst copious distractions, Lily could feel an imbalance in her body that threatened to toss her to the floor. As always, her working day ended at 7pm and she stumbled through to bed as though on the deck of a rocking ship. Within seconds she had become a crumpled heap on top of the covers, soothing her head beneath a thin, cold pillow.

Though Lily’s body stilled, her mind continued once more to fizz through fitful sleep, tightening and unfurling itself relentlessly. Against the background of a faint, guttural exclamation of thunder, Lily’s dreams took her to Adcock Farm and the small brook that laced along the lower field.

Her brother is there, aged ten or eleven, his trousers rolled up to his scuffed and tanned knees. He’s bent over in the middle of the brook, allowing the water to run through his fingers and spit against his calves. He chats away to her manically, about everything and nothing, whilst she sits on the bank feeling a vague damp climbing into her skirts from the grass. She can taste lemonade at the back of her throat.

Suddenly there comes a metallic roar and a wall of water appears around the bend, crashing into her brother and blowing him out of sight. Lily leaps to her feet and screams, feeling black, cold water racing into her lungs. As quickly as it had arrived the wave moves on, washing all the water from the brook and leaving nothing but a sodden trench lined with stones, weeds and the thrashing of dying fish. Leaping into the mud, Lily races after the water, screaming her brother’s name. Within a few steps her feet lose traction and she is flying, swooping after the trail of vapour and high into the sky. And then the water disappears and Lily is left suspended in mid-air overlooking a near-perfect, unbroken field of barley, stretching as wide as the eyes can see. In the middle of the field there is cut a tiny spread-eagled shape.

Lily drops to the ground and kneels beside her brother, now beyond twenty, and wipes thick, purple blood from across his face. His eyes open slowly and he smiles, showing her the redness of his teeth and tongue. Lily lifts her skirt and wipes it hard across his face once more, scrubbing, but the patches she clears are quickly swamped again. Rain arrives over her shoulder, creating wide grey circles in the blood-soaked white of her clothes. With soft fingers on her brother's lips, she feels his breath run meekly up to her wrist, where it falls away, exhausted. Clambering to her feet Lily backs away from the small clearing and turns to run for help.

The crops grow and grow as she runs, slapping against her thighs, her chest and then her flushed face. Soon she is buried by it, losing any sense of direction or purpose. Spinning round like games of old she catches sight of her mother standing at the end of a long corridor. Lily cries out to her but before they can touch the corridor collapses, folding her mother up in an ocean of dirty yellow. Then there is a man behind her and then another and another.

"I'm your brother," one of them says, his face smooth, grey and featureless. He drops a hand between her legs and lifts her with strong fingers, causing Lily to fall hard against his body and then to the floor. Scrambling on her hands and knees, Lily watches large filthy feet march around her in a circle, getting closer and closer, suffocating her with their number and their intent. Curling herself as tightly as she can Lily feels their hands in her hair and across her face and throat. In desperation she bites down on a finger, tasting its calloused skin and mud-sketched nail. Blood runs down her chin and across her tongue. She bites harder, growling furiously and twisting her head. Something gives, warm liquid splashes across her face and the images crack, break and fall away.

Lily's breathing settled to the rhythm of slapping rain. Sweat sat in beads on her forehead and along her top lip. Her jaw ached and cool saliva soaked the corner of her pillow. Such was the chaotic normality of falling awake. She slowly lifted herself from the sheets and swung her legs over the side of the bed.

Her head still felt tight but hunger shifted in her stomach. Edging tentatively down the stairs and into the kitchens Lily saw the large clock ticking purposeful towards 1am. She found a small husk of bread and drove into it greedily, revelling in its heavy, tired flavour. As she ate she felt some of the drag of the day slip away, softening her shoulders and easing the pain that had burned to the very tips of her hair. Refreshed, Lily padded out of the kitchens. The stairs to her bedroom curled upwards in front of her but after a brief pause she slipped to the right and through the door of the main hall.

Lily ducked into one of the many strips of darkness and swept with well-practiced softness to the back of the vast room, passed the nurses' table and into the small warren of side rooms. As was more often the case during the summer, just one of the rooms was occupied. Moving blindly along familiar walls Lily guided herself to a door handle and, easing her weight against the door, ghosted across the floor, beneath the blanket and into the chair. For a few moments she caught her breath and let the stillness re-fill the room.

"Harry?" she whispered once, and then again, hypnotically into the darkness.

"Harry?" she said for a third time, more insistent, and there was a noise of shifting blankets and stretching bed springs. "Harry, it's me."

"Lily?" Harry responded; a deep grumble from somewhere asleep. And then, with more animation, "Are they here?" The bed shrieked as he pushed himself quickly and uncomfortably to sitting.

"Not yet, it's just me for now," Lily whispered in the direction of the hardening edges of Harry's shadow.

"But it isn't morning yet is it? What time is it Lily?"

"It's one o'clock in the morning Harry," Lily replied flatly.

Against a background of mighty nothingness, Harry allowed his nocturnal visitor to become real and true. Something unthought had brought Lily to Harry's side once more, like a migrating bird turning for home, and to Harry it was just a simple, aimless truth. He was here and she was here and that was that.

Lily's uniform was still damp from the sweat of her dreams. She shuffled the chair forward with her heels, bringing her knees to within inches of Harry's bed. For a moment she considered reaching forward to touch the cool, cloudy fingers forming on the bed in front of her but better judgement intervened. Harry shifted noisily but still didn't speak. Lily held her breath to hear him, her heart popping too solidly between her ears.

"Harry," she spoke finally. "Harry, will you tell me again?"

"Again?" Harry replied in a whisper.

"Please. Please tell me the story again. Tell me about you and the boys."

"About how we were heroes?" Harry replied, dreamily.

"Please." Lily felt the skin on her left cheek change slightly and only when something traced the line of her chin did she realise she was crying.

"You'll be able to ask them yourself one day of course. Soon, probably this week, maybe even tomorrow." Harry looked towards her for the first time and, despite the darkness, Lily blushed deeply.

"I know, I know. But until then…" Her words caught slightly and she hoped that Harry hadn't noticed.

Lily heard Harry's breathing change. From the shapes emerging in the night she could see his head tilted to the ceiling, where raindrops were smearing stains of light onto the dirty paintwork. There were a few more moments on the edge of the cliff and then he drew a long, deep breath and started to speak.

Chapter Two

Walter was the one that had always been there.

My first memory is sitting up in a pram, the sun flashing on the metal handle. Just across from me there is another pram, just like mine, and a yellow-haired baby is looking at me, waving and squawking happily. On the floor I can see the shapes of ducks fussing about on the grass, occasionally bouncing off each other in the pursuit of scraps. If I close my eyes I can be there as though it were yesterday. I can even feel the coarse lines of a blanket running underneath my tiny fingertips. Sometimes, if I concentrate enough, I can smell the sweetness of my mother drifting on that warm summer air.

For a long time I thought Walter was my brother, even though I kept being told that he wasn't. He lived next door with his mother and father in a house that was usually quiet but rarely peaceful. Mr Croucher worked with wood and you could taste it hanging in the air. He spent most of his life in the yard, forearms bared to the elements, tongue poking out of the corner of his mouth. Some days Walter and I would sit at the kitchen window and watch him work, painstakingly, making every line smooth and immaculate. He was a nice man Mr Croucher but I got the impression, even as quite a young child, that he was never completely happy with anything. They nearly had to postpone his brother's funeral because he wasn't happy with the job he had done on the coffin. My mother once said that she thought he was more upset about some unfinished joinery than he was about losing his brother.

In many ways, my father was similar. As the vicar of our small parish his work never ended, or even paused. Aside of the formal business of the church, he was forever tending to the emotional and practical needs of his parishioners. My mother would become frustrated with him sometimes and, just occasionally, she would suggest that he had an important role to play at home as well as in the community. But to argue with my father was to argue with the will of God, and so we seldom found fault with either his behaviour or indeed his thoughts. As I grew older, I did begin to wonder about how little joy my father got from his work. I had read much about the light that God brings into our lives but my father forever wore a look of severity about him, like his service was a penance.

Walter's mother was a wonderful painter, although only people that visited the house would ever have known. Their small home creaked and leant with her beautiful paintings, many of which were hung above furniture made in their own back yard. Mrs Croucher had an eye for colour – we thought it rather shocking at times – and she produced works of great magnificence and glory. I remember that above their fireplace there hung a bright yellow picture of a corn field, swaying against a deep blue sky. The bottom of the frame had been stained somewhat by the heat of the fire but the picture was undamaged and unrelenting. I told her once that I would love to run through her picture all the way to that blended horizon. For a moment I thought I had spoken out of turn until a broad smile stretched across her face.

"Maybe one day you will," she replied softly.

On the face of it, my mother's contribution to life seemed less significant, but that simply wasn't true. There was something magical about her, and even now I'm not sure I can find the words to describe it. She was a deeply pious woman but chuckled and smiled her way through services and Bible stories like she knew a secret. And she would play with us like a school friend. So often, when the weather curtailed outside games, she would chase me, Walter and my sister Betty around the house, with the threatening roars of an escaped lion or the soft curses of an angry witch. We would hide and seek, peek and boo, kiss and chase and the house would rock with shrieks and laughter. My mother was the essence of life, rolling with the seasons and wrapping us all up in a big, creeping blanket of joy. We lived our childhood around her, beneath her, like she were the happy madness of a big top.

Then, at the end of the day, she would set us down and tell us a story. Sometimes it would be from a book but often the characters would be her own, taking shape in front of us, whipping the air into the rich fragrances of a Moroccan bazaar, royal palace or filthy Tudor street. The tales themselves were masterful and as sharp as a tangled thorn, but it was the words that seduced me, the sound of them, the shape of them, the bursting alliteration and bouncing rhymes. Each night as she took me to bed I would thumb through the story like it were a dictionary, asking her more about the characters and what happened next; all just to hear her say the words again. She would protest at my endless questions, but we both knew that she loved it just as much as I did.

She loved my passion for it, my compulsive appetite for language. Sometimes I am asked about my favourite authors and each time I tell something of a lie. Because I never tell them about my mother; I never tell them about the very best.

As young children Walter and I would ape my mother's every move; her mannerisms, her phrases and her footsteps. But as we grew older I started to find it less natural to see life the way she did. Before long, I was rather forcing myself to be like her, copying her like a sad mimic and feeling nothing but mild, questioning embarrassment. That was where Walter and I divided. Over the years, my best friend became more and more like my mother, morphing into her growing reflection and suckling on her instinctive and glorious recognition. People would tell me that I reminded them of my father which I took as both a compliment and an instruction. Those same people never linked the personalities of Walter and my mother, but then they never saw what I saw.

*

There was a quiet street outside our houses where Walter and I would spend hour upon hour inventing and playing games. I would prefer the fantasy games, where I could become a hero from one of my books, whilst Walter just wanted to be a sportsman – dashing and triumphant. We would play in the winter, when the wind would lace between the houses and threaten to cut you clean in half. We would play in spring's damp, crotchety air and we'd play through the summer and into autumn using the longest of the light for our favourite pursuit – endless, glorious cricket. We'd up-turn our old tin bath and play with a tightly wound ball of string and an old bat my father brought home one day from the church. I have no idea where it came from but we used it for years and years, until it was held together by hope as much as anything else. We were devastated when it finally broke but the very next day Walter appeared from his house with a beautiful bat immaculately carved from a single piece of wood. It lacked the authenticity of our old one but on that autumnal morning it was the best bat we'd ever seen.

Walter really loved to bat and so I would mostly bowl. I liked to bat too but there was something about watching him hitting the ball that meant it just seemed right to let him stand there, sometimes for hours on end, with the dark tin bath looming behind him and a thousand seagulls calling his name. He was so controlled, so elegant, and he would move his feet so softly, like my little sister tip-toeing up the stairs. I could hit the ball harder than he could but however far it went, it never made the sound off the bat that it made for him. He made that ball sing. I suppose I sometimes felt a little in awe of my best friend. Somehow the things that I was better at seemed empty and meaningless whereas his talents were important and magical.

We held hands on our first walk to school. That seems so strange now, but we did. I was a little bigger than him in those days and I remember my thumb and middle finger meeting behind his hand. The closer we got to the school gates, the harder I pressed those two small pads of skin together. Inside the building, everything appeared so impossibly vast, loud and frantic and, given the chance, I would have turned and run all the way back to our beloved street. But Walter had no such doubts and, with him at my side, I stepped into the madness.

By the time we returned home that first afternoon I was almost paralysed with tiredness and my feet were glowing from the harsh lines of new shoes. It had been interesting; an adventure of sorts, but I also think it bewildered me a little. In time I would come to cope with my new world reasonably well but, however hard I tried, I could never completely shake that initial sense of discomfort; it was like I was wearing new shoes every single day.

*

It was only a short walk from school to home, but often our return trips would take the best part of an hour as we weaved aimlessly along the street, pausing to examine insects or hit fallen fruit with outcast sticks. When we were young our mothers would constantly be scolding us for our lateness but over time they mellowed and saved their energies for other battles.

One autumnal afternoon our journey home took us into the fields of Adcock Farm. In the farthest corner of the lower field was a small copse of trees and we wandered into it absently. At once the atmosphere felt different. The heavy foliage cut the light sharply and gave the sense of being inside a vast, high-ceilinged room. There was a weighty silence and that pervading sense of being watched. We looked at each other, pulled mock-scared faces and laughed. Within a few moments we were tearing around in-between the trunks, shooting each other with outstretched fingers and sending raucous yelps up to the canopy and down again with a soft echo. Eventually we ran ourselves to a standstill and collapsed onto the floor in a small clearing. There we lay, our eyes flitting backwards and forwards and our chests dragging air into our lungs.

"I bet you wouldn't dare jump from there," Walter said eventually when his breath returned.

"Where?" I asked, flipping myself over onto my front.

Walter pointed upwards to a short, stubby branch that, in curling back on itself, had made a small, rounded ledge. It was probably three times my height. I brought myself to my knees and cocked my head to one side.

"Neither would you," I responded, standing up and brushing myself down. Walter didn't speak. He simply disappeared from view behind the tree and reappeared a few feet up. He climbed easily and boldly and within just a few seconds he was standing on the ledge. For a moment it seemed he was going to step straight off but then he paused, looked down and in an instant his whole demeanour changed. He breathed out slowly.

"Are you *going* to jump then?" I asked, shielding my eyes from a strip of sun that was poking through the leaves. Walter was quiet for a while.

"Maybe tomorrow," he said eventually. "We'd better be getting back now."

"Yeah, I'll do it tomorrow as well," I replied, hoping he wouldn't remember. I turned away, picked up my bag and began walking out of the copse, but after a few seconds I realised that Walter hadn't yet dropped into his normal stride beside me and indeed, he hadn't reappeared from behind the tree. I waited for a few more moments and then called back to him.

At first, I didn't hear his reply. I heard something, certainly, but I couldn't make it out. I stepped slowly back towards the tree, suddenly aware again of that sense of unease we had initially felt when we'd entered the copse. This time the noise was a little clearer, but still very weak.

"Harry?"

I walked a bit closer.

"Harry?"

"What's the matter?" I asked, edging slowly towards Walter's whisper.

"Help me Harry."

A chill ran through me. The balance of my life shifted uncomfortably.

"Please hurry," I heard him say again in a voice I barely recognised. I placed my hand on the tree, for stability as much as anything else, and edged my way round it like I was blind. All my saliva ran away and I swallowed a thick click of air.

Walter also had his hand on the tree. He was leaning against it somewhat, angling his upper body towards the trunk. I met his eyes. His pupils were huge and deep and the colour had fallen from his face. His thick blonde hair seemed grey in the shadows. He returned my stare and then motioned his eyes towards the ground. I followed those eyes. As he had climbed down the tree he'd apparently dropped his left foot into some sort of bag, burying it almost to the knee. Looking closer, I could see the contents of the bag beginning to climb his leg.

When you're five years old, maggots are one of the worst things in the world. They're like little monsters; strange, faceless creatures that only stop moving when they're dead. Maggots are the stuff of nightmares and there they were, thousands of them, marching their way towards my best friend's face.

"Ugghhhh!" I shouted, "Maggots!!"

"Do something!" Walter shouted with such feeling that I was sent spinning round and round like the ballerina on top of Betty's old music box.

Just a few yards away there was a big stick – almost too heavy to carry – but I picked it up from amidst a patch of nettles and dragged it back to Walter. My hands rang with a dozen stings. With some effort, I lifted the stick and pointed it towards the bag, but the weight was suddenly too much and I dropped it, dragging the splintered edge down the outside of Walter's calf. He yelped in pain and my arms began to shake.

"Come on!" Walter encouraged and I lifted the stick again, this time lowering the sharp end cleanly into the bag. The material fell back, freeing Walter's ankle and his trapped foot. Walter's leg was alive with maggots and his shoelace was matted with vague, greying pieces of slime.

Bouncing away from the tree Walter stamped his foot repeatedly on the ground like it was on fire and brushed his hands as quickly and lightly as he could across his leg. When he could no longer see any movement on his foot he swept his satchel off the floor and sprinted out into the field. I raced after him and caught him up as he attempted to vault the fence back into the street. He made three attempts to get over before flopping onto the floor with his face buried on top of his knees. I shuffled next to him and dropped my arm over his shoulder. He didn't lift his face up for a while but eventually he turned to look at me again.

"I couldn't move," he said hoarsely. "I tried to but I just couldn't. It was horrible." His voiced tailed off again and we stayed silent for a while. I could feel his body vibrating.

"Why would someone put a load of maggots in a bag?" I wondered aloud.

"I don't know," Walter replied, checking his leg again for any sign of activity. "Maybe they were fishing in the stream. My Dad said once that you use maggots for fishing."

"How?" I asked.

Walter shrugged his shoulders and we sat for a moment longer, the heat running slowly out of the day. After a while, Walter looked up at me, a freshly painted expression on his face.

"Shall we go back?" he asked.

"Back? Back in there? Why?"

He flipped to his feet in a flash and began to stomp back down the hill.

My mother had always told me that I was a thinker, a quiet thinker, and it's true that I very rarely acted on impulse. I did however sometimes act on Walter's. I stood for a moment and watched his slight frame became smaller and smaller. Watching him move pulled at me, like I had a magnet buried in my stomach and, forgetting myself, I bounded in his wake.

I was a few feet into the copse before my eyes adjusted again to the change in light. In front of me I could see Walter, crouched, dragging the bag from behind the tree with that same heavy stick, even more unmanageable in his smaller hands. Occasionally the end of the wood would slip from the bag, tossing Walter to the floor but each time he would climb to his feet again, re-insert the stick and continue with the job. Within a few minutes, he had pulled the bag completely away from the tree. I moved tentatively to his side.

We stood, feet apart, looming over the dirty mass like hunters over a kill.

"Do you want to look?" Walter whispered, lowering the end of the stick into the bag. I stepped back instinctively.

"No," I said firmly.

"I'm going to," Walter replied and, not missing a beat, he flicked his wrists like an accomplished conductor, turning the bag's small opening into a vast, gaping chasm.

The cat had been dead a few weeks. Maggots writhed ceaselessly through its flesh and we could hear their frantic movement. Once-green eyes had popped and disappeared and ugly pinches of flesh hung loosely from the exposed skeleton. Then there was the smell. We brought our arms up across our noses, leaving just our eyes to take in the scene. I could feel an image for every dark and lonely night being burned instantly onto my eyes. For so many reasons we should have turned and fled but somehow neither of us did. We just stood there, watching this small, shifting pool of death unfurling in front of us. Silently, Walter lifted the stick and laid the two edges of the bag together again. For a moment the cloth wriggled and writhed with life and then it was still, murky and sad.

“Was that a cat?” Walter said eventually, his eyes still fixed on the bag. I made a tiny nodding movement with my head and blinked repeatedly in an attempt to wash away the image. Without speaking further, we slipped back from the copse, the field and the farm and melted into the streets around our homes. At the end of our journey Walter, his foot resting on the front step of his house, turned to me and smiled.

“Tomorrow,” he said, “I’m going to jump Dead Cat Tree,” and I never doubted it for a minute.

Chapter Three

As a young boy, I can't really remember having any friends other than Walter.

But as we grew older, and school became so central to our lives, so other faces drifted into focus. Some arrived with an alarming bang whilst others simply and easily blended into our shared childhood.

Although he never realised it, Walter was the one that held them near. He attracted them with an effervescence that was difficult to place; a vibrancy impossible to replicate. He was never the biggest, the strongest, the funniest or the cleverest but he had a wild, captivating determination and a pervading charm that instinctively brought warmth out of everyone he met. For so long it seemed that I only ever knew people through Walter, like he was my gateway to the rest of the world.

Gordon Stokes was the first. He was a thick-set and dark-skinned boy whose face always looked like it needed a moustache. His father, like a lot of local men, spent most of his time at sea and Gordon's upbringing was pragmatic, physical and dominated by three older brothers. Walter and I found him one wet Tuesday crouched behind a tree watching a dirty, mottled seagull plod around in small circles.

"Shhh!" he hissed sharply as we walked past. "Don't move!"

Gordon edged on to the balls of his feet and stole a quick glance around the trunk at the ungainly gull. And then, after a short pause, he threw himself forward like a cat, extending his legs and throwing his arms out in front of him. With Gordon's shadow looming heavily across its future, the bird snapped into life, launching upwards in a noisy flurry of wings. For a moment they were one, boy and bird, and then they separated distinctly, one moving towards the sky and the other inexorably towards earth. Gordon's horizontal figure slapped hard onto the ground, sending a small fountain of brown water across his bows. Momentum carried him forward a couple of feet before he stopped, abruptly, with mud on his chin and the disappearing outline of a seagull reflecting back in his eyes.

Walter moved from my side and offered Gordon a hand, pulling him up with an indelicate, wet, ripping sound. Mud lay in a thick strip down his torso and a large flick of bird excrement ran across his forehead and deep into his hair. He looked at Walter and then me.

"Nearly got him that time," he coughed through rasping breath. He brought his hand to his face and looked longingly at a small fistful of white feathers.

"Very nearly," Walter agreed, patting him on the shoulder and guiding him away from the shimmering slick on the grass.

We spent the rest of lunch time trying to make Gordon a little more presentable and our efforts, along with his typically ragamuffin appearance, were enough to ensure he escaped punishment. Of course, we never asked him why he'd been trying to catch a seagull with his bare hands. Such questions seem irrelevant to young boys.

*

Peter and Donald Peacock were always fighting. They were twins, but they didn't appear to share a single physical characteristic. Peter was tall and thin with small features and a high forehead. Donald, his junior by about five minutes, was short, wide and rounded in every way possible. In fact, the only thing they appeared to share was an unrelenting irritation with each other. Their parents, a timid older couple from a nice part of town, wore permanent expressions of bewilderment and fatigue. The relationship between the two brothers was intense, all-consuming and contradictory. It was as though they still hadn't worked out if they were one person or two.

It's hardly surprising that our first encounter with the Peacock brothers came in the middle of yet another petty conflict. We were sitting in a classroom during a wet lunchtime – me reading, Walter doodling impatiently – when Donald appeared at the open doorway and fizzed a bright blue school cap straight towards our desks. Vast and colourful lights burst in front of my eyes as, for an instant, I was unsure as to what was hurtling towards my head. By the time I had recovered my composure, Peter was in the doorway, flushed and dishevelled.

“Where’s he put it?!” he snapped, scanning the room. I held the cap out towards him and he snatched it from my fingers smartly. Squeezing his head beneath the peak he turned on his heel and hurtled in the direction of Donald’s slapping footsteps. Walter laughed heartily.

Moments later the desperate gallop of feet filled the air once again and Donald arrived tumultuously, thundered beyond us and threw his bulk heavily into the corner of the room, barricading himself imperfectly behind a couple of desks. His ill-fitting shadow Peter was gasping for breath when he returned to the room, and his red face was starting to pale. Using the door frame like a boxer uses the ropes, he propelled himself across the room until he towered over his brother’s hiding place.

“Come out!” he demanded, to no response. He repeated his call, slapping two palms painfully on the desk in front of him.

“Not a chance!” Donald eventually replied, sliding yet further into his corner fortress. Peter’s patience was wafer thin and so he bounded into the forest of wood in front of him. Unfortunately, after just a couple of steps he lost his footing and tumbled over, bringing desks and chairs down on top of him in an ungainly heap. He struggled briefly but, like a fly in the web of a spider, he only succeeded in trapping himself still further. So there they were; two brothers, locked in place, too close to be on their own and too far apart to be together. Within seconds, they were both in floods of tears.

It took us quite a while to pick through the nest of wood and free them from their self-imposed captivity. They stood looking at each other fiercely and unhappily for a few moments after their release, twitching and jerking involuntarily with emotion. Walter chatted to them softly, as though he were coaxing them from a tree. After a while, the gathering calm fogged the memory of what had come before and a lightness descended onto proceedings. The brothers joined us at our desks and together we shared simple, happy and familiar tales of boyhood until we found a fair patch of common ground and, within it, a lasting friendship.

Not all the connections we made in those first few months were as dramatic as the turbulent arrival of Peter and Donald Peacock. Indeed, my first memory of Tommy Parnell is finding him asleep at the foot of a tree. Walter and I were too fascinated with this slight absurdity to walk away and so we stood for a few moments staring at him like he was in a museum.

"Do you think he's dead?" Walter asked in a whisper.

"He doesn't look dead," I replied confidently, trying to convey wisdom in such matters.

"Do you think I should poke him with a stick?"

"Of course not!" I replied quickly but Walter wasn't listening.

He looked on the ground around his feet but all he could find was a small and rather limp looking tulip. He looked at me and I shook my head nervously. Smiling tentatively, Walter edged towards the sleeping figure and prodded him softly with the flower. I flinched. When no response came, he did it again, bending the poor plant's head back almost to right angles in the process. As a last attempt, he drew his arm back and rattled the tulip impressively across the boy's face, with a surprisingly loud slap. I heard myself gasp in horror.

Tommy's eyes popped open and he leapt to his feet, batting both the flower and the attacker handsomely to the floor.

"What are you doing?!!" he shouted, glaring at Walter accusingly.

"We thought you might be dead!" Walter replied quickly.

"You hit me with a daffodil!"

"A tulip," I added pathetically, for no reason that I could explain.

Poor Tommy looked terribly confused to be woken up by a couple of flower-wielding strangers. His face was a flushed triangle of confusion, anger and distress.

"Why were you asleep under a tree?" Walter asked after a few seconds.

"I was tired," Tommy responded and we all nodded sagely as though we were wise old men discussing the changing weather. "I've got a sister…a baby, she cries all the time so I don't get a lot of sleep."

"I've got a sister," I added quickly. Tommy and Walter both looked at me so I felt I should say something else. "She doesn't cry much really, so that's good I suppose." They turned away from me again like I'd blown away in the wind.

It turned out that Tommy's street was quite close to ours and so we walked together for a while, looping all over the road with the imprecise awareness of young boys. We got to within about a hundred yards of Tommy's house when he stopped dead in the road.

"Oh no…can you hear that?" he exclaimed.

"Hear what?" I asked.

We all stood still, softening our breath and brandishing our ears to the wind. It was mostly hidden at first, but after a few seconds a rolling, repetitive sound sought us out. It could have been anything really, but Tommy knew it like he knew the hum of his own tired mind. It was a baby, crying.

We edged closer and watched the colour run out of Tommy's face, down his clothes and into a pool at his feet. I was reminded of the organist at the church practicing pairs of notes, over and over again. Walter tried to smile but it warped quickly into a grimace. By the time we stood in the street before Tommy's house, it seemed the noise was coming from everywhere – relentless, raw and angry. We turned to look at Tommy. For a moment I feared he would cry.

We plopped ourselves down on the side of the street and tried to pretend that we weren't too scared to step into the house. We invented an elaborate hopping game involving a piece of chalk, we argued about whose feet were the biggest and we staged dramatic sword fights with long, once proud daffodils. Eventually we ran out of distractions and just sat together, letting the increasingly hoarse cry of a baby girl stab into us from every direction. The sound would peak and fade, shout and whisper but it never stopped.

We were focused so intently on wishing the sound away that we didn't notice my mother striding down the street. She suddenly appeared in front of us, as happy as a rain cloud. She held her hands out to her sides as a bewildered question.

"We were just listening to Tommy's sister," I pointed out, feeling the wetness of the words as they left my mouth.

"Home!" She said simply. We stood up and gathered our things together. As we did so a striking silence landed. We all stilled, fearing that we might upturn the peace. A small blush of colour returned to Tommy's face and a half-smile cracked on his lips.

"Do you want your new friend to come for tea?" my mother asked kindly, perhaps pitying the crumpled boy in front of her.

"No. No, thank you Miss," Tommy replied smartly. "When she's not crying, I quite like her really."

My mother found a smile for Tommy and then turned her stony face to us. She pointed towards home and we marched away with her. I stole a quick look back as we turned the corner and saw Tommy climb softly in through the front door, his school bag in one hand and the sad remnants of a much-broken daffodil carried tenderly in the other.

Our group of friends leapt in size one October Sunday as Walter and I were rowing his father's small boat down the river. It was the first time we'd been allowed out on the boat without an adult and we were having a great adventure, bouncing unsteadily from bank to bank and lying flat on our stomachs to avoid overhanging trees.

Just as we were starting to get the hang of things there was a large scraping noise and the boat ground to a complete halt. The sudden stop threw us hard to the floor and my head thudded into Walter's thigh. He yelped instinctively but made little fuss, rubbing his leg briskly and hopping from foot to foot. We looked into the water but couldn't see any obvious obstructions and our prodding with the oar produced nothing but the occasional spout of disturbed river water.

"We're stuck on some mud I reckon," Walter said, dipping his head almost into the water to try and see.

"Hold tight," he warned, grabbing the edges of the boat and rocking it dramatically from side to side. Before I could shout at him to stop, I was thrown to the back of the boat, desperately spreading my legs to try and stop the world from see-sawing across my eyes. Balanced on his knees, Walter threw the boat first left and then right, sending heavy ripples of water smacking into the banks on either side. At first I held on but then, as I attempted to change my grip, my right hand fell away and I dropped heavily with the boat, causing it to overbalance and climb suddenly towards the sky.

Walter looked over his shoulder at me with alarm as the vessel teetered at the vertical, lost its grip on the water and plunged heavily downwards, burying us underneath its upturned hull. For a second, I was lost in the shock, the weight, the darkness and the water. When I opened my mouth the entire river descended deep, deep inside me, filling me up and rinsing my insides. I waited to see how it would feel to die.

Within seconds Walter's hands were upon me, face pressed hard against mine, his hands groping for my head. I felt my ears being grabbed and then I burst through the surface of the water. We were still beneath the boat but suddenly I could breathe again. Warm and uncertain air filled my lungs, laced with the increasingly familiar smell of river water slowly eating wood. Walter's screeching, rasping lungs called out right next to me. I turned to look at him, just inches from my face and I imagined his wide, desperate eyes, running into mine. There was water, air, darkness and Walter, and I thought that would be it. But then, from nowhere, the rest of the world returned.

Light flooded in from every direction. There was a huge sucking noise followed by the slightly despairing sound of lungs learning how to breathe again. Arm in arm, we clambered to our feet to see three boys laying the boat back upon the water where it bobbed innocently. I was suddenly aware that the water barely came above my waist. I looked at Walter and saw his blonde hair streaked across his forehead, a deep bruise developing below one of his eyes. He coughed heartily and spat the memory of water back into the river before making a sharp noise – half-roar, half-laugh.

“Are you two all right?” asked one of the three boys, putting a hand out to steady me. I nodded weakly and gesticulated in the vague direction of the nearest bank whilst the largest of the three boys tethered the boat to a tree.

“Did you see what happened?” Walter asked, crawling up onto the grass. “She went right over on top of us.”

“Yeah,” the third boy responded. “She flipped right over. Was it some sort of big wave?”

“On the river?!” I replied, a little curtly considering.

“Well, my brother told me once…”

“Thanks for the rescue,” Walter interrupted sheepishly. I smiled my agreement. The other boys studied their sodden shoes in embarrassment until the moment passed.

In the soft, friendly sunshine of an autumn afternoon we had met Rupert Randall, Charles Lucas and Johnny Black. They were boys that we had seen at school but never really approached. From a distance they seemed so different but close up they were just boys like any others. Like us. On that day, we were their adventure, their excitement, their tale to tell. In the years that followed we would be again, many times, but they would also be ours. As evening gathered with intent we peeled ourselves away from the grass and, with a slight breeze bringing a chill to our damp clothes, we went home with our stories; some tall, some short but all happy enough.

It wasn’t until the following January, 1901 I think, that Terry and Sid became attached to our group. Terry was just there one day, arriving quite unobtrusively at the edge of our circle and never leaving. Sid was different though. He’d not made many friends in his first year at school. He was very lively, too lively really, and many of the boys were intimidated by his frantic and excitable demeanour. I later found out that many parents had discouraged their sons from playing with him, no doubt fearing he would inevitably end up bouncing his way over to the wrong side of the law. But of course they hadn’t allowed for Walter. Almost without anyone else noticing, Walter had started speaking to Sid, nurturing him and bringing him towards us. Sid responded at first by becoming bigger, with a larger audience to entertain, and many of us avoided his attentions. It took a few weeks before Sid became universally accepted but Walter won us round, just as he always did.

My childhood memories are largely of books, summers, and the occasional Christmas, and I have this recurring, timeless image in my mind from one warm day after school. The patch of grass is quite small but very green. We're playing cricket and I'm batting. Donald Peacock is crouched behind me, repeatedly telling his brother that he's standing in the wrong place. Walter is about to bowl and in front of me they all wait. Some are crouched, others stand with feet set apart for balance. Rupert and Charles are leaning on each other in the distance and now there's Terry and Sid as well. We're all there.

Walter bowls and I strike the ball cleanly, through the air and into space. I run and run, pushing off the hard ground with the bat. I can feel warmth bouncing off me and my ten friends are shouting and gabbling all around. I make it home before the throw and turn to receive another ball. But that memory isn't just one moment or even one day. It's every moment of every day. It's my childhood.

Chapter Four

My old sports master used to say that he could tell what season it was simply by looking at a schoolboy's hands. In the spring they would be shaded with mud, in summer they would be red with the polish of a cricket ball, come autumn the palm would be full of horse chestnuts and for winter they would be pink to almost blue from the constant exchange of snowballs.

Before long, we were the only calendar he would ever need. We lived our young lives amidst the elements, good and bad, and although we were different enough, we shared our experiences genuinely and wholeheartedly.

In the February of 1906, when snow lay in suffocating depth, we slipped unceremoniously into the roles of Eskimos and adventurers; cutting through the snow, piling it up, living in it and hurling it at each other. Our favourite game during those few hard, grey days was to line-up along the sea wall, strap on Mr Peacock's waders and plummet into the drifts of snow on the beach. It was an activity fraught with just the right amount of danger; just enough peril to make it thrilling but not enough to cause the more careful among us to shirk away. Predictably, I would pick my landing area with plenty of thought but the others seemed to thrive on the uncertainty and the ambiguity, emerging from their freezing holes colder, wetter and happier each time. Occasionally the snow would be much deeper than it at first appeared but it was only Sid that ever really needed rescuing. Once he dropped himself off the side of the pier into a drift so deep that only his woollen hat remained visible. We clambered dramatically and inefficiently to his aid. When we eventually lifted him clear he was gabbling with enthusiasm like a champion fisherman but his lips were purple with cold and panic.

Sid was also a champion fruit picker, skills he mostly honed in other people's gardens. Sid would climb trees all day, as though that was his purpose of birth. I didn't mind heights but, as Walter would often remind me, Betty could climb a tree quicker than I could. My role was usually to stand at the bottom of the tree and catch the apples as they were freed. I loved that job, staring up into those yawning branches, spotting my friends and timing my move. I loved how they would call my name before they dropped the fruit and how good I was at catching those apples. No-one else ever caught the number of apples I did.

I can still remember however the sound of a dropped apple hitting the floor, that chilling sound that only apples make. You knew that when you found the fallen fruit it might look fine, but inside its flesh would be destroyed, already beginning to fail and putrefy. Eventually I could tell a bad apple just by the feel of it in my hand, the weight of it, the shape of it and like a doctor looking into the eyes of a dying friend I could tell that, somewhere along the line, I had failed.

It was the summer that truly brought us to life. Long happy days spent challenging the world and warm, sweet-smelling nights spent jumping from Dead Cat Tree. Living by the sea made the summer wider somehow, like it would reach out to the horizon, spreading and stretching each sunny hour, and into that vista we continued to pour endless bucketfuls of adorable cricket. My love of cricket had come from father although, typically, his rare appearances at the wicket were more likely to make him grumpy and childish than relaxed and joyful. Walter, I rather suppose, had taken his interest from mine, an interest polished and sharpened by a natural talent for the game.

By the summer of 1909, as we moved through the middle of our teenage years, our weekends were dominated by games of all sizes and shapes. We played on the streets, on the beach, in fields, in gardens and, on one long-regretted occasion, in Mrs Black's kitchen. Sometimes it would be all of us but more typically we would come together in pockets of convenience and a game would break out as easily and effectively as the dawn.

Not all our friends initially considered themselves cricketers, indeed some never would. Rupert, for example, had art in his blood, not sport, and it would be the beauty of the game and of the surroundings that he would enjoy. Unfortunately, a well-struck drive would often find him staring wistfully at dancing butterflies and crack him on the shin, knee or even worse. Eventually we got into the habit of shouting "Rupert!" whenever the ball was so hit, just to warn him that it might be on the way.

Charles and Terry were both vast and powerful men but neither of them had the grace or touch for a game like cricket. Terry could run like a branded pony and Charles had the strength to carry three of us on his back but neither of them could control what God had given them. Terry could run down a ball that most of us would give up but, like us, he never knew where his throw would land. We knew that Charles could hit a cricket ball nearly 100 yards because we had seen him do it – but only twice. Such was the legend of Charles' hitting ability that local children used to coax him into trying to hit balls over barns, across fields and high into trees but, for all the encouragement in the world, it rarely happened, and a legend it remained. For Gordon, cricket was a complete stranger, its secret subtleties and etiquette bewildering to a man educated by necessity and nature but, like everyone else, he threw himself into the game and tried not to drown. Cricket meant different things to us all, but the one truth we all understood was that the game was just the wrapper for something deeper and more important; something we would later understand to be friendship.

It was Walter and Johnny that could really play. Johnny's father and grandfather were both members of the MCC and cricket ran through the family like the fine stitching on the fraying family crest. Johnny had been able to bowl before he could walk, or so he would tell us, and he could do things with the ball that we could neither predict nor explain. More than once there was talk about Johnny pursuing the game as something more than a pastime but the millstone of dynastical expectation always dragged him towards more conventional professions.

One scorching afternoon in August, we were approached whilst playing on the promenade by a couple of smart looking strangers. A short cigarette stub wobbled precariously on the lip of one of the men, threatening it seemed to light his moustache. He spoke out of the side of his mouth.

"What are you boys doing tomorrow?" he asked with a curling local tone. We looked at each other, searching for an appropriate response.

"We've got a game all set up at Norton Park," the stranger continued, a small fragment of ash falling softly unto his tie, "and the opposition have pulled out. We've seen you lads playing around the place, is there enough of you to make a team?"

We looked at each other once more, this time with more electricity and urgency. We nodded all the heads we had.

"Are you any good?" the other man asked, surveying our sweaty forms like a farmer sizing-up cattle.

"We can play," Johnny replied, flipping the ball confidently from hand to hand. Beside him, Walter turned the bat over and over in a smooth, well-oiled motion. Between them they looked like some sort of cricketing machine, threatening to spew runs and wickets all over the seafront. The rest of us looked far less confident.

"Good, excellent. 2pm then," the first man said smartly.

"We'll be there," Johnny agreed.

The two men lifted the ends of their caps in our direction, turned and disappeared into the crowds. Walter's face was smeared with a vast smile.

"We've got a game!" He said once and then over and over again before sensing his excitement was a little lonely. "What? What's wrong?"

"A real game, against proper cricketers?" Rupert asked.

"It'll be fine, we'll do really well," Johnny reassured, still spinning the ball through the air.

"It'll be wonderful, I promise," Walter added.

"Harry?" Gordon asked, all eyes suddenly turning to me. I looked at all their faces, all their different hopes and fears. Walter's eyes were the brightest, always.

"It'll be good. It's what we've always wanted isn't it? A proper game? It'll be good." I replied, gilding my own trepidation with the excitement I could feeling tickling the ends of my fingers. Walter smiled broadly and the doubters acquiesced.

*

The hours that marked our journey to that first ball fell away at a pace. Our preparations were frantic as we raced around the streets, begging and borrowing kit. Cricketing whites were the main problem. Johnny had enough kit to share out among a few of us but none of it fitted Terry or Charles. Rupert borrowed a pair of his father's cream trousers only to find that one of the legs had torn all the way down the outer seam and for a while it seemed possible that Sid might have to play wearing one of his mother's less decorative blouses. But by the time the sun set, late on that Saturday night, we were ready to go. Scruffy, ill-matching but ready to go.

Walter and I sat shivering on the steps outside our houses. The smell of heat remained but a thin lace of mist had descended to dampen the temperature. We leaned back against our front doors and let our imaginations run a little wild.

"I rather think we'll win," I said, "we've got some good players." I felt Walter nod in the dusk.

"I shall dream of making a hundred," he replied softly. I looked at him and saw the way the warm glow from the house lights shone on his profile, marking out his familiar features. He looked so grown-up, so well-formed and mature. His nose had rounded slightly as he'd got older, bringing a pleasing symmetry to his face. He caught me looking.

"What?" he asked with a light accusation. I shook my head sharply as though to wake myself from a daze. We shared a thin smile.

"I'm sure you'll do well," I said eventually. "I think it'll be a super afternoon."

*

Even in the valley of night, the darkness of summer lacks the teeth of its winter cousin. I lay in bed as Saturday became Sunday and, with happy nerves as my companion, I surveyed the blue shapes and shadows of my small room. Then, in the familiarity, a foreign crescent of orange appeared near the window, swinging back and forth as though on a string. I pushed my covers down past my shins and climbed out of bed. I followed the orange arc down from the window, across the wall and into the Croucher's back yard where I found Walter, his silhouette vague against the shaded light of an oil lamp, practicing his batting with empty hands. I watched him for a while, an amused smile growing on my face. He went through his full range of shots – front foot and back foot, attack and defence – with such elegance and balance that you could almost hear the orchestra in his head.

I unhooked my father's old dressing gown from the back of the door and picked my way through the house to the accompaniment of a dozen yelping floorboards. Walter froze as I opened the back door, hoping to remain undiscovered. I climbed up and over the wall with practiced ease, landing softly in the glow of the lamp. Walter smiled, dropped his hand onto his chest and let out a long, slow breath. I reached into the dressing gown pocket and pulled out an imaginary ball, tossing it from hand to hand as easily and effectively as Johnny had done the day before. Walter nodded in appreciation and stepped towards the back gate, setting himself up to receive my delivery. I took a single step run-up and bowled. Walter treated the ball with respect, patting it back to me gently. The next ball though he chased, clattering it through the covers with a flourish. I mimed a short round of applause before rubbing the ball on the front of the dressing gown to develop the shine and then beating Walter with a ball that swung away late. And so it went on.

For about half an hour we played, without a sound. It was like theatre, but without the endless rehearsals. We never needed to query what I had bowled, or where Walter's shots had gone. Twice I got him out (once bowled, once caught) but more often than not he looked in imperious form, as effortless and smooth as migrating birds. From a distance we must have looked quite queer, but within our little world it was as normal as the dropping sun and the rising moon. Eventually Walter stepped forward with a big smile, shook my hand and leaned his imaginary bat against the shed. I tucked the imaginary ball back into the pocket of the gown, and climbed back over the wall.

"Goodnight Harry," I heard him whisper, putting out the lamp.

"Goodnight Walter," I replied, "sweet dreams…"

*

We got to Norton's Park early of course, but Peter and Donald Peacock were already there, throwing a ball at each other with unnecessary aggression. They both wore stinging red bands on their foreheads which bore testimony to both their efforts and the unrelenting sun.

"How long have you been here?" I asked them.

"Since just after breakfast," came Peter's reply. Walter and I just laughed.

We were all ready to go at 2pm with the exception of Gordon, who hurtled into the park at the very last minute, his legs trailing over the top of a small bicycle. He was closely followed by a scruffy looking young boy with tears cutting clean lines down his face. Approaching us with purpose, the child grabbed the bike, aimed a kick at Gordon's shins, swore appallingly and then rode off in a haze of dust. Gordon smiled sheepishly.

Our opposition were a decent enough bunch of chaps from the nearby hospital. Some were porters and others were doctors but they were all happy enough to play occasional games of cricket together. They were also rather good.

We fielded first and quickly saw that there would be no rest from either the heat or their confident batsmen. We had a few moments of good cheer, most notably when Johnny bowled their captain, but for the most part we chased our own shadows along the hard, bobbling surface, only occasionally getting close to the ball. We all had a turn at bowling, although most of us wished we hadn't, and I seemed to spend half the afternoon on my hands and knees, trying to retrieve the ball from hawthorn bushes or thirsty streams.

By the time they declared their innings, we were broken into little pieces. Rupert was nursing three ugly bruises on his left leg, Sid had torn his trousers through the crotch and the Peacock brothers were nauseous with sunstroke. We were starting to feel a little embarrassed by our naïve optimism and our attempt at batting didn't improve the mood. In the end I was our top scorer, which was pleasing, but not much to celebrate when you only get seven.

Walter was out first ball trying an attractive looking drive and I spent a few unhappy minutes watching my team mates walk enthusiastically into the line of fire, as though their self-belief could alone defy the weight of evidence. Their walk back was typically slow, bewildered and sloping.

With our innings lying in tatters all around me, I tried desperately to fend off the bowling and lengthen the game. Tommy and I batted together for about half an hour, putting our bodies between the ball and the stumps. We didn't achieve anything pretty, or even effective, but at least we felt we'd been in a contest. Eventually I ran out of luck, deflecting an aggressive bouncer to the grateful hands of slip and a short ripple of applause rolled out of the pavilion as I returned – a pale acknowledgment of a pale achievement.

By the time the game finished there was still plenty of light left in the day; the heat barely limited by the marching clock. In the space of just a few hours we learned that our vast and colourful cricketing dreams had been nothing but a house of cards. Our changing room was quiet as we packed our bags and wiped the sweat from our faces. The only noises to be heard were the soft cluckings of physical disappointment.

"We'll be better next time, you'll see," Walter said eventually. Not many eyes met his.

"There's going to be a next time?" Rupert asked, his pale face running with sweat.

"Of course," Walter replied, suddenly tossing some enthusiasm into the room. "Isn't there?" The response was short and barely audible, but it was unanimous enough. There would be a next time.

A light tap on the door prevented any further debate and one of the senior opposition players curled his face into the room and looked around nervously.

"Bad luck chaps. Do you want to have a look through the scorebook?" There were a couple of soft snorts at the back of the room. The head nodded with understanding. "I'll just leave it here on the side – have a look if you want."

"Thank you sir," Walter responded eventually, long after the bespectacled face had withdrawn.

For a few minutes, the leather-bound notebook sat alone on the bench, yawning with unsettled scores.

"Well I think my bowling figures were all right," Johnny said after a while, walking across the room to pick up the book. Gradually, the rest of us joined him and, quickly enough, the sombre mood evaporated into light chattering and the occasional ribbing. It hadn't been much of a game, but it had at least been a game.

The book was passed from hand to hand. Some people held it barely long enough to see the stark and unhappy truth scratched in pencil on its wide leaves whilst others perused it more carefully, almost lovingly, as though their single run would prove to be rare and precious. When it eventually returned to Walter the room was all but empty and the book was haunted by a dozen sweaty fingertips.

"Oh Harry," he sighed, "it wasn't meant to be like this. Do you think they'll play again, really?"

"I think so, if you ask them nicely. Anyway, it wasn't as bad as all that."

"Wasn't it?"

"No, not at all. After all, I got seven…"

"So you did Mr Hobbs, so you did!"

Walter clapped me on the back and we left the changing room arm in arm. We did indeed play again, a few weeks later, on a day that could barely have been more different. The heavy, sullen dampness of that September Saturday should have stopped us even starting the game but start it we did and, by the time it came to an end, the clouds had drawn so tightly together that it was almost impossible to see through the gloom. We lost, of course, but although our defeat was comprehensive, it wasn't embarrassing – at least not by the standards of our first effort.

"We probably shouldn't have played," I reflected to Walter later, "not in those conditions."

"Nonsense," he replied firmly, "the game must go on – always. The game must go on and on."

Chapter Five

The following summer we managed to beg and scrounge ourselves seven full games of cricket, and we even managed to win a couple.

Playing cricket together proved to be every bit as fulfilling as Walter had promised. We had a wonderful time on those sunny afternoons, and after a while we started to attract a fair crowd as well. Parents, siblings, family and friends followed us where they could to enjoy the spectacle, the sport and the happy weather. By the end of the summer we had also become accustomed to seeing a small group of young ladies at our games, taking picnics on the mound in front of the stream. I recognised most of them in a vague sort of way but many of our friends were shockingly enchanted with them, as though they were of a different land or, perhaps, species. Some of the things Sid in particular did to attract their attention were nothing short of embarrassing.

It wasn't just Sid though, not at all. Indeed, I had started to notice that even Walter was talking more about those girls. Up until this point, we had barely even acknowledged their existence but, seemingly overnight, Walter had developed an unquenchable interest in those things we used to ridicule; the way they looked, moved, spoke. It was like he had developed a sixth sense. He also seemed to behave differently towards my mother, more deferential if that were possible. I asked my mother about it once and she threw her head back, laughed with a slightly dreamy air and just walked away, muttering something about how practice would make perfect.

Walter would sometimes tease me by asking when I planned to get married. I would always tell him that I had made no such plans yet and neither should he. He knew how to get under my skin though and sometimes I am sure he did it on purpose. One evening after a game he asked me if I had ever wondered what it would be like to kiss a girl. I have to say that I was rather rude in my reply and refused to engage further on the matter, but before we were halfway home he had apologised, lolled an arm over my shoulder and promised he would be better behaved.

It wasn't like us to bicker and we remained very close throughout our time at school and, later, as we took up jobs. Walter started to work with his father and although he didn't really have the passion or the patience needed for carpentry he did nonetheless appreciate the time they spent together. I took up an apprenticeship at Harvey's Printers in town and although I disliked the repetition, I did rather thrive in the physical environment. I enjoyed pushing myself to work harder and harder, even on days when the temperature in the workshop was stifling. For some reason, I found the creeping fatigue, running sweat and throbbing feet almost pleasant, like I was being cleansed.

Gordon, Terry, Peter and Donald took a predictable enough route into the fishing trades of their fathers whilst Johnny Black went off to a school in London, only to return within a few months due to some sort of ill-health. Charles also took up an apprenticeship, this time with one of the local builders whilst Tommy and Sid worked on Adcock Farm. Rupert was the only one that seemed genuinely happy to be working, delivering bread for the baker in town. He could often be seen during the day, hurtling through the streets on his bike, with a heavy basket and a happy tune playing on his lips.

The evenings were different when we were working, shorter somehow, and even on summer weekends it was hard to guarantee that we would all be able to get together for cricket. We occasionally roped in friends, brothers and colleagues to help out when we were short but they were only ever temporary replacements.

Walter and I would always try to share a smoke at the end of each day and over the months, over those hundreds of woodbines, we must have posed and solved just about every question known to man. We spent one particular autumnal evening lying on our backs on the roof of Walter's Dad's shed, staring at the vast and varied collection of stars that were spread out across the purple sky. We lay there for a time, watching small clouds of smoke unfurl into the air.

"It's beautiful isn't it?" Walter said eventually, in a barely audible whisper. I turned my head to look at him and could see a hypnotic film lying across his eyes. He was lost somewhere, among the stars perhaps, and I stayed quiet until he returned.

"You know," he continued eventually, "if I were to reach up right now and pick a star out of the sky then people as far away as France would be able to see me do it. Did you realise that? Isn't that remarkable?" He dragged out the syllables of the last word luxuriously, his breath snaking through my fringe.

I turned and nodded in agreement but in truth it all made me feel rather dizzy. Such was the vast and sweeping depth of the sky. Such were the untold tales of its immense, suffocating breadth. I could feel my body rocking on the roof, swaying and turning beneath the endless night. To me staring at the world above my head felt like walking on the edge of a cliff. One wrong step and I would fall.

Most young children are frightened of monsters or ghosts. My sister hates spiders. But ever since I was a toddler I was haunted by the idea of falling into the sky. Not jumping, but falling, like the earth could suddenly be turned upside down. I would watch birds flying through the air and be wracked with anxiety, terrified that their wings would fail and they would be sucked upwards, until they were too small to see.

As I got older, the fear faded a little until, as I became a teenager, I realised something else. One day that vast, clear sky, and all its many mysteries, was going to watch me die. It was going to see the end coming, watch it happen and then remember it for as long as it chose. And there was nothing I could do about it.

I took a long drag on the woodbine and breathed warm air into a thick cloud above my head. Walter's eyes were still on me.

"It frightens you doesn't it?" Walter asked me suddenly. I tried not to look at him but failed.

"What makes you say that?"

Walter didn't reply. Softly, he edged himself a little nearer to me, shrinking the gap between us and making the roof whinge lightly. What it was, I thought at that moment, to be that known, that understood. I felt ready to tell this young man almost every thought that lived in my head but I also knew that I probably didn't need to, as he'd put most of them in there himself.

"The stars are interesting," Walter said softly.

"If you say so."

"You'd be less scared if you looked at them properly."

"Walter, I am not scared of the sky."

Walter didn't respond, he just edged his body nearer to me again and pointed upwards, encouraging my eyes to climb his arm, his hand and his long, thin finger. "That," he began, "is the North Star. That one over there is Hercules and that one is some sort of bear I think, or maybe a dog."

"Right," I replied, feigning disinterest.

"And there's a hunter here somewhere as well, on a horse I think," his finger drifted along the stars, flicking and circling them tenderly, looking for a pattern or shape.

"There's a cross there," I said, spotting a large, six point crucifix directly above us, almost perfect but for a slightly sloped cross-bar.

"So there is," Walter replied, patting me tenderly on the arm. He drew his finger over it slowly and deliberately, up and down, left and right before shifting himself back over to his side of the roof.

"Being afraid doesn't make you weak," he said eventually. I neither agreed nor spoke, keen for the conversation to take a turn. "You don't realise how strong you are Harry," he continued.

I snorted my disagreement but Walter's eyes were on me in a flash, fixed and wet.

"I get scared too you know," Walter spoke calmly, but with weight.

"What have you got to be scared of?" I asked, knowing the tone of the question would irritate him.

"You don't want to know."

"Tell me."

His eyes refused me.

"Tell me," I repeated, hearing an unwelcome whine in my voice. For a while it seemed as though he was going to leave me there, lying on that roof forever imagining the very worst that it could be, but he didn't.

"Do you remember," he began, "about six, maybe seven years ago, when we did that school nativity and I was picked to play Joseph?"

"Yes...why?"

"And do you remember what happened in the end?"

"No. Oh hang on, yes; you were sick, weren't you? Johnny had to step in at the last minute. He loved that if memory serves." Walter nodded heavily. "So," I prompted, "what's that got to do with anything?"

"Well, I wasn't sick Harry. I pretended to be so mother wouldn't make me go. I'm not sure even to this day that she believed me but, in the end, she let me stay at home in bed."

"Oh. Why did you do that?"

"I wasn't scared of performing, you know how much I loved being on stage when I was that age. I'd been in the summer play that year hadn't I?"

"I can't remember exactly but..."

"It wasn't performing that scared me Harry, it was the role."

"Sorry Walter, you're losing me. What do you mean it was the role?"

Walter took a deep breath in and pushed it out in a sharp succession of short puffs, like a train struggling up a hill. I sat up and looked at him, my head cocked to one side in a question. He sat up himself, studied his fingers for a few seconds and then looked at me sadly.

"I didn't want to be Joseph."

A crack of laughter burst out, forcing me to slap my hands across my mouth to stem the noise. Even with my mouth gagged, my eyes continued to cackle. Walter's face didn't change.

"Sorry, so the part wasn't *big* enough for you?" I blurted. Walter held steady.

"It wasn't about how *big* it was," he replied, suddenly quite quiet. "It was about how *real* it was."

"How *real* it was? What does that mean?"

"I'm sorry Harry, really I am."

"Sorry? What for?"

"I didn't want to be Joseph because I didn't *believe* in Joseph. I knew that I should but I didn't and I felt sure that everyone would know it the moment I stepped on the stage."

My laughter, still echoing a few streets away, now seemed foolish and misplaced. I rubbed my face to try and break up the confused expression it was doubtless displaying.

"I'm still not sure I understand," I said eventually. Walter held his palms out to me in a gesture of submission, or maybe regret.

"That was when I realised Harry. That was when I realised that I just didn't believe in God. And I don't think I will ever be able to explain how that felt, and how frightening that was. How frightening it still is."

I stayed sitting, but a significant part of me blew off the roof, across the yard and fell into a million tiny pieces in the cracks between the flags. Walter looked even more shocked, like a simple game of kiss chase had ended in marriage. He'd always asked questions, even when we were little, but I had always seen it as part of his healthy curiosity, nothing more than that. It wasn't unheard of to have doubts about faith, not at all, but there's a big difference between knowing something occurs and seeing it occur right in front of your eyes. In the space of a handful of words, Walter had shrunk in front of me like a deflating balloon.

"I'm not sure what to say to that," I said eventually as his face searched me for some sort of resolution. Walter fell back onto the roof and covered his face with his hands. I suddenly felt quite tired, like I had been lying on that roof for days. I started to notice the stiffness of the wood beneath me. A thin shiver of cold ran through my body. "I'm not sure I really understand Walter. What makes you start thinking something like that?" Walter's shoulders made a shape.

"I really don't know, it's not something I can explain. Do you...do you think it matters?"

"Of course it matters!" I replied sharply. Walter ran his hands through his hair a couple of times before cupping them around his mouth as though he feared being sick.

"But if I don't believe that God exists then...?"

"What do you want me to say Walter?" I snapped. "If you want me to say that I think it is okay for you not to believe in God...well I can't, I don't. How can I say that? How can it be okay? It...it just doesn't make sense to me."

"People can be different though Harry can't they? Different from everyone else, different from what you'd expect?" I felt something substantial snap silently inside me.

"This isn't being different Walter. Growing a beard would be different. Wearing a top hat would be different. This isn't about being different. This is...wrong. You need to get better; you need to sort this out." I found myself pointing at him, almost prodding the side of his face. He looked at me sadly.

"You're right of course," Walter replied gently, "I want to believe, really I do, but sometimes..."

"You've just got to stop thinking these things Walter, they're not real. Sometimes we all think things which are strange or...or just wrong. We usually know they're wrong."

"Like you and the sky?"

"Well, I don't know about that, you just have to stop thinking these thoughts. Just make yourself stop and then one day..."

“What?” Walter jumped in as I paused. “Then what?”

“One day you will be better.”

A new degree of darkness seemed to wrap around us at this point. I kept my eyes facing the sky, a sky that looked a little more like home than it did just a few moments earlier.

“You’re a good man Harry,” Walter said eventually, from what seemed like a thousand miles away. “A very good man.”

With that he hopped off the shed, rubbed his arm hard across his face like it was covered in dirt, and skipped up the back steps into the kitchen. I sat up, watching the space where he’d just been. I laid my hand on the wood and felt the heat of his body melt into the night. I had felt many things in the company of my great friend over the years, many incredible things, but this was the first time I had felt pity.

*

One Sunday afternoon late in August 1912, we were in the final throes of a game against Lord Cromer’s XI at Norton Park. It was a keenly contested match against a much-weakened opposition and we were endeavouring to defend a modest total.

The general sense of competitive urgency was heightened by the fact that the morning’s light sea breeze had started to whip itself up into a near gale and, in the mid-distance, there were deep, wide clouds gathering across the sky like ominous bruises. Within just a few minutes the clouds had come together to form an endless, grumbling mass over our heads and then the rain arrived with real purpose. The drops thudded heavily against the hard ground and a huge, scraping cry of thunder burst just a few hundred feet above us. To a man we turned and ran for cover with wide strides and lowered heads. We skidded and crashed our way into the pavilion like startled cattle and turned to watch what remained of our game disappear behind a curtain of rain.

“I thought the game must go on and on?” I smirked at Walter, rainwater running off the end of my nose.

“I’d have carried on,” winked Walter, “it’s just this lot, you know what they’re like.”

We sat for a while to give the storm a chance to pass, but it didn’t. Instead the clouds anchored themselves for the evening and threw great walls of water down upon us, unrelenting and tireless. After an hour or so, when any chance of resumption had long since been washed away, we began to talk about making a run for home, but this clearly wasn’t going to be easy. There was a hearty stream running across the front of the pavilion and, behind the building, the seasonally dry brook was heavy with water.

Gordon stepped out of the pavilion and his foot immediately disappeared up to the ankle, making him curse. Cringing, he tried a second step but found himself unable to dislodge the first. He stood there for a moment, balanced improbably on the toes of his feet before dropping sideways to the floor. Amidst raucous laughter we pulled him back under cover but there wasn’t a great deal we could do to help him dry off. Seeing his friend in such a state prompted Walter to reminisce, not for the first time, about our first meeting with Gordon and for a while the weather was forgotten as we paddled our way instead through puddles of nostalgia.

The darkness came early that evening and the lights on the pavilion porch were fizzing and spluttering unhappily when we finally decided to make a move. By this point the rain was less dramatic than it had been earlier in the afternoon. It was falling more gently but somehow it had become almost solid, like we were sitting behind a waterfall. We prepared as well as we could, rolling up trousers and leaving larger items for collection another day before, staying close together, we stepped into the sodden greyness.

There was much merriment and high spirits early on, but even before we had left the park the complaints had begun. The slope from the field to the road was rolling noisily and white water was visible where the gallons from the park met the gallons on the road. With our shirts pressed against our bodies we struggled onwards, kicking our feet through endless rolls of mud. The dust of a dry summer had been folded into a sopping cake and it climbed effortlessly against us, coating our feet and shins. Progress was horribly slow but eventually we were able to guide everyone to within a few feet of their homes. Some were able to clamber straight inside but we had to help others mop a route to their front door. Poor old Charles had to strip down to his underwear on the doorstep before his mother would let him enter.

Walter and I walked the last few yards alone, struggling for breath and words against the elements. Turning the corner into our street we faced yet another battle, as the gale threw water at us, down from the sky and up from the running road at our feet. My mother snapped the front door open and, shielding us ineffectively with her apron, she dragged us into the house.

"Don't move!" she ordered, leaving us shivering and filthy in the hall. She returned within a few moments with towels and, a little later, a couple of bowls of warm water. We peeled off our clothes and wrapped the towels around our bodies whilst mother loudly and passionately berated us for being out in such conditions and, more importantly, coming home in such a state. By the time we were allowed to take a seat in front of the fire my chest and jaw were starting to ache and my feet throbbed with discomfort. The small glimpses of flesh that I could see on Walter looked hard and pained and his knuckles were white across the edges of the towel. Shortly, mother returned with a better humour and some warm bread. We sat eating into the night, listening to the rain hammer against the window. And that sound remained with us for three more days.

It was the first day of September before my father came home again. He spent almost a week in the parish, helping people deal with the terrible flooding. Where possible, Walter and I would help him with his work, bailing out cellars, shifting sandbags and cleaning the badly damaged hospital kitchens. But people wanted more than practical help. My father also had to deal with parishioners that were angry or frightened by what had happened. Three people had died during the storms, including a two-year-old boy who had been washed away when a bridge collapsed in Westwick Street. They never found his body.

One day I found my father with a bloodied handkerchief pressed to his nose. He explained that he had fallen over a submerged pot but I have always suspected that someone struck him that afternoon. They were angry you see, and in my father they saw someone to blame.

So the glorious summer of 1912 came to an end earlier than we had hoped. September was miserable and the few days of good weather we had in October did nothing to lift the prevailing mood. But the town recovered, as towns tend to do, and Christmas was a big community affair. Thus, by the summer of 1913, we returned to the cricket field again with a fair bounce in our stride.

Chapter Six

For a lifetime, my relationship with Walter had been effortless. As babies, we had been laid side-by-side to kick together against the air and, as boys, we had developed an understanding that was so rich we could communicate through silence, through stillness, round corners and through walls. I've met a few sets of twins in my time, but none of them shared more fragments of life than me and Walter.

But at the start of May 1913, as the sweet smell of dried sweat and tired wood once more entered our lives, I began to realise that something had changed. We had talked very little about our conversation on the shed roof all those months before and, for the first time, I felt there were parts of Walter that I was unable to access. My mother was full of platitudes and reassurance but we both knew that something small and significant had broken and there was no guarantee that it would ever mend.

If change could have a name, then for me it was called Hattie. Hattie was prominent in the relatively harmless group of young ladies that had become a feature of our games, as consistent as Rupert's bruises and Johnny's over-confidence. Hattie was popular enough but she also had a hardness about her – you could almost call it fierce – and I knew a few people that had felt the sharp and effective lash of her tongue. Hattie's parents were elaborately wealthy in a non-specific sort of way and for me it was evident in her demeanour. She was confident, classical and gilded with the attractive veneer of the well-heeled. And in the summer of 1913, she caught Walter's eye.

He had this look, almost like his face was shining from the inside. I'd never seen it before, not like this, and as soon as I saw the way he smiled at her, I knew. For a while, I tried to snap him back to life but in time I realised that I was becoming to Walter like I felt I was to everybody else, largely invisible. Seeing them together made me feel strange, like there was a tight belt across my chest and my stomach was full of lead. My mother told me it was probably jealousy but I very much disagreed with her. I asked her whether she felt I should go and see Doctor Lavender but she told me that under no circumstances was I to do such a thing.

Walter and I had always walked home from our weekend games together, but increasingly I was trudging back on my own whilst he spent time talking to Hattie. After one particular game in early July I walked out of the pavilion to be confronted by Walter, Hattie and another girl whose face was vaguely familiar. Her name was Ruth. It had been decided that Walter was going to walk Hattie home and that Ruth and I were to accompany them, as chaperones of a sort. My instinct was to refuse but one look at Walter's pleading face was enough to make me change my mind.

Hattie's impressive home was some three miles away and we strolled slowly in the fading sunshine. Walter and Hattie walked a few paces in front whilst Ruth and I exchanged long, drawn-out pleasantries behind. For much of the time our eyes were focused forwards, onto the backs of our friends' heads. We would take turns to speak and break the spell. Ruth was pleasant enough, sweet even, but it was hard not to be irritated by her simple existence.

Walter was beaming later that night as we trotted back home. He chatted incessantly about Hattie, her life, her thoughts, her looks and her family. I listened as patiently as I could, but made no effort to keep the conversation rolling. As we parted at our front doors Walter grabbed me lightly at the elbow.

"I really like her Harry," he said with great fondness, making me more upset with myself than with him.

"I know you do Walter," I replied quietly, with an expression that was as genuine as I could muster.

"And Ruth?"

"You never stop do you?" I replied, my face hardening. Walter gave me his best guilty smile, punched me firmly on the arm and disappeared. I opened my mouth to call him back but no sound came out. I didn't sleep much that night.

Over the next few weeks the long walks to Hattie's house became more frequent. Ruth and I began to accept our roles with more grace and we would amuse ourselves by swapping stories about our childhood friendships.

She would tell me the soft focus adventures of young girls and I would respond in boyish comparison with snails, dirt and sport. Ruth, it turned out, was a fine listener and she had an endearing thirst to learn more about our meek adventures. So I told her about the time that Walter had jumped upon Farmer Rumpole's old mare and held on for dear life as the frightened animal tried desperately to throw him to the floor. I told her about the night we spent in the graveyard and the desperate terror I felt when my foot disappeared into a crumbling grave and I told her about the games we would invent and the challenges we would set each other.

But her favourite story was the one that I told a lot. The one where Harry and Walter go out on a boat and Walter saves Harry's life. Ruth listened open-mouthed to that tale and when I'd finished she all but made me tell it again. Almost without noticing I embellished my story to meet her awe. At every turn the boy that was me took yet another step towards an early death and the boy that was Walter emerged yet further into the heroic light. Other boys were there of course but the more I told it the more it grew into a simple story of how my best friend gave me back my life.

*

We played our last game of the summer of 1913 in early September. The evenings carried a more comfortable air but the days were still hot, dry and ominously heavy. We fielded first in chapping sunshine and by the end of a sumptuous tea we would probably have chosen an afternoon nap rather than a stint at the crease. For most of us, unsurprisingly, batting was lethargic and heavy-footed, but there was something about Walter that afternoon that was unavoidable. He seemed a yard taller than the rest of us and he batted gloriously. Walter had always been our best batsman but he'd never really shown everyone else what I had seen of him so many times in the street outside our homes. Well they got to see it that afternoon.

Just a few yards to my right I could see Hattie and Ruth. They had eschewed their normally relaxed postures and were instead perched on their knees, leaning forward towards the action. Like the rest of us, their faces betrayed their admiration. If anything, Ruth seemed even more engrossed than Hattie. If my mother had accused me of jealousy at that point then I would probably have denied it, but she would have been right. To hold people in the palm of your hand like that; to be so loved, so worshipped. I challenge any man not to be jealous of that.

Shortly before six o'clock, Walter turned the ball elegantly to the longest boundary and completed his century. We clapped and cheered with all our might and Walter offered a short and humble smile, acknowledging our acclaim with an exaggerated doff of his cap. A few minutes later, the game was won. The energy was bouncing off my best friend as he returned to the pavilion. Even before I had a chance to shake his hand and slap his back, he was striding across to Hattie. After a short exchange he went onto one knee and, with great theatre, presented her his cap, like a medieval knight handing his colours to his queen.

I stole away to walk home on my own that night and when Walter knocked on my door at dusk I made an excuse that was so feeble it evaporated before it reached his ears. He wanted to talk, to share and to remember and so I let him. We sat smoking on the front steps once again and I listened to his memory of every moment, every shot and every kind word. It was one of those moments in life that makes the daily grind manageable. It was the sort of day that I knew we would both remember forever and yet I was holding back. I grew up expecting days like that to be ours but it wasn't ours, it was just his…or maybe theirs.

*

For as long as I could remember, the churches of Cromer had held a fundraising dance on New Year's Eve. My parents used to go when I was little but mother had long since stopped attending and father's role had become more of a helping hand than a reveller. In truth, the event had become a little controversial in recent years, as many Church elders complained that there had been 'unsavoury incidents' involving some younger people. Certainly my father made sure that Walter and I fully understood the expectations he had of our behaviour when, at the end of 1913, we were first given permission to attend.

My father insisted that if we wished to take Hattie and Ruth to the dance then they must both have chaperones – they were not to chaperone each other

– and their parents' permission had to be sought. It took a little while, and a handful of letters that Walter made me write, but eventually the arrangements were made. I had to admit that even I was a little excited, and certainly curious, but Walter was almost uncontrollable. Our evening smokes were dominated by Hattie's dress, Hattie's hair, Hattie's shoes and he became obsessed by practicing his Waltz.

"I just can't get it right," he said to me one night, chewing his fingernails savagely.

"It's easy," I replied, demonstrating as best I could in my work shoes.

We had both been taught to dance by my mother. One school holiday, I think it was a Christmas but I'm not sure, we spent hour after hour dancing with her in the front room. That was a special time actually, and it's amazing how easy it is to forget. She had a balance about her which was difficult to describe, like water; still but always moving. I had always taken to it a little easier than Walter, although somehow he always seemed to look better. My mother once said that whereas I had learned to dance, Walter had learned what it *meant* to dance and I had no doubt she was right. It was during that time in our lives that mother taught us so many things, *fine things* she would call them, about art and music in particular. I seem to remember there was even one weekend she enthralled us with a lecture on architecture, complete with a long walking tour of Cromer. I once asked her how she came to know so much about so much and she just smiled at me and said that the key was to listen rather than ask questions. I didn't mention it again.

"Show me," Walter asked. I chuckled with embarrassment but duly obliged with a perfectly reasonable, if somewhat limp, demonstration.

"No," Walter said, stopping me. "*Show* me..." He held his arms out towards me, indicating that he would lead.

"Walter!" I sniggered. "You are joking?"

"I'm not, really, come on."

"I don't really know the lady's part."

"Come on."

I looked into the shadows and across the line of gardens for mocking eyes, but no one else was braving the bitterness. I looked at him again, standing there, ready to dance with me. I swallowed nothing and stepped into his arms.

His face was close to me, allowing me to whisper my instructions and corrections. He hummed a passable tune and, on a cold and unfriendly English night, we danced together. There were moments when I wanted to laugh, others when I wanted to run away, but mostly I was happy just to be where I was, where we were. Walter's eyes barely left me and I reciprocated, playing my role as best I could. After a few moments he stopped making the tune but we kept dancing, kept moving together. Walter closed his eyes for a while and I watched the way his pupils made little mounds under each eyelid, casting richer curves across their lashes. Eventually, he broke himself free of me and laughed.

"You know what Harry?" he said with lightness, "I might just be able to do this. Let's just hope Hattie smells better than you!"

He laughed again and I pushed him playfully, but perhaps quite hard, to the floor.

*

When my father had first gone to the New Year's Eve dance it had been expected that the men would wear full evening dress and in many cases that would also include a top hat. In more recent years the requirement had been relaxed slightly and by 1913 a gentleman's best suit was largely deemed sufficient. Only Johnny wore a hat.

Hattie's grandfather had a glorious old motor car and we waited outside Hotel De Paris for the sight and sound of its impending arrival. When it did so, there was an audible gasp from my companion as Hattie stepped out of the back.

Hattie was quite a pale young lady with scratches of colour on her cheekbones. She had angrily curled hair that sat on her shoulders and there was an undeniable femininity about the way she moved. I thought her a little plump but that was never a view I shared with Walter. That night, Hattie was wearing a sleeveless golden dress with long white gloves and from the moment she stepped into view, she held Walter in the palm of her hand. I waited for Ruth dutifully and offered her my elbow as she approached. Ruth was wearing a similar dress to Hattie but in crimson and her thin blonde hair had been conjured into a many-tiered pile of gold and flowers.

Our dance partners drew compliments throughout the night and I was struck as they took their turn with other suitors at how similar they had become. When I first met Ruth in the summer she had been softer, more child-like than Hattie and her personality was pleasant but somewhat small. I had liked her that way. I liked her dignity and her simplicity and I liked the way that she could become translucent when it suited her. If she wanted to, she could choose to disappear.

But things had changed. Ruth had become more colourful, more substantial over the previous few months and there was a familiarity about her behaviour and her mannerisms that it took me a while to place. It was only that night that I fully realised what I was witnessing. I watched Ruth as she danced, as she spoke, as she smiled and as she sparkled and I realised; Ruth was becoming Hattie.

Predictably enough, Walter need not have worried about his Waltz, or indeed any of his dancing. He wasn't impeccable, but what he lacked in technical skill he more than made up for in enthusiasm, commitment and something approaching elegance. He also looked so good with Hattie, so comfortable and so convincing. When young men, including Sid and Johnny, wished to dance with Hattie then they always asked Walter first. No-one asked for my permission to dance with Ruth, not that I ever really felt it necessary. A happy formality had entered into Walter and Hattie's relationship and it radiated from their every move.

Walter had hoped that he would be given the chance to walk Hattie home after the dance that night but her father would not consider such a thing. As the party broke up in the simmering minutes after midnight so the overbearing black car appeared once more and whisked our companions away, into the unfamiliarity of 1914.

We spent a short time helping my father to break down tables and straighten chairs but at the first opportunity we slipped back into the night and, with our feet hanging over the end of the sea wall, wrapped ourselves eagerly around a woodbine. Over the years, our dangling feet had dropped closer and closer to the beach and, in the twilight of our teenage years, my toes hung just a shoelace length from the sand.

As was often the case in the early hours of a new year, the air felt heavy and significant. Walter shifted uncomfortably for a while, occasionally looking over his shoulder to follow a shout or bang. He looked a little sheepish to me, embarrassed even.

"Another year then," he said eventually, to no-one in particular. Passing me the smoke for a final time, Walter shoved his hands under his legs to keep them warm and lifted his knees up and down quickly like he was driving some sort of machine. I worked the woodbine over carefully, feeling its warmth and the reassuring scrape in my mouth and throat. I knew I was waiting for something to begin, or perhaps to end.

"1914. We'll be twenty this year Harry. Twenty!" I smiled at him and flicked the butt onto the beach. It looped pleasingly through the air and I watched it to see which way it would turn when it landed.

"No more jumping out of trees!" he added.

"And no more disturbing perfectly innocent maggots," I replied instinctively. Walter laughed heartily, maybe a little too heartily, and the sound fell quickly short.

"Harry?"

I turned to look at him, properly, and I could see something very unusual in his eyes, something very rare. It was a look I had seen many times before, but always in a mirror. It was a little like fear.

"Go on," I instructed softly. He studied me for any hint of doubt but I didn't offer him any.

"I'm going to see Hattie's father sometime in the spring. I'm going to ask him for Hattie's hand. I'm going to be married Harry. I'm going to be married."

A small handful of sea air shot through my hair, sending it swirling in all directions. I placed my hand on my forehead until the wind passed. By the time I was able to let go, I found myself nodding.

"Would that make you happy?" I asked simply.

"I rather think it would Harry."

"Then I'm very pleased for you," I stated simply. Walter's face didn't change.

"You've never said much about Hattie, Harry. What do you really think? It's important to me what you think."

I took a few seconds. I thought of everything in an instant, but most of all I thought of something my father had said to me many, many times over the last few months. I thought of Corinthians 13 and I thought of setting aside childish ways.

"I think she's a handsome woman Walter who would make you a splendid wife and I think you will make a fine, fine husband."

The anxious mask of Walter's face broke to dust and disappeared. He smiled with that light he had been nurturing for so long and slapped one happy, grateful arm across my shoulder, shaking my hand warmly with the other.

"To 1914!" he toasted happily.

"To 1914," I agreed.

To 1914. The first year of the rest of our lives.

Chapter Seven

Some of us knew more about the situation than others.

My father had a fervent interest in politics and he would spend many hours poring over newspapers. I knew, from the little that he had said, that war was a possibility but we never truly talked about what that might mean. Johnny's father was loosely associated with various important businessmen in London so that grapevine also bore the occasional fruit but on the whole the spring of 1914 arrived unimpeded and unobtrusively.

For Walter, life was dominated by one unfortunate event in early March. Hattie's mother, an unquestionably confident rider, fell from her horse whilst galloping in the grounds. For a while it seemed that her life may be in danger but after a few days she rallied and by Easter she was back at home with both family and serving staff at her beck and call.

Unfortunately though, the inevitable turmoil and distress upset Walter's smooth proposal plans and he had no alternative but to wait until Hattie's mother could be considered fit enough to play the central role she would no doubt command. As you can imagine, this left Walter heavy of foot and heart. For a few weeks, he barely saw Hattie and his usually perky demeanour was clipped slightly, like a songbird that had lost its voice.

In contrast, that spring saw Ruth and me spending more and more time together, often reading in the park, sat close against the hustling breeze. We no longer needed Walter and Hattie to initiate our meetings and we were establishing ourselves as a couple in our own right. We may have lacked the glamour of our friends but we became an expected and welcomed fixture among our peers. It also seemed that Ruth had ended her mimicry of Hattie and had reverted back to the manner I had first admired in her; soft, quiet and demure. It was like she had tried something out for size and found that it simply hadn't fit.

I also became aware that a slight frostiness had developed between Ruth and Hattie. It was only subtle, and I don't think Walter ever noticed, but it was there nonetheless. It was a bristling, a slight changing of the air between them and whereas many of the conversations I'd had with Ruth in the previous summer had been around the common threads we shared with our two friends, we had come to speak of them only rarely. Indeed Ruth would often steer us almost abruptly away from such talk, as though it troubled her to think about them. I never asked her what had happened, what had passed between them, but it was real enough and I rather suspect it is still there today.

Ruth was orphaned at quite a young age and she had been brought up in relative comfort by her elderly but spritely Aunt. My world seemed for a long time like it was too different to share; too simple, too complete, but eventually the look on my mother's face began to scream at me and I dutifully invited Ruth and her Aunt to tea one clean, sweet-smelling Saturday afternoon in April. My mother was polite and courteous to the point of charming, just as I would have expected, and she moved and swooped around us, smiling brightly and catching crumbs before they left the cake. Like so often in the past, she grew in front of my eyes and Ruth saw, just as I knew, what a remarkable and different woman my mother could be. Like something from another world, or maybe another time.

Above this, beyond it all, was my father.

For as long as I can remember, father had saved his best side for his God. His contribution to our lives had been full but restricted. He had educated us, guided us, advised us and scolded us. He had shown us the many paths of life – those that were lit and those that were not. He had given us everything he had at his disposal, doing the very best with what he appeared to have. All our other needs would be met by mother. I wouldn't say that father didn't love Betty and me but maybe his capacity to show it was narrow. He showed his affection and his commitment through service and strife. Perhaps this is what allowed him to become a complete clergyman but only a partial father.

But then Ruth stepped gently through our open door and, just for a couple of hours, he was a different man. His skin started to colour and his tired, dry eyes began to move around their sockets with surprising vivacity. Something approaching warmth gathered in the air around him and he showed Ruth a face and a personality that I barely recognised. Even mother was taken aback and at one point I caught her looking at him with bewildered adoration, as if recognising a long lost friend. When Ruth and her Aunt left towards dusk, you could almost see the light passing from him, like a lamp flame clinging to the final drops of oil.

He left within a few minutes to make some house calls but before he did so he dropped a hand hard on my shoulder, pulling me lightly towards him.

"I look forward to seeing Ruth again," he said with little trace of anything. I nodded firmly and half a smile climbed from his mouth towards one ear.

His fingers left my shoulder with a little drummed goodbye and ran away through his modest hair. He replaced his hat and disappeared into the gathering gloom of the cool, spring evening. I stood and watched the back of the door for a while feeling a crystal-clear realisation wash over my face like a freak wave. My father didn't just *want* me to have Ruth in my life, he needed me to. I might even go as far as to say he was desperate.

As always, all these new truths of my life took their turn on the carousel in my head. As I grew older, I found many things made more sense. They started to fall into their place and fit together in a manner that I never thought possible before, but other pieces were more confused, more inconclusive and I disliked the way these uncertainties made me feel and sometimes behave.

Many of those mixed feelings were about Walter, mainly because of the relationship he had with Hattie. I could never quite put my finger on what bothered me so much, but it felt like I was trying to cough something up from my throat, to remove something that was constantly irritating me, some days more than others, but constantly. My mother told me that I would just have to get used to the fact that we weren't little boys anymore.

I'd love to say that there was nothing about my relationship with Ruth which caused me such turmoil and such doubt but that, unfortunately, would be a lie. I liked Ruth, and I liked myself more when I was with her, but I was also aware that that wasn't necessarily enough. There was something about our relationship which was unseen, unexplored, like we lived some of our time separated by a thin piece of glass.

Often we would go for many days, sometimes a couple of weeks, without meeting-up and although this seemed strange to others, it never presented us with any questions or concerns. Indeed there were occasions when we could be quite cold to each other and anyone watching from the sidelines would doubt if we were a couple at all and yet the next day we could just as easily be great friends and companions again, without a cross word ever being shared or even considered. We simply accepted that this was how our relationship would be and, on the whole, I never questioned it.

"Do you think you could be married to Ruth…forever?" Walter asked me one day, lounging across 'forever' to emphasise the weight of the word.

I told him that I very much thought I could and the conversation ended as quickly as it had begun but I knew what he meant, and why he had asked. There was an absence in my relationship with Ruth, an absence of heat, of need, of wanting and I think the truth is that we were both happy with that, riding a smooth and unflustered path through our lives. I knew that there could perhaps be more, even that there *should* be more but I also knew that someone like me should be very grateful and very proud to be with someone like Ruth. It was not for me to expect or demand anything beyond.

And did it bother me that Ruth's body seemed to angle away from mine when we danced? Maybe it did, but it bothered me more that my body, with a simple mind of its own, seemed to do exactly the same to hers.

*

By this point our cricketing exploits were firmly established, not only in our lives but in the wider community as well. We had about a dozen regular fixtures pencilled-in for the 1914 season and although we were still more likely to be second-best, we were earning something of a reputation as decent competitors and hosts.

Walter, whose mood improved steadily with Hattie's mother's health, started to make runs regularly and attractively. The rest of us tended to play supporting roles but no-one seemed to object. It was a simple time, but I'm not sure we realised it. We didn't realise that things were starting to change either, not until they were practically on top of us and the whole of the town was buzzing with rumour and accusation.

My father spoke earnestly to me and Walter one night that July, for over an hour in fact, about what was happening in Europe and what it would inevitably mean. He told us very sincerely that there was going to be a war, a very large war, and in some way we would all have to be involved. To be honest, although we listened respectfully, I'm not sure how much of what he said we actually *heard.* It wasn't that we were complacent or casual as such, I just don't think we could match what he was saying to what we were seeing in front of our own eyes. We walked the following day along the beach front and saw exactly what we had been seeing for weeks; wide swathes of sunshine, many hundreds of holidaying people and the rock-solid edges of England.

I remember the day that we read about what was happening in Europe and how their armies were getting ready for war. I remember thinking back to what Walter had said about people in France being able to watch him reach out and pick a star from the sky. That night I lay awake, my heart a more pressing thud in my chest, and allowed my mind to tip-toe among my fears. England would soon be at war and, as a coastal town, we may one day meet an invader face-to-face. It seemed to have happened so quickly, but father had of course known it was coming for many months. The night before everything started, he gathered me, mother and Betty in the front room and we prayed together. It was a short and simple prayer. He begged God to forgive us all for our sins and to have mercy on our souls and then he went to bed.

Chapter Eight

The more I thought about it, the more I warmed to the idea of becoming a soldier.

There was something about the duty, the serving, that seemed to fit and in spite of all my flowing fears I wanted to feel the weight of a uniform on my shoulders; I believed that it would fit rather well. Walter was different but the same. He was bouncing like a teased dog, happily looking for a direction to run. Suddenly our lives had a purpose beyond Hattie, beyond cricket and beyond Cromer; a purpose for the King, a purpose for God and a purpose for history.

There was a peculiar sense of dislocation in those first few days after the declaration of war. In many ways the sights and sounds of Cromer were just the same, but then we would find small corners of our once predictable lives had suddenly changed. The privileged and carefree had been joined on the beach by the responsible and the weighty. For some people, the sense of threat and suspicion left them prone to both sinister self-preservation and distracting titillation. As a family, we tried to ignore it but we also couldn't help but play the game. Some people would tell us that to be complacent was to be vulnerable and we had no ambition to be either. My father barely slept for a fortnight, rushing forward to be a guarantor for the worst fears of his parishioners. He'd never been busier.

The call to arms came about a week after the start of the war. Many people thought the conflict would be swift, successful and over by Christmas but there were clearly some who were less optimistic. The general sense of urgency suddenly had a focus and all around me my peers babbled with excitement and hope like they were queuing for Cup Final tickets. Walter called us together at the cricket pavilion one evening after work with a heavy sense of urgency. Peter and Donald were at sea but the rest of us came together, breathless with energy.

Tommy was the last to arrive, with his barely teenage sister at his heel. We all looked at him with questioning eyes.

"Don't…I'm supposed to be looking after her. She'll be fine."

We all acquiesced politely enough but insisted that she sat on her own, right on the edge of earshot. This was, after all, very definitely the business of men.

We sat there together for several hours, until nearly midnight in fact. Some of us mainly listened, others mainly spoke. Between us we shared every hoped-for adventure that ever there was. I'm sure we all sat there wearing our own particular scarves of doubt, but we kept them tucked deep inside our shirts, out of sight. The bells of our youth were ringing loudly that night and we all heard them. Different notes and different sounds, but the same steady, calling beat.

Sid wanted to join the cavalry and gallop down the promenade with a sword. Terry wanted a medal before Christmas and Johnny seemed to think, somehow, that joining-up would make him a fortune. Charles wanted to marry a French woman and live in Paris whilst Gordon was thrilled at the opportunity to spend more time on dry land and Tommy had promised his sister the finest dress in France. Through the electricity of that night we chuckled at our imaginations, our fantasies and our long-held secrets. This was the adventure that we'd spent our lives rehearsing for and we all seemed ready to play our part.

We all noticed that Rupert was quiet that night, but we never drew any attention to him. Rupert never saw the opportunities in war that the rest of us did and there is little doubt that he would have rather picnicked in the fields of France than fought in them. But he was also a proud and loyal member of our group, a real friend, and just as Rupert had made himself into a cricketer, of sorts, then so he would become a soldier.

As night reached its peak and began the slide down to dawn, so we slipped back into the core of our lives. We all shook hands with hearty satisfaction, like businessmen agreeing a deal. Walter and I walked slowly home allowing everyone to pass through. Rupert was the last, a deep cut shadow moving swiftly on his bicycle. We could both hear his familiar whistle, but he never made a sound.

Like so many times before, our day came to an end on the doorsteps of two modest and anonymous terraced houses in the farthest corner of England.

"We're going to be soldiers Private Parker,"

"Who are you calling Private?" I joked softly.

"Harry, what do you think war will be like, really?"

"I think it'll be everything you ever dreamed of Walter," I replied with half a wink.

"No, no I mean it. What do you really think it will be like?"

I leaned back against the windowsill and looked up at the roof-tops of the houses opposite.

"Well, I expect it will be…"

My voice tailed off as I felt the air change in the space beside me. I looked over my shoulder to see my mother standing in the doorway, still dressed, with a strong but ambiguous look on her face.

"Don't let me stop you Harry," she whispered firmly, "what do you think it will be like?"

I looked at her, and then at Walter, who in turn took a lingering glance at my mother. I suddenly felt an embarrassed heat rise through my chest and into my face. An imprecise tension had slipped out of our house and into the thick summer air.

"Go on," she urged, in a manner which made me feel scolded.

"It's late and we're disturbing you," Walter interjected, motioning towards his door. Mother reached smoothly across and caught his elbow. Walter stopped still, body half-turned towards his home. Both of them looked at me hard.

"Go on," she said again, slightly more softly.

My mother lowered herself down onto the front step and motioned for us to join her. From the pocket of her dress she produced a tin of woodbines, lit one and drew on it strongly. Like obedient dogs, we carefully took positions either side of her, our thighs bunched all together like six, long fingers.

“Well, I expect we will learn a great deal,” I stated brightly, feeling it was a good answer. My mother’s nod suggested that she agreed but I should continue.

“I think that we will come back as men; more intelligent, more cultured and more aware of the world. I think we will serve our country very well. Very well indeed.”

I studied the splitting fibres of my cuff for a while but no-one else spoke. When I turned to Walter and my mother they were both looking at me with distant, far-away expressions. Mother blinked a couple of times and then turned her head to look at Walter.

“Has my dear Harry answered your question Walter?”

“My question?”

“It was your question Walter, you asked him what war would be like didn’t you? Well now you know. Harry has answered your question hasn’t he?”

Walter looked lost. He tried to glance at me for some sense of grounding but my mother’s eyes drew him back like a dancing snake.

“I suppose so,” Walter said slowly and unconvincingly, clearly hoping this was the right answer. For an uncomfortably long time, we avoided my mother’s stare as though we had something to hide.

“Well that’s good! Excellent. I’m sure you’ll both make fine, fine soldiers. And Harry, your father *will* be pleased!” Mother chirped suddenly, popping to her feet like a schoolgirl and ripping a hole in the discomfort like a farmer snapping the neck of a dying bird.

She flicked the end of the woodbine across the street, kissed us both on the cheek and disappeared back into the house, closing the door very gently behind her. Like was often the case, my mother’s departure left a gap far greater than her body should command.

"Sometimes, your mother…" Walter began.

"I know," I replied, following her in.

*

Two days later, the nine of us donned our best suits and boarded a train for the short ride to Norwich. Nearly all of our employers had accepted our sudden departure with good grace, even enthusiasm, although the fishing community was a little irked that their boys weren't joining the Navy.

Our mornings had been a collection of goodbyes, some of them perfunctory and others affectionate but all of them weighty in one way or another. My mother's hug had been tight but cold, like an uncovered mattress. My father's handshake had been short and tidy, but his left hand had cupped my elbow with something approaching affection. We all felt a sense that this goodbye was more ceremonial than substantial, and we would ultimately be given another chance to get it right.

We disembarked onto a busy, bustling platform and as we walked to the recruiting office we saw many familiar and friendly faces. There was something of the expectant in all those faces; some stern, some joyful but all deeply aware that this was, of sorts, their moment.

The queue slowed our feet to a shuffle before we got within 50 yards of the front door. Some of the lads were jostling each other playfully and more than once a cap was ripped from a head and thrown across the road. A smart looking old soldier strode up and down the line, pointing at things absently with a cane. We all quietened and stilled as he passed us, and for a few moments we were back at school again.

"I hope they're not full up before we get to the front," Johnny said, craning his neck and roughly counting the heads he could see bobbing in front of us.

Within a few minutes there were as many men behind us as there were in front and little verses of song were bursting into the air. There was a terrific atmosphere, proud and excited, and we joked and japed our way to the front of the queue.

“You lads all together?” we were asked by a slightly overweight man sweating into a heavy grey suit. He counted us quickly with his pencil, scrawled some sort of record in his book and then waved us into the building. I bounced up the steps with the others, only to catch my toe at the top and drop heavily to one knee. High-spirited acclaim rang in my ears and, in an instant, hands were under my armpits and I was dragged into the room.

I hopped into the main hall, rubbing my knee with spitty fingers, and looked in awe at the bustling officials and controlled chaos. Old soldiers of the Norfolk Regiment stood all around, directing the fidgeting crowds and barking with half-baked venom at any lapses of concentration or order. We formed a tight and curious queue once more and waited our turns to be measured, questioned and evaluated.

Gordon’s face suddenly snapped round to us from the front of the queue. He motioned towards one corner where a doctor and soldier were talking sternly to a man of about thirty. The man was clearly distressed and eventually the portly soldier eased him out of the room with a combination of reassuring arm and instructional cane.

“Too short,” Gordon hissed back at us, his jaw made prominent by the clenching and unclenching of teeth. We tried to make reassuring noises to Gordon who, after Donald, was the shortest of our group. Frankly we couldn’t tell whether Gordon or Donald were taller than the man that had been sent away or not, it was too close to call, but before the issue could be discussed any further, Gordon was ushered to the table and his medical examination began.

The doctor listened to his heart and his lungs, asked him a few questions and peered at him with suspicion over the top of his glasses. Gordon kept trying to smile and appear relaxed but we all knew him too well to be fooled by that. The eight of us were transfixed as the doctor checked Gordon’s teeth and eyes before moving onto his weight and then, with the finest of attention, his height. The doctor removed his glasses and motioned once more to the portly old soldier. Our collective hearts fell and Gordon’s eyes opened broadly, pleading. There was a short discussion, during which time the soldier spoke and then studied the list he had in his book. A short question then prompted Gordon to point at us, almost one by one, and both old men nodded slowly. The old soldier then snapped his book closed, nodded to the doctor and walked away, leaving Gordon where he was. The doctor handed Gordon a small piece of paper and pointed him in the direction of another queue. Our friend's face returned to its normal colour and a smile grew beneath his moustache.

One by one, we moved from queue to queue. Rupert's rasping lungs and then Sid's eyesight detained the doctor for a few moments but in the end he seemed happy enough. Soon the nine of us were back together in a small side room. I watched my friends as they burbled excitedly about the various inspections and laughed heartily at the happy absurdity of the day. I stood to one side with Rupert.

"Were you worried for a while there, with your chest?" I asked him. He was watching the others when I spoke and he turned his face to me slowly. He was a picture of contentment, although he also seemed very, very tired. Rupert had doubts, we all knew that.

"My lungs are weak Harry," he replied, "and the doctor knows that very well."

"But he passed you?" I queried. Rupert nodded.

"He did, but he could also have sent me home."

"And you could have taken yourself home couldn't you?" Rupert's eyes fixed on mine.

"And leave you lot to look after yourselves? I don't think so my dear boy. I don't think so one little bit."

With that he grabbed my shoulder and shook me warmly. I hooked my arm over his elbow and we stood there for a while, our arms embracing, and watched our friends bounce around the room.

"You're deeply fond of Walter aren't you?" he said eventually as we watched Walter and Sid mimicking the old soldiers. The question affected me somewhat but I couldn't quite identify why. At that moment I saw Rupert in much clearer focus, like I had previously been viewing him through dirty glass. He had always been a quieter one of our party, quieter even than me, but I wondered then whether he had quite a lot that he could say, if he chose so to do.

"Of course," I replied, after what was probably too long a pause.

At that moment a couple of men entered the room through a door we hadn't noticed. A short cough brought us to attention and as one man introduced himself as the recruiting officer, the other handed us each a copy of the New Testament. We eyed the Bibles shyly and a couple of lads flicked through them as though they wanted to be reminded of the contents. The room fell silent.

"Take the book in your right hand," the recruiting officer began, his thick voice ringing around the room. There was a brief pause whilst nine young men checked they could remember their left from their right and then, slowly, nine Bibles were lifted into the air. We then repeated his words, finishing together, "...so help me God!"

We were invited to kiss the book, which we did. Walter laid his lips on the leather cover without flinching and as he did so he looked over to me and reached out to my right hand with his left. I took his fingers in mine for a moment and, in a manner more reminiscent of childhood than adulthood, we shook hands.

At that point of course we had expected to be given our uniforms and maybe even our rifles but we quickly learned that we would have no such fortune. We were handed a piece of paper to confirm our oaths and our battalion. We had joined the 7th Battalion of the Norfolk Regiment and, for whatever 'the duration' would be, we were soldiers.

We stepped out of the hall that hot August day and were surprised to see the sun already starting to cast long, tired shadows across the street. We had been in Norwich for many hours but our day was not quite over yet.

A younger and fitter looking officer corralled all the new recruits together into tight lines in the middle of the street. Passers-by were stopping and lining the pavements to watch this queer and impressive spectacle. When we were all grouped neatly enough, the officer cracked a few orders into the air and, with the older soldiers mingled among us for guidance, we marched erratically towards the station, spurred on by an enthusiastic reception from the expanding group of spectators.

It was quite a moment for us, and even without uniforms, our chests heaved proudly before us. Had Fritz been at the end of that street he would no doubt have got the very best that the Norfolk Regiment had to offer and between us we would have sent him scurrying back to Berlin in double-quick time. Waiting for us at the station was a train, breathing heavily with anticipation. We dropped upon it to be swept to an unknown depot; our first step on a long march to France. Almost as soon as we had found our corner in the carriage, the weight and length of the day landed upon us and we drifted into quiet, happy and sleepy reflection.

I sat with Walter on the way and we spoke about the day, the march to the station and our shared concerns for the diminutive Donald. We also talked about our parents and Hattie and Ruth.

"I think father was pleased," Walter said, "he mentioned something about his grandfather once nearly joining the Navy so I know he was listening."

"What did your mother say?" I asked him.

"She said she was very proud of me, but I'm not sure she meant it. She's been very…very dark lately Harry, like something is troubling her very deeply."

"I hadn't noticed," I replied quickly, hoping that such an observation would, in some way, be reassuring.

"When did you last see her?" Walter asked me.

I thought for a while and realised that it may easily have been weeks, possibly months. How easy it is to overlook people that were once so constant in your life. I changed the subject.

"You wait until Hattie sees you in the uniform! You are going to look like a very fine young man." I nudged him gently in the ribs. His smile returned and he shifted himself round in his seat to face me.

"That will be quite something won't it Harry? Do you think I may be able to get married in the uniform? Do you think that would be allowed?"

"I don't know."

"She's very excited for me Harry. A little nervous, of course, but on the whole she's nearly as excited as I am. We talked last week that maybe I could become an officer one day."

Walter spoke for a few more minutes. He gushed with enthusiasm about the war and the splendour it would bring into our lives, but mostly he gushed about his beautiful Hattie, her fast improving mother, the impending engagement and subsequent marriage. I found my eyes drifting over his shoulder and into the near distance. As the sun set behind me so all manner of burned orange shadows began to recline across the fields and between the trees. Every few miles a blanket of water would break into view and the sun's colour would leap back from it like fractured fire.

Whilst Walter took us onwards aboard his happy dreams, so my mind found the day before, and Ruth. Just as Walter had talked to Hattie about joining-up, so I had been to see Ruth. Her Aunt had been resting in bed and so we had sat in the garden, enjoying tea to the sound of the summer birds. For a long time we stayed quiet, allowing the sounds of an English summer to dress and dominate the air. Every so often, Ruth would look at me and, shielding her eyes from the sun, offer me a small, deliberate smile.

"I am very pleased to have you in my life Harry Parker," she said suddenly, catching me somewhat off-guard and unprepared.

In hindsight, I know it as one of the kindest things that has ever been said to me but at the time I didn't recognise it at all. I reached for a reply but nothing came to hand. As the seconds raced on so I realised that the gap between her words and my reply was becoming too large, vast, immense. And still I had said nothing. Just as the moment became unbearable, a large bumble bee drifted lazily across the table and onto my lap. I leapt to my feet, catching my knees heavily on the iron table and tossing many items of crockery onto both the tablecloth and the grass. In the confusion and repair that followed the moment was lost and the direction changed.

For the remainder of my stay Ruth seemed distracted and heavy with fatigue. We passed time, like a river passes beneath a bridge, but we neither marked it nor made it memorable.

Later, her Aunt returned to join us and as the afternoon became the evening so the elderly widow walked me to their front gate.

"Ruth tells me that you're joining the Regiment tomorrow."

She spoke politely yet with purpose, as was her way. I said that I was. With an appreciative nodding of the head, she closed the gate behind me and then leant on it with pale arms, once taut skin hanging grey at the elbows beneath gathered sleeves.

"You must go," she said dreamily, "but you must come home as well, you and the other lad. You must both come home when you're finished, that's very important for those of us that will be left behind."

"Sorry, which lad?" I asked.

"Walter."

"Of course," I replied before bidding her good day and heading home.

It was at that moment that I saw a little of the other reality of war. For Ruth, for Hattie, for our mothers, for Betty and even for Ruth's Aunt there would be something different to deal with. There would be the impotence of their sex and the ancient female burden of marking time until their men folk returned.

"...and maybe Ruth could be bridesmaid, wouldn't that be a fine thing? Harry? Harryyy?"

I drifted back into the train carriage slowly. Walter's face was beaming out at me.

“Sorry,” I managed eventually, “bit sleepy I suppose…” Walter smiled and patted me on the face.

“You rest then soldier,” he laughed, “you’ll need to save your energy for Fritz!”

I smiled back at him, closed my eyes and drifted away to erratic dreams and the safe, grey land of the semi-conscious. And there I stayed for some time until the high, plaintive shriek of brakes brought me back to a warm and crowded station platform, with my friends around me, just as it had all begun.

I thought later, much later, that no-one ever asked me what made us join up, what led us to the decision we made, what took us to that place on that special day. It was almost as though it didn’t need asking, it didn’t need to be talked about. It was just nature, like the chirping of the birds, the tides of the sea and the soft, warm sunshine bleeding away at the end of the day.

Chapter Nine

We spent a couple of days at a holding depot somewhere near Bury St Edmunds.

There we huddled together with hundreds of other men, all with their own storybook dreams of what lay ahead. Our excitement made us tolerant of the discomfort and chaos but we were all nonetheless delighted when it was our turn to ride buses and trains to the permanent camp at Colchester. There we found an enormous, swirling mass of men that moved with a purpose and understanding we couldn't yet share. Sounds bombarded us from every direction and distance; some human, some mechanical and some the pleading protestations of nature. The reality of our situation was coming home; we were backstage at the theatre of war.

At the centre of all this movement there sat vast communities of huts and tents, many of which already bore the stains, strains and signatures of their inhabitants. Each tent held five men so we split ourselves across two vacant abodes – Tommy, Rupert, Walter and I in one and the others next door. The beds were simple strips of wood covered with a thin mattress and a single blanket. They looked like they knew something that we didn't.

The pattern for our first few weeks at camp was set very quickly. Every morning we were woken early by the painful sound of a bugle and, after a decent enough breakfast, a fierce band of retired soldiers with voices like tree trunks would roar us to within an inch of utter physical collapse. We were all allocated to the same Company, which helped, but none of us were prepared for the relentless nature of the training and the constant burning sensation in our lungs and legs. Every day featured at least one long run, often more, and our instructors seemed able to find hills and obstacles in the most featureless of landscapes. We all did our best but Rupert and Gordon both found it particularly hard and they would often be chased home by the heel-snapping snarls of the veterans.

Any dreams we may have had of horses, rifles and gleaming bayonets soon seemed foolish. It was weeks before we saw anything that even resembled the paraphernalia of war. Instead our bodies became the army's weapon of choice.

So many times that first week I left my bedtime reading untouched, fell onto my wooden bed like it were the deepest of mattresses and slept until the scraping bugle would drag me back to life from many, many miles away. We were starting to move about like old men, folded into quarters by the tightening of virgin muscles. There could scarcely have ever been newer or greener recruits.

Harder even than the constant physical jerks were the parades and the inspections. We were forever being told how to stand, how to carry our heads, where to place our feet, hands and eyes. At the time, we simply couldn't piece the pains and inconveniences of those first weeks into the various jigsaw dreams we had of army life. They seemed so incongruous with what we felt we had promised when we took our oaths. Our instructors watched our development, if that's what it was, with knowing and arrogant smiles. They had, we would come to learn, seen it all before.

Each evening a new group would arrive and add to the ever-expanding population of this loosely contained field. To me it was one of the most amazing things, the sheer vastness of the situation and the seemingly never-ending supply of young men. As with any crowd, there was an energy and an elegance to its movement, like the intricate workings of a gargantuan grandfather clock, and occasionally it was possible to glimpse a little something of the whole. But mostly our lives were small, intimate and intense, staring as we were into the cog next door.

As you would expect with vast groups of men, the atmosphere was boisterous and brazen. I suppose that up until this point many of us had been a little sheltered by our small communities and to suddenly be thrust into this sprawling environment was shocking, exciting and raw. I'm afraid to say that our language quickly became that of the factory rather than the field and although I endeavoured to be careful, cursing simply soaked into our skin from the rich pools around us. Many of the men, including some of our small group, also blasphemed without care or implication, which I certainly did not, but it would have been churlish to take this too seriously. These were, after all, extraordinary times.

Very occasionally we would see a young woman in the camp and her presence would shoot through the men like a sickness bug. They would become like animals – preening, dancing and competing fiercely for her lukewarm and fleeting attention – but in the main, women were confined to the thousands of photographs trapped in pockets, wash bags and diaries. Some sisters, many mothers and countless sweethearts smiled loyally from within their confinement, with sharp white folds cutting across their chests and muddy fingerprints glazing their soft, pale skin. Hattie was one such sweetheart, pinned above Walter's bed, her unsmiling image looking down with the cool, refined dignity of a Duchess. She haunted us a little from there to be honest, her eyes rolling endlessly around the inside of the tent, watching, judging and, I always felt, disapproving. My small, modest picture of Ruth stayed hidden, just as I think she would have wanted, between the pages of *Robinson Crusoe.*

Hattie and Ruth, like all the other living mementos, would no doubt have been sharp with indignation had they seen some of the other photographs the men carried with them. I don't know where these pictures had come from and their ability to reproduce was staggering. Many of the women in these pictures were reclining but others were seated, standing and, in one example I saw, riding a bicycle. Some of the women wore hats and some wore smiles but none of them wore any clothes. In some instances wide waves of silk or cloth had been used to hide their more intimate of areas but many were simply as God had made them and only their husbands should see them. I remember one picture very, very clearly; a lady perhaps in her early twenties, draped across a neat pile of cushions. Her hands are behind her neck, gathering up all but a few strands of her light hair. Her pale skin falls down her body as though it were running milk, over her breasts, her hips, down her thighs, knees, shins, to her toes. She is slim but womanly and her eyes are locked in place, holding the gaze of every man that touches her. I imagined that they were green, like the rich tangled weeds of a pond. She was at once both beautiful and sad, perfect and flawed, complete and yet broken. Her happy tragedy stayed with me for a long, long time.

To everyone else it seemed these pictures were a great source of entertainment and in some instances currency, but it never sat right with me. To see the men with such a crude card in one hand and a picture of their dear mother in the other seemed an unmanageable equilibrium, like life was in danger of over-balancing and falling out of control.

*

We didn't really notice how we were changing, physically and mentally, until the evening the Peacock brothers drifted back into our lives. Their most recent stretch at sea had ended in late August but they had spent many weeks trying to convince recruiting officers that Donald was tall enough to be in the army. After a few fruitless attempts in Norwich, they heard that one particular recruiting officer in Kings Lynn could be persuaded to approve just about anyone – if the price was right. It cost them more than a week's pay but, in the end, Peter and Donald Peacock jumped off a train on our new doorstep and, with their usual brand of bumbling drama, raced to be with us again. Before we'd had a chance to welcome them properly they both stepped back to look at us, with expressions of surprise and awe.

"Look at you boys!" Peter said grandly, spreading his arms out wide.

"What?" Walter replied.

"You're...you're huge!" Peter laughed, grabbing at Tommy's arms and feeling the rough iron beneath his shirt.

In a few short weeks we had shed our youthful flesh and replaced it with armour of sorts. Our shoulders were wider and our necks thicker. We didn't all wear it well, indeed Rupert now cast the shadow of Frankenstein's monster, but we had nonetheless started to make our long-awaited metamorphosis from country boys into soldiers. Once we had noticed these changes, so we began to champion and review them at every turn. During a time of near constant novelty, our bodies took their turn as our source of fascination.

Peter and Donald caught up, slowly, as we continued our daily development. Before long, those things that had been so difficult to master became second nature and the miserable parts of soldiering became acceptable and bearable facts of life. We saluted when we were supposed to, and who we were supposed to. We stood upright, marching firmly and in time. We drove imitation and then real bayonets into sacks of fibre with constantly improving vigour and efficiency. We fired unloaded and then loaded rifles at still and then moving targets and, one fine day, the fragments of uniform came together into a full and throaty chorus of khaki.

We looked at each other like a teacher might look at her favourite class; proud, admiring and happy. And I was right about the uniform. It fitted me well, completely. I found a moment in a mirror and reflecting back I saw a man with more air in his lungs, more shape in his chin and more depth in his eyes. The army had taught me how to stand again and I felt taller. I was definitely taller.

"My God, what have you done with my Harry?" Walter's image cracked over my shoulder, wide with smile and warmth. I blushed with gusto.

"Look at you as well," I replied sheepishly, "look at you."

*

As the winter set in, so our training became less about drills and marches and more about the day-to-day realities of war. One of our oldest instructors, who we called Snowy on account of his uncontrollable white hair, took us to High Woods to help us prepare for the battlefields of France. Here, in a small clearing, he instructed us to dig a line of trenches.

"Well I don't know about being a soldier, but I'm going to be a bloody good gardener," Gordon complained as we worked, cutting into the hardening ground as best we could.

After a few hours we had completed a decent enough trench and began the job of reinforcing the sides and laying the duckboards. The work was difficult and the cursing terrific, most of which was aimed at Snowy who strutted around the wood with his hands clasped behind his back. When Corporal Harvey considered our work complete he presented the trench to the old soldier proudly. A short discussion followed before the Corporal returned and Snowy marched smartly off into the distance.

"Get comfortable men, we're staying the night," Corporal Harvey announced, betraying no obvious opinion on the matter. "We're to defend the trench and prepare for a possible attack." We exchanged sharp and unhappy expressions in respectful silence and waited for the descent of night.

"What's Old Snowy going to do, run at us with a broom?" Johnny joked over a reasonable supper.

"Are we allowed to bayonet him?" somebody else asked.

For all our tiredness and irritation, there was still a sense of excitement in the air as the night soaked in through the trees. In-between the hard and incessant training, small but definite pieces of soldiering were taking shape. It may have been a bland, anonymous wood in Essex and our enemy may have been a single, eccentric old man but it was nonetheless starting to feel real.

The darkness was certainly real enough and by midnight there was no natural light anywhere beneath the advancing trees. My turn on sentry duty came just after 2am. I crouched on the fire-step with my unloaded rifle, my eyes and ears desperately seeking something to track.

Every few seconds I would sense movement in the clearing, like black curtains being opened and closed, but I could never tie it down, never make it mean anything. Every shadow had its own shadow, and every tiny sound had a thousand echoes. To the others, gathered together in bundles all around me, there were only the soft sounds of uncomfortable sleep but to me, with their safety in my hands, there was a riot of roaring danger. At one point, I was convinced that I'd heard the surprised exclamation of metal on metal and my finger grew hot against the futile trigger. I stared harder and harder into the dark, pressing myself into the earth to feel it vibrate, to hear it talk to me, but it had nothing more to say.

My duty done, I took Tommy's warm gap in the huddle of men. Sleep came in thick, heavy and definite lumps, separated by wide periods of pressing pain and something approaching cold. Each time I came to consciousness the light was different. It was something that I sensed rather than saw and it marked my slow progress towards morning. Still no alarm, still no attack.

It was a hand on the shoulder that woke me, shaking me with short, sharp intent. From all around me dull packages unfurled into men, gained faces and then personalities. In the final gasps of night, we stood-to, shoulder-to-shoulder, bayonets fixed. We took turns to keep watch although I don't think any of us knew what we were watching for. Time went by and light began to silhouette the branches around us, but still there was no sign of Snowy or his Octogenarian army. Each minute brought more of the night's secrets to life, exposing them as phonies and phantoms.

"Corporal Harvey," Johnny hissed with urgency from the fire-step.

Our eyes shot to Johnny in a flash, our bodies beginning to bristle with anticipation. Corporal Harvey drew near and carefully looked out across our self-imposed No Man's Land. He drew his eyes away and dropped them to the floor of the trench before stealing another glance, and then another. We could do nothing but wait. Eventually Corporal Harvey stepped down from the step, rubbed his eyes hard with his fingers and said something quietly to himself.

"What did he say?" Peter whispered forward to Johnny.

"I think he said 'shit'," Johnny replied as Corporal Harvey bustled past us in great agitation.

"What's going on?" Walter asked, edging along the back wall of the trench. Johnny motioned his hand towards the fire-step. Walter clambered up and looked for himself. He repeated Corporal Harvey's routine before a huge, broad smile split across his face.

"Oh dear, oh dear, oh dear," he chuckled with embarrassment. "No wonder Harv is cursing, he's going to get roasted for this. Gentlemen, we've been had."

For the next thirty minutes, we took turns to look out and each time, in the rising light, we saw more of Snowy's work, more of his masterpiece.

Snowy was sitting just thirty yards from our trench on a straight-backed dining chair – one of six dining chairs to be precise. In front of him there was a large table laid with tablecloth, candlesticks, condiments and table settings for dinner. There was even a floral centrepiece of autumnal colour. It was utterly, incredibly and inexcusably immaculate.

“How on earth?” Sid wondered out loud.

When the light made the situation indisputable, a disconsolate Corporal Harvey clambered out of the trench and approached the table. We watched with morbid curiosity as, with barely a movement, Snowy invited the Corporal to be seated. I felt sure that, at any moment, a servant would arrive with the starters. As it was the two men, as far apart in stature as they were in years, spoke for some time, with little animation or emotion. When Corporal Harvey finally stood his chair was listing heavily, losing a leg into the damp earth. He scuttled back to us swiftly and hopped down into the trench.

“What the hell were you lot looking at last night?” he exclaimed, his face purple at the edges. “Do you see what he’s done out there? Do you? How the hell did you not notice that? For God’s sake men, he’s set up a sodding dinner party in our back garden. Jesus!”

He waddled away again in a fragile silence as dozens of tongues were bitten almost through. When he was finally out of earshot C Company all but fell about in the trench with laughter. We saw the seriousness of course but it was drowned by the absurdity. As we were to appreciate, accepting absurdity was also an important part of being a soldier.

After breakfast, not alas served at the table but in the mess tin, Snowy gathered us in the trench. Striding up and down the parapet he gave us a predictable but doubtless deserved lecture on the importance of observation and the various skills we would have to master to survive and thrive on the Western Front. He told us how much more we had to learn and how easy it would have been for him to kill every last one of us.

“What, with a soup spoon?” Sid replied with a tiny whisper to the once more stifled amusement of his old friends and his new comrades.

Chapter Ten

The war didn't end by Christmas and our break from training was short; just a few days snatched among muted festivities, but it was long enough for Walter to become engaged.

On Christmas Eve there was a party, an announcement and much rejoicing. Hattie's mother was gloriously centre stage and the happy couple were displayed in front of her many important friends. Walter wore his uniform and he was every inch Hattie's equal. Ruth and I hid ourselves among the commotion, feeling utterly watched and completely ignored in equal measure. Ruth stayed close, in a special way, and each time I looked at her, she turned a stony disposition into a shining waterfall of contentment.

Walter was immense, bursting from his uniform, and delighting all those that he met. The last few months had been so significant, so weighty, but it seemed to me that Walter had found where he belonged, with those people, polished, paraded and acclaimed. And I was beginning to wonder if I had also found somewhere that I belonged. I had thrived in the white heat of physical effort and in our cardboard scenes of war I had made quite a toy soldier. So many pieces were dropping into a shape, of sorts, and it made me pleased in a way that I struggled to express. It made me feel more complete.

We all wore our uniforms, of course, and we received such attention and affection that many of the boys wondered why they hadn't thought of joining up sooner. We were toasted alongside the King and the band played Auld Lang Syne in our honour. We were kissed by countless elderly ladies and one of Hattie's many Aunts acclaimed us as the pride of Norfolk. It was all a little overwhelming and for every handshake or kiss came twice as many questions about our departure to France. Everyone wanted to know when and where we were going but we still had no idea. For all our development we clearly still had so much to learn and the wild zephyrs of rumour brought only false hope and contradiction.

Walter and Hattie were to be married in the spring, or whenever his army commitments allowed. It was never said explicitly but the arrangement was like so many others being made by families across the country. Whatever it took, Hattie and Walter would be married before active service called.

I didn't see much of Walter that Christmas, and my time at home was quiet and subdued.

When I returned to Colchester my friends were buoyant, although a few hearts bled for sweethearts that first, bitter day of 1915. Within just a few hours everyone was back into the swing of camp life and by the end of the week there were fresh rumours of our departure to France. One such claim even had trains arriving that very night to take us to Dover but no trains arrived, not that night and not for many weeks to come.

Walter was the slowest to relax after the Christmas leave. He was clearly finding it hard to readjust to life without Hattie and his earlier excitement about the war had started to wear away to reveal a more thoughtful and questioning man beneath. Our infrequent free evenings were often spent catching up on sleep but one crisp, brutally cold night in February I found Walter outside, some yards from our tent. He was sitting on a large crate and, as casually as I could, I sat myself down next to him. He turned his head to acknowledge my arrival but didn't speak. I blew hard on my gloved hands and patted them together softly.

"The rumour is that we'll be in Boulogne by morning," I quipped.

"And in Berlin by the end of the week no doubt," he replied.

"You'll be married before any of that Walter."

"But then what?" Walter replied, "Then what happens?"

Walter didn't say anything else on the matter. We passed the time with a couple of woodbines and then the heavy veil of tiredness descended once more, leaving us almost unable to drag ourselves back to our beds.

As spring began to fight back against the frost, so our training moved onto more sophisticated matters. We were frequently finding ourselves in forms of combat against other Companies and, on more than one occasion, Battalions from the Suffolk Regiment. We were encouraged to be competitive and before long our intensity spilled over in to arguments and fist-fights. For the most part we avoided such petty conflicts but one afternoon after a bombing exercise Tommy was attacked by a couple of reprobates from A Company. Within a few seconds a veritable brawl had developed and when the scrap was eventually broken up there were a fair few bruises and punishments on each side. Although I didn't dare admit it, and I was scarcely proud of it, there was a sense of camaraderie about leaping to Tommy's defence. Perhaps this was always the way it was supposed to work, friends joining up together, fighting for each other and with each other. As individuals, as small groups, as Companies and as a Regiment we were becoming fighters and we were becoming impatient. We were nearly ready.

*

It started as a rumour like any other, a whisper overheard from a vague conversation possibly had between two unnamed officers at a time and place no-one could confirm. At first it appeared to be just the background noise to another day but the rumour wouldn't go away and, after a week or so, it became clear that something definite was brewing. Then, in the second week of May, came the announcement we had all been imagining for nine months. We would be travelling to France on 31st May. We were going to war.

We were granted two weeks leave to make the necessary arrangements, although many of us had no idea what arrangements they had in mind. Walter didn't wonder though, for he had wedding plans. For the first few days of this strange fortnight, I barely saw Walter. He flitted infrequently into my life and more often than not he was just passing between errands, between thoughts and between happy, ill-formed dreams.

Ruth and I were together often, enjoying the bold spring weather and avoiding all but the most trivial issues and topics. I also passed a lot of time at home, running my fingers along long-ignored bric-a-brac like a man that had fallen blind. Betty was well-established in the hospital kitchens by this point and I spent many long hours sitting reading alone in the front room whilst my mother busied herself around our small home. On the mantelpiece the clock that had been my great-grandfather's nagged away at me; steady, consistent and unshakable.

“I was nearly thirty hours in labour Harold; did I ever tell you that?” My mother said to me late one afternoon in that first week. It had been more than fifteen years since she had called me Harold.

I pressed the palm of my hand hard on to the open pages of my book and looked at her. My mother had many tones to her voice, some safe, some dangerous and others mysterious. This one was not to be treated lightly.

“I am certain that you did not.”

“In the back bedroom at Grandma’s house. I walked across that floor maybe ten thousand times, listening to the noise the floorboards made under my feet. It got light and then dark and then light again. It was freezing outside but that little room was roasting. Grandma would come in occasionally and tend the fire, bring me tea and endless plates of toast, smeared with her homemade plum jam. God I hated that stuff. And I read, book after book after book. Just to be anywhere other than where I was.”

Mother slid herself over the arm of a chair and into the cushions, her hair spilling over from the careless attention of a handful of pins. Her eyes were fixed into the mid-distance, dreamy and unseeing.

“Wuthering Heights was my favourite. I can’t say how many times I read it during my childhood and when I was Betty’s age. How many times I woke to the half-dreamed sounds of Catherine at the window, how many times I imagined a desperate Heathcliff hammering through the fields near our house. I read it time and time again in that tight, hot room; even when Cathy is born and Catherine dies, I read it all, over and over and over again. Hour after hour after hour. Until, eventually, you came.”

I smiled weakly, out of duty rather than happiness. My mother didn’t smile back, she just kept staring into nowhere with hypnotising intensity. I felt sure that there was something I should say but I had no idea what it should be.

“Doctor Lavender came of course but he didn’t stay for long. No-one did really, not even your father.”

“But he was pleased wasn’t he?” I asked quickly. Mother snapped out of her trance and turned her silver-grey eyes onto me.

"Of course Harry, of course he was. It was just what he wanted. You were his gift from God Harry, his affirmation, his approval. You were his proof."

"Proof? What does that mean?" I asked, feeling a warmth in my chest, like tea swallowed too quickly. Mother's eyes threatened to glaze again. "Mother?" I asked sharply.

"Nothing, never mind. I didn't mean it that way."

"What way?"

"The way it sounded."

"How *did* it sound?" I asked, shifting forward in my seat. Mother's face changed subtly, like it was caught in a sudden breeze. She opened her mouth to reply but her words were lost beneath a sharp rapping on the front door. A glorious and delighted Walter had arrived with fresh duties for his best man and an electric impulse that reignited my mother like a discarded, smouldering coal.

*

My parents didn't take alcohol.

Father always said that he had seen too much of its 'bitter sting' to be attracted to even a simple wine whereas my mother side-stepped it more furtively, carefully, and kept her reasons to herself. Personally, although I had known the occasional glass at parties, I had never seen it as having anything more than a medicinal role, easing a heavy cold or the claustrophobic compulsion of introductions and small talk.

We sometimes got a tot of rum in Colchester, but only when the cold was particularly crippling. It would always be taken quickly, forcing a thick block of heat down the throat, across the chest and then into the guts. Some men would find their way to some sort of oblivion by claiming additional shares but their demeanour the following day served as a stark warning to everyone else.

I had therefore, never been drunk. Not, that was, until Friday 28th May 1915 – the day Walter and Hattie were married. The sumptuous party at

Hattie's copious and manicured home was out of kilter with the tone of the period but even her most exquisite planning couldn't control the weather. It rained steadily all day, with the sort of dogged determination that made you wonder if it really was bad luck to be married in May.

According to the local paper, Hattie's dress was of a 'cream silk' and everyone said she looked stunning. Walter wore his uniform, as we all did. A picture was taken of the eleven of us together, in our uniforms, but I can't remember ever seeing it.

My memories of the service itself are unstable and threadbare. I performed all my best man duties carefully and solemnly and I can still picture the look on Walter's face. Happiness, certainly, but also unquestioning and committed. A look of almost stupid contentment. Other than that I remember the damp odour of the church and the sound of the rain beating away at the windows. Looking to the ceiling I even thought I could see the heavy, all-conquering clouds gathering with menace beneath the eaves.

I wasn't the only one to enjoy the wine at dinner but no-one else seemed to be so affected, so moved. As the evening progressed, the dancing became more jovial and the music louder. At this point, my memories dip in and out of focus, like salmon in a stream.

I can remember Ruth being there, of course. I remember that I thought her beautiful, but also strangely inane. I remember that I told her that we would soon be married. I remember laying my hand on her hip and I remember that she shrugged me off like a damp shawl. And I remember that, throughout the day, her face never changed. It was as though she didn't hear a single word that anyone said. It was as though none of them were even there or, perhaps, she wasn't.

Many people were fascinated when I told them about our camp and I seem to recall answering numerous questions about our drills, training and plans. I also told them about how I had thrived and how I felt sure that I would spend my life being a soldier, travelling the world. I then remember Tommy and Johnny telling me to stop, which annoyed me I think and I seem to recall that we exchanged strong words. I don't know why they told me to stop my anecdotes but at the time I was almost sure that they were jealous of the attention that I was getting.

There was definitely a conversation with my father at one point, who seemed very agitated. I told him that his nostrils were flaring when he spoke and he became angry. He told me that he had been worried that this would happen, that he blamed my mother for my 'schoolboy fantasies' and that the sooner I went to war the better. He was halfway through a sermon of some description when Hattie's mother came over, all jewellery and happiness. Father slipped effortlessly into sparkling banalities and I slipped away.

The married Walter moved around the room as though he were on wheels, effortlessly bringing small periods of charm into the lives of his doting guests. Occasionally I felt the flap of his wings as he rushed past. I can vaguely remember grabbing his arm. His face met me with warmth and happiness, yet it quickly faded and fell. He asked me if I was drunk, over and over again. He asked me if I was all right, over and over again. I can still picture his face as a jumble of wavy lines, like a children's game. I think I was a confusion to him, a question, a doubt. That felt good I recall, knowing that I still had the power to affect his life in such a way, to continue to be influential, important.

The other things I remember are isolated and small, memories so fine that they might fall down the back of an armchair. I remember those guests that, at Christmas, had lauded and demanded our departure for France were quieter, more hidden, as though their simple naivety had started to bear heavily on their shoulders. The back-slaps remained but they were gentler, more considered, with more weight and more feeling. Talk of war was no longer the swollen gossip of a community. It lived only behind hands, in quiet corners and across those small, smoky tables that our fathers had made their own. Already, there were people for whom the war had become personal, tragic and very real. There was nothing idle about the tales, no thrilled speculation, no effervescent dreams. One by one, they were learning that war wasn't about the winners and the losers, it was about the sad, broken and bewildered mess in-between.

I remember the smell of the curtains, the light catching Johnny's forehead, the feel of the lace at the cuff of Ruth's dress and the sound my nails made as they scraped up and down the fabric on my thighs. I remember the lights, dancing and rolling in a reflection of the revellers beneath. I remember the feel of Rupert's hand in the small of my back, supporting. I remember the noise, but not the sounds. I remember moving very slowly, the sense that my head was filled with water and the nagging, persistent fear that I would cry. I don't remember having that much to drink and, to an extent, I don't really remember being drunk. I just remember that someone pulled apart the jigsaw of my life and forced it back together in the wrong order; uncomfortable, ill-fitting and utterly unrecognisable.

The party still had life when I departed, hooked onto mother's arm like an over-filled shopping basket. We walked slowly and quietly along well-worn paths, familiar even in the damp night. As we walked, mother pulled at flowers, leaves and long pieces of grass and worked them in her hands until they crumbled and fell to the floor. Every few steps she lifted her hands to her face to enjoy the rich, fresh mix of smells she had made.

In the cool, damp air I began to unravel a little and, for the first time, felt a genuine sense of fear about what was to come. I stared rigidly ahead as, all around me, the shimmer of bayonets threatened in the midnight. Things moved, changed shaped, became threatening and dangerous. Sweat beaded on my forehead and then ran, crazily, down my face and neck, into the collar of my uniform and across the plains of my back. My breathing suddenly became complicated and I could see the outline of my pounding heart climbing through my ribs.

As we neared home, so I found myself praying desperately to be a child again. To be racing through innocent and uncluttered streets. To be bowling over after fruitless over at a young, glorious Walter and to be chasing him through the fields, gold forever beneath a cloudless, azure sky. To be hunting for biscuits with Betty. To be singing in church on Christmas Eve. To be chewing pencils in school lessons. To be playing soldiers.

As we reached our street, mother tucked herself tighter into my flank as though suddenly cold. She nestled her head into my neck and a happy, familiar scent filled my mind. Flowers, baking, soap, Betty and the slightest hint of kissed skin. The smell of my mother and of my childhood. The unsurpassable, irreplaceable smell of belonging, of loving, and of home.

My mother moved to the front door and opened it wide. She stood herself on tiptoes, took my face in her hands and kissed me on the lips. She moved back to look at me, tears scratched into the bottom half of her eyes and then kissed me again. She dropped her forehead heavily against mine and whispered straight into my mouth.

"Harry…my precious, darling Harry. My beautiful, precious boys."

We stayed there for a few moments, our heads pressed together, until rain started to fall again with cold, heavy intent. Mother kissed me once more, on the cheek this time, and disappeared into the house. I waited a moment, allowing the rain to rinse the sweat from my face and hair, appreciating the taste of nature dripping into the corners of my mouth. In spite of the alcohol, the emotion of the day, the disorientating darkness and the ugly weather, in spite of everything, I realised what had just happened. A mother had just said goodbye to her son.

*

It had been Tommy's idea to return to Dead Cat Tree.

The day before our crossing we gathered in the leaf-filtered wet sunshine of the afternoon, with that old tree to our backs, to eat a picnic, smoke woodbines and bring to an end that part of our lives which happened before we went to war.

Before meeting the boys, I made one final trip to see Ruth. I hadn't seen her since the wedding but if my drunken failings had affronted her in any way, she didn't make it known. We walked for a while through the fields near her home and whilst she knew the dangers that lay ahead for me, she spoke confidently and openly about the future. Indeed, as my anxiety had developed in recent days so it appeared that Ruth's had faded and she spoke dreamily at times about weddings, new homes and even children. I was happy to hear her talk in this fashion although I found it difficult to throw myself fully into her enthusiastic stride. My mind had slipped onto the battlefields of France by this point and my future lay there. Beyond the war, I simply couldn't say.

Being with Ruth made me think of my mother and her courtship with father. I had asked her once what it felt like when she knew that she wanted to marry my father. She paused for a while and then said, "appropriate". At the time I was left, as was often the case when speaking to mother, both fascinated and bemused, but in recent weeks I had felt that my relationship with Ruth could also be described as 'appropriate' and every day that word seemed to mean something different to me. Sometimes it made me happy, sometimes it made me sad and sometimes it made me downright angry.

As we arrived back at her garden gate, Ruth embraced me with sincere affection. We held each other for a few moments before, tilting her head backwards and closing her eyes, she allowed me to kiss her softly on the lips. At the end of the kiss we both looked away, unsure as to what should come next. I took her hands and shook them gently as though I were holding the reins of a horse.

"I will see you soon Ruth," I said, earnestly looking into her pretty eyes. She nodded purposefully.

"And I will see you soon Walter."

My friend's name curled into the air like a ribbon of smoke, weaved in-between our bodies and then gathered in a cloud above our heads. I watched great roses of colour gather in Ruth's cheeks and her mouth opened and closed quickly like a dying fish. I tried to retain my expression but I could feel various fibres in my face betraying me; contracting, twisting, fighting for attention. I dropped her hands from mine and they flopped pathetically against her sides. She looked as though she may cry.

For a moment I felt as though my body had vanished and I was just a head, floating in the air without substance or support. The first sensation to return was in my legs, which began to twitch and jerk with a barely suppressed desire to run. Then my stomach returned, swilling with burning metal and I felt my mouth; dry, empty and impotent. Ruth seemed desperate to react, to do something to change what had happened but she didn't, she couldn't.

I lifted the brim of my cap softly and stepped away. I heard her make a small sound of protest as I departed but when I looked back over my shoulder a few yards later she was gone. I walked swiftly to Dead Cat Tree, almost marching, with four words and one sinking realisation parading around my head.

'She called me Walter...'

I was early, and at first it seemed as though I had Dead Cat Tree all to myself. But as I ducked my head beneath the branches and stepped into the clearing, I could see the sharp colour of a lit woodbine peeking through the shade. At the other end of the woodbine stood my finest, my oldest and my very best friend. My Walter.

I was about ten yards away when he saw me. He raised his eyebrows in half a smile and extended the woodbine out towards me between two fingers and a thumb. Instinctively I took it, and I was immediately annoyed at myself for doing so. Walter slid his way down the tree and sat at the bottom, his jacket riding up his back and his knees gathered too closely to his chest. He shuffled a little until he was comfortable. I looked at him through narrow eyes, finished the woodbine and flicked it to the floor. I waited for him to acknowledge my stance, my irritation. I waited for him to ask what was wrong, but he didn't.

"For so long Harry I was thrilled by the idea of going to war. I really wanted to fight. I really wanted to but…I'm sorry to say that now I'd rather it all ended tomorrow. All things considered, I'd really rather stay here." He lifted his head towards me, "Don't tell the others though, will you? Please."

"This is our adventure Walter," I told him, my voice wooden and lifeless. "This is all we ever dreamed of."

"I know, I know. But things are different now."

"You don't need to remind me of that."

"I don't want to leave Hattie. Oh Harry, what would happen if I were killed."

“Oh I imagine there would be some sort of statue,” I replied instantly, an energy of sorts flowing into me. Walter peered up at me as though he had reading glasses balanced on the end of his nose.

“What’s *that* supposed to mean?” he asked, with a little menace.

“You’re a very popular young man Walter,” I stated, making it sound like failing. Walter shielded his eyes against a rod of sunshine and looked at me more closely.

“What’s the matter with you Harry?” There was a gram of concern in his voice but it was mostly an accusation, a poke in the ribs.

“Nothing’s wrong with me, you’re the one that’s suddenly turned coward.”

Walter’s face flashed with a mixed expression of surprise and anger. I was hurting him and I’m ashamed to say it felt good.

“I’m no coward Harry, you know that. Why would you say that? It’s not about that.”

For a second an image flashed into my head from our childhood; Walter marching back down the hill to this very spot, on the day Dead Cat Tree got its name. A deep swell of nostalgia hit me but I suppressed it fiercely.

“My Walter wasn’t a coward, not at all. But of course you’re not *my* Walter anymore.”

“Harry, you’re starting to scare me now. You’re not…you’re not *drunk* again are you?”

“Of course I’m not bloody drunk.”

“Well you sound it, you’re talking nonsense.”

“That’s rich coming from you. What are we now, a Conchie?”

“Oh grow up Harry.”

“Fuck off.”

"Nice Harry, very nice. You really are ready to be soldier aren't you?"

"Yes damn it I am and I'm proud of it too. You should be ashamed talking the way you are."

I don't know at which point Walter had got to his feet, but he had. He seemed calmer than me, but his fists were balled tightly. We were close by this point, just a few feet apart and I suddenly felt a lot taller than him. But there was also something else, a nagging sense of role reversal.

"I've just got a bit more in my life now," he poked at me with his words.

"More than who? You're not better than me!"

"I didn't say I was. Anyway, a few minutes ago they were going to build me a statue."

When the raised voices stopped there was one of those special silences that you only hear after too much noise. A couple of birds spoke into the gap.

"Look Harry," Walter started softly, "it's only natural that you should feel a little jealous…"

"JEALOUS?!" I screamed, bouncing forward towards him, "what on earth have I got to be jealous about?" Walter looked a little scared.

"I'm a married man now and Hattie's really special…"

"So is Ruth!"

Walter scoffed in my face and I suddenly realised that at some point soon I was going to hit him.

"Ah yes of course, Ruth. Has she let you kiss her yet Harry?"

"Yes she has…but that's none of your business. Anyway, Ruth is worth ten Hatties. I've never known what you see in her to be honest. I've never said anything before now but I'm not having this. She's utterly self-obsessed, dim-witted and fatter than her horse."

At this point I felt a puff of air pass by my ear and a fist land firmly on the side of my head. I was knocked to one knee but bounced up instantly and charged at him, driving my shoulder into his midriff. His frame bent over my back and I threw him into the tree. His body made a soft thud as it impacted followed by a solid knock as his head hit the bark. We both ended up on the floor and I thudded the side of my fists repeatedly into his chest, tearing at his shirt. He pushed a free hand under my chin and prised me off. His feet swung into me and I retaliated with my knees into his thighs. He scrambled to his feet and punched me hard on the side of the face. I felt my jaw move, grating my teeth into each other. There was blood in my mouth. I cracked him on the shin with my elbow – once, twice and then again until he stepped away and allowed me up. As soon as I was free I aimed a huge punch at his head, missing wildly and banging my forearm into his neck. He stumbled and as he fell I drove my foot into his ribs. I stamped on his arm and, with teeth clenched in fury I fell upon him, pinning his body beneath my thighs. He writhed beneath me, twisting desperately. I grabbed his wrists and held them high above his head. I flicked my heels into his side and twisted his hands until he screamed out in pain. I released one hand and raised my fist high above his head. He drew his free arm across his face and cowered beneath me. Three times I began that punch but I never finished it. He looked at me through the crook in his arm and, half-hidden, he could have been a child again. I dropped my head and rolled myself onto the floor.

We lay there for a few moments, breathing hard, staring towards the obstructed sky. There was blood on my lips and a deep sense of futility in my heart.

"I'm scared Harry." Walter spoke softly and carefully, as though he had something unexpected in his mouth. Tears balled heavily in my eyes.

"I know you are," I replied, feeling like an absolute beast.

I straightened my body and, reaching out, eased my arm under his head and encouraged it onto my shoulder. We kept our faces apart and cried as silently as we could. I can't be sure how long we lay there, but it was long enough for the sunlight to change shape in the canopy and for me to forget today, remember yesterday and think about tomorrow.

“I do want to have our adventure Harry, really I do.”

“And what an adventure it will be, how they will love us in France,” Walter nodded his head enthusiastically into my arm-pit.

“Hattie will be fine,” Walter said to himself. “And after the war there will be…”

“...ever after,” I finished.

By the time Rupert and Tommy arrived, laden with picnic baskets, Walter and I were leaning against the tree, three woodbines away from the fight I thought we’d never have. Rupert was phlegmatically resigned and Tommy was haunted by leaving his unhappy little sister but, in the kindness of our shared company, we all stepped clear of our troubled paths and moved into the collective light.

Within the hour we were an eleven once more. Sid produced a knife from his pocket and as final family meals beckoned, we chipped our initials into the tree – neatly, cleanly and permanently. But not before we had all performed the ritual jump from the crooked branch. Walter first, me last, and everyone else in-between.

We emerged from the copse with a fruity light behind us and long shadows in front. We walked slowly away, hands in pockets, kicking absently at chuckling grasses and loose earth. It could have been any day from the last decade but it wasn’t. It was that day, the day before we went to war.

“We’ll always do this won’t we?” Gordon asked as we walked away.

“Of course we will,” someone replied. “Always.”

Chapter Eleven

Walter's mother had lived in France for a while when she was a child and I had always imagined that the vibrancy of her art had been cultivated there, amidst colours brighter, bolder and more outrageous than we knew at home.

My mother had taught me that France was about Paris, music, mystery and that edgy, hedonistic sense of a life more lived. I dreamed of visiting Paris one day and sampling this more cultured world. The thought thrilled and intimidated me in equal measure and I hoped that my first visit to France would be long, leisurely and indulgent. My mother would come to visit me and I would show her all the finest galleries and patisseries and when I eventually returned to England I would be a man that had known the world.

As it turned out of course, my relationship with France began not on the Champs-Élysées but in Boulogne where we docked after the short, heavily reflective journey across the channel. Our first sight on disembarking was of a very familiar canvas world. The rows and rows of tents we had vacated in Colchester seemed so modest in comparison to what appeared on the horizon as we approached French soil. We had left a tented village and arrived in a tented city. For me, there was nothing French about this world, nothing Gallic, nothing foreign. To all intents and purposes we had not moved from one country to another, but from the edges of a war to the middle of it.

Just a few hours earlier we had taken our final, ceremonial march through Norwich. The streets had been packed and it had been difficult to maintain our new military bearing whilst also dutifully scanning the fascinated flock for friendly, loving eyes. Father was there and I held his gaze for a time, watching his hands pump firmly together in appreciation. There was something in his face that I couldn't quite decipher – it may have been pride, it may have been relief. Just as we reached the station there was a slapping of petite feet and Tommy's sister was suddenly swinging from his neck, all kisses, flowers and tears. We laughed, cooed and whistled as she was lifted softly away. As we disembarked in France I noticed that Tommy still had thin, petal fingers laced through his hair, like tiny memories of home.

Many of us, myself included, rather expected that we would step off the boat and stride straight into the front line. Indeed some of the men had been mentally preparing for this to be the case and when it became clear that we would be fighting guy ropes and tent pegs rather than Germans, there was an almost palpable sense of frustration and ire. Over the days that followed those feelings were nurtured and refined in drills, jerks and practices. We were pushed further and harder than had ever been the case in England and once again our minds and bodies responded with fatigue, failure and eventually acceptance.

But it wasn't the same. This wasn't a jolly outing to the Essex coast. This was war, and everywhere we looked we could see its fragmented legacy. Like the wounded men who moved slowly through our ranks, re-tracing their filthy steps back to Blighty, and the shining shells that raced in the opposite direction to return the misery in kind.

I threw myself into the training, almost wrecklessly, in a barely conscious attempt to stop my mind from exploring that last, sorry exchange with Ruth. I was curt with Walter for a while, but the absurdity of it all was too strong and soon the only animosity I retained was directed back home and even that was thin and frayed. There was just too much life dropping into the palms of my hands to consider what was beneath my nails.

I shall never forget that moment when, as we rested between exhausting drills, we first saw a group of those wounded men scratching their way back to the port. There were about a dozen of them, and they carried their proud bounty of war around limbs and heads. There is no question that in those few, frozen seconds, as we looked into that warped mirror, we shared a moment that was pure pity. They saw our pity for them and disregarded it. We saw their pity for us and didn't recognise it.

We didn't look at the stretcher cases, but we knew that many of those men would not survive to see England again and that others were going home less of men than they had been when they arrived. But for all the crumpled heaps beneath mottled blankets, it was the men that walked in darkness that upset us the most. Individuals usually, but sometimes groups of men, hooked together like a caterpillar, with bandages bound tight across useless eyes. Sometimes it was shrapnel, sometimes it was gas and as we watched those men begin their journey home we shared a single, silent, shameful thought – *better off dead.*

Then there were the graves, the final resting places for those sad fellows who had expired at the very last, just a few sailing miles from home. There weren't that many, a few dozen at the most, but there was no hiding from them. Early on, it was hard to get them out of your mind but after a while they became an accepted fixture of a background that changed constantly and erratically. Only when a fresh pile of earth appeared did we feel that vague sense of foreboding, like the war was closing in on us before we could close in on it.

We'd been in France for a few weeks when, in the middle of the night, we were roused and told to prepare to move. Our equipment had become vast and varied and our fully-laden weight was substantial. We dragged ourselves aboard filthy trains and then, bizarrely, what appeared to be belching London buses. We travelled through the long stretches of dawn and onwards into the heart of the day. Having been shaken to distraction by the bus ride we were grateful to be thrown back to our feet and asked to carry ourselves once more, on and on through faceless France. After a while, it became necessary to think about the marching, such was the fatigue. I felt myself having to count my steps, watching my feet land and lift, land and lift. It was an almost dream-like state; a haunted, shapeless cocoon that left me oblivious to all but the most pressing of sensations.

It wasn't me that first noticed the noise. I'm not entirely sure who it was, maybe Sid, maybe Peter, but someone ahead of me twitched and then turned, cocking their ear to the night air. One by one, we lifted ourselves out of our living slumber and sharpened our senses. Nothing for a few paces and then possibly something. More steps, more noises; some nearby and some distant, and then definitely something. A few more paces and then a clear, unequivocal sound. The sound of guns. Huge guns, making huge sounds, rolling across miles and miles of flat, French countryside before arriving softly to the tired ears of tired men. Back then, there was a strangeness to the sound, like it was being made by something of another world. In time, we would learn how it was made, why it was made and what it meant but if I'm honest, I never stopped finding it strange.

We were finally allowed to rest deep into the night of the second day, falling immediately to sleep in one of the hundreds of barns that littered our painful journey. Scores of men, draped, lumped and curled together and not a single dream between them.

Rupert shifted beneath me and my head fell from his shoulder, clipped a trenching tool and hit the straw. My eyes shot open but it was a few seconds before I woke. I lay there, listening to the morning separate from the night. Walter was asleep on my thigh, the dawn breeze rippling through his fringe. His hair, which was once almost white, had become permanently dull, dirty and unkempt. Back home, where he belonged, Walter was still beautiful and young but in Colchester and in France he was ageing faster than any of us. He was changing. He retained an elegance, a grace, but his movements were more reserved and considered, like a retired racehorse. He looked like a man that had already known the best of his life and his fatigue was different from ours. He wasn't just tired of marching or tired of digging. He wasn't just tired of the orders or the discomfort. He was tired of everything; tired of life.

I thought back to the Walter I'd fought with at Dead Cat Tree. I thought of his apparent composure, arrogance even, but the fragility he'd exposed when I scratched at him. Back then he still yearned for life, life with Hattie and their golden future, yet now it seemed that he didn't yearn for anything, the sad turbulence of France had shaken him to the very core. That deep, unwelcome sense of pity gathered in the air again.

Our breakfast was surprisingly leisurely and we made the most of it, drowning ourselves in weak tea, chewing our way through fistfuls of dry bread and devouring small lumps of fatty bacon. All around us were other young men, other groups of friends coming to terms with the seismic shift in their lives. We eyed them suspiciously, watching some of the louder characters balloon in front of their growing audience. Had it not been for Hattie then I'm sure one of those balloons would have been Walter, bobbing in the morning air, floating around us, the string that tethered him to the ground running through my fingers. But Hattie's Walter was different.

Dawn spread into morning over a broken land. In-between the dull normality of Northern France there were blotches of war splitting through the surface; broken machinery, discarded supplies and abandoned tracks. There were no guns to be heard that pretty morning, but the tension crackling in the air was arguably louder, more intrusive. We'd been backstage, we'd been in the wings, and our next move was going to take us right out beneath the lights. The war of storybooks and films was paling beneath a bright, scratching reality.

Back in the training camp we'd seen wounds from a safe, sanitised distance beneath a muslin blanket of protection and modesty, but that security had long since been taken away and the blood we saw as we approached the trenches was warm, thick and glistening in the sunlight. The graves were more frequent and more hastily arranged and the smooth, curved shell holes were strewn with lives ended and bodies broken.

It's hard to describe how we felt in those final hours. There was a touch of thrill, certainly, but moreover there was a sense of boundless desperation. My breath came in short, incomplete gasps and my whole body was coated in a cold, clinging sweat. So many times I closed my eyes to fight back an urge to vomit and each time it came closer, gathering in my throat and mouth. I kept my face forward, not wishing to look at any of my friends, but I could hear their soft, sad reactions escaping from tight mouths.

We passed the scattered remains of a wagon and, in a few steps, we nearly stumbled over the bloated and broken body of a large horse, split down the middle like an over-stuffed cushion.

"Jesus..." breathed someone to my right.

A few steps more and the human victims of the direct hit began to appear, pressed into the earth amidst strips of uniform and equipment. A couple of unhappy looking souls were moving nervously among the remains, like young boys avoiding nettles. With careful deference they brought their lost comrades back together, piece-by-piece, into small, bloodied sacks, bulging meekly. And then there was the smell; that smell.

"They wouldn't have known a thing about it Don..." Peter said in front of me, turning his head to his brother in an unusual show of affection. Donald kept his eyes forward, fixed.

We were no longer marching, not in the way we had been so religiously taught. Such was the traffic flow on this once simple country lane. Supplies were grinding along in vast, winding columns and men found space where they could. For long periods we would be still, waiting for some unseen blockage to be removed or relieved.

"Messy, this war business isn't it?" Rupert said sadly as he arrived at my shoulder. His face was tired and flabby, his breath furious.

"Not the place for dodgy lungs," I replied, surprised to hear a smile in my voice. Then Tommy was suddenly behind me, scraping too many different shades of mud from battered boots. He was smiling broadly and so was Sid. Terry, just behind them, was chuckling with real feeling.

"What?" I asked them.

It was at that point that Gordon appeared, mud layered down the front of his tunic in thick fingers. I shook my head in disbelief, a wave of something near happiness climbing through me like a warm fire on a winter's day.

"What happened?" I asked him as the queue ahead of us began to break.

"Just stepped out for a piss. Fell in a fucking shell hole or something. These bastards just laughed."

How we laughed at that. That typical, truculent moment of happy friendship. That slither of normality in a carnival of the incredible, the horrendous and the absurd. That echo of our beloved homes.

Within an hour we had reached the outskirts of Carnoy, just a few hundred yards behind the line. The roaring guns we had heard on our approach were silent and we were surprised by the calm organisation. We were given simple, time-consuming tasks to pass the evening knowing that, come nightfall, we would be going into the line.

Walter and I were left to sort huge piles of discarded uniforms. We tried not to think too much about how they came to be there. In the quiet normality of a simple task, the tension in my bones began to ease.

“You’ve been really quiet these last few hours,” I said after a handful of monotonous minutes. Walter made a short sound of acknowledgement but said nothing else. “I’m trying not to think too much about any of it,” I continued. “It’s not quite how I imagined it.”

“Aren’t you *scared?*” Walter asked, looking up at me suddenly and incredulously.

“Of course I am.”

“But you seem so in control. I expected…” Walter tailed off but I knew where he was going.

“You expected me to be in pieces didn’t you?”

“Not in pieces but…”

“If I’m honest, so did I, but…I don’t know. I guess you can only be so scared for so long and then it all just gets…blurred.”

“But all those bodies; all those poor, poor boys. That could easily be you, easily. One moment you’re folding trousers and then gone. Gone.” He shuddered so violently that he had to move his feet to keep his balance. I nodded and closed my eyes as a wave of fatigue crashed against me.

“Walter, we knew people were dying.”

“Yes, but not…not like *that.*”

“Look, there are 11 of us. We’ve just got to watch our backs that’s all. When we get in those trenches and get a shot or two off at Fritz we’ll be fine. I’m sure we will.”

“You’ve changed Harry. You’ve really grown up.”

“So have you…” I began unconvincingly. Walter shook his head.

“No Harry, I’ve grown old.”

“Don’t be daft…”

“I have. I don’t know what has happened to me but I just feel so old, so FUCKING TIRED,” he shouted the last two words, causing some of the old hands nearby to scoff behind stumpy cigarettes.

“You do know why,” I stated carefully. He looked at me. “Your heart’s not in it Walter. You want to be at home with Hattie and you can’t seem to think about anything else.”

Walter’s face darkened suddenly and for a second I feared a repeat of our final night in Cromer but it didn’t happen. Instead he let out a long, soulful sigh and lugged a pile of boots into a three-sided crate.

“And you?” I asked when I felt it was safe. “Are you scared?” Walter looked away for a few seconds and then slowly turned towards me.

“I just hope it doesn’t hurt,” he replied in a voice scraping to a whisper.

“Hope what doesn’t hurt?”

“When it happens.”

“When what happens?” I squeaked in irritation. Walter took me in a calm, firm stare.

“When I’m killed.”

It would have been easy, and probably right, to dismiss his words immediately, aggressively, but they paralysed me for a moment like a small electric current.

“Don’t say things like that Walter, that doesn’t help anybody,” I replied after a few seconds.

“There’s no point pretending otherwise Harry. I’m not as well prepared as the rest of you, my mind is elsewhere, you’re right and…well you know your God will keep you safe Harry. He’ll get you home in one piece.”

“Is that what all this has been about? About you doubting your faith?”

“It’s not doubt Harry. I’m not in any doubt.”

“But…” I started to speak but with little idea of where I would end up. I suddenly felt like a child trying to excuse a broken vase. “We should pray together,” I said eventually, falling back on to an old line of my father’s.

“I don’t want to pray,” Walter said firmly.

“You *need* to pray,” I replied, in a voice that I hoped seemed firmer still.

“Praying won’t keep me alive Harry. He knows.”

“He knows what?”

“He knows I can’t find Him. And, worse than that, He knows I’ve stopped looking.”

Walter was crouched down in front of me, shuffling substantial piles of khaki. There was a bold stain across the back of one vest and he hurried it beneath some others. I reached forward and placed my hand on Walter’s shoulder. He flinched at first before quickly standing, bringing the back of his head swiftly in line with my mouth. He began to turn away so I wrapped my arm around his neck and softly pulled him back onto my chest.

“I’ll keep you safe Walter. If God can’t then I will.”

“Harry…”

“I mean it Walter.”

“I know you do, Harry, I know you do.”

With that he twisted gently away, lifted a pile of broken boots and went back to work.

*

We entered the support trenches under the cover of night, shuffling along the narrow passageways, clambering passed unfortunate debris and indistinguishable mounds. Although the fear still sat heavily on our shoulders, it had been joined by a sharp taste of anticipation and a sense of purpose. After days and weeks of physical and emotional travelling, we had, to some extent, arrived. Ahead of us we could sense activity and adventure as in near silence, experienced soldiers scampered and scuttled about their business. We peered at each other, unsure as to what would happen next. There was clearly some waiting that needed to be done, but for a while we didn't know if we were waiting for Fritz or he was waiting for us. Within a few minutes a young, fastidious officer decided that we were in the way and quickly found us work to do – repairing trenches, fetching supplies and, in the unfortunate case of Terry and Rupert, emptying the latrines.

Peter and I moved up and down the trench, straightening the duckboards and stamping loose mud firmly into the damp floor. Even though we'd barely seen rain since arriving in France, there was nonetheless a definite tackiness about the soil, a thickness to it like it had spent a long time as a constantly shifting paste. We had passed through a couple of traverses when I became aware that the air had changed, warmed perhaps, moved certainly. Then there was a sound, an unhappy, complaining and miserable sound. Peter and I looked at each other, shock splattered across our faces, before hurling ourselves to the ground, covering our heads and waiting for the descending shell to make one giant hole where our lives had once been. Moments later there was a thud, like a heavy pillow hitting the side of a barn, and the earth wobbled softly beneath my chest. I lifted my head from the ground just as two pairs of boots stepped over my shoulder and disappeared around the corner.

"You'll learn!" one of the boots hissed back at us as they departed.

Apparently we'd all done it, all us new lads, throwing ourselves to the floor as a bored Fritz shell sought out a transport line way beyond our position. It didn't take us long to work out whether a shell was going to trouble us or not; you tend to pick these things up pretty quickly when your life depends on it. In those first few weeks we learned about two wars – the war during the day and the war at night. That first night was relatively quiet in comparison to what would come as, like nocturnal animals, we lived our entire lives beneath that deep, purple, terrifying carpet to forever.

As day broke the next morning, we were confronted with an unimaginably foreign environment. We had long since become familiar with the basic structure of a trench but nothing could have prepared us for the strange blend of horror and domesticity that faced us that morning. Practicality and survival had a made a mockery of the normal expectations of a civilised society. There were things in those trenches that belonged only on bonfires and in nightmares but those men that called this world home didn't look twice at their macabre surroundings. For all the visions of Hell, the lanes of this filthy land also wore strange, misplaced badges of the old England – street signs painted onto fractured wood, familiar novels, and the sad carcass of a split football. Amidst it all, tucked away in unnatural crevices and scruffy holes, men slept, many of them boys, just as we were, lifted on a wave of happy delusion from the arms of their ageing mothers. I didn't sleep much that first day. Instead, I crouched in the sweet-smelling dug-out and listened to the sounds of aliens, monsters and ghouls dancing fearlessly in the bright, shocking and unforgiving light.

Chapter Twelve

As young boys, we spent forever playing war.

We raced between trees, through bushes and across the streets, chased by an invisible hail of bullets, the futile slashes of wooden swords and the thundering hooves of imaginary steeds. Time and again we would fall, slain, our bodies shattered and bleeding over the soft grass and yet each time we were cured, climbing bullishly to our feet knowing that this time it would be our turn to strike the telling blow. Eventually, beyond the dramatic battles of the dusk, the darkness would come and save us from each other, until the next day of course. Those naïve and happy days were all about noise, running and wild imagination but as real soldiers we spent much of our time quiet, still and considering nothing but stark, striking truth. We had played war endlessly and we were learning that reality, as is its way, was making fools of us all.

Trench life was dominated by the sort of routine that was so mundane it had to be good for you. We bookended our days awaiting an attack that never came, we shaved our thin, stretched skin in half-an-inch of what we had come to accept as tea and we fought an endless and unwinnable battle to keep ourselves and our equipment clean. The dirt got everywhere, seeping into our uniforms, through our uniforms. At times I was sure that I could feel it coating my tongue, filling my nose and scratching wildly behind my eyes. And when it rained we became wet in a manner that no-one could have understood back home. Once you were wet in the trenches, you were wet for days.

On the better days, when kinder weather coincided with letters from home, life had an almost holidaying air but such moments were rare and short. Ruth's first letter came through on one such day, and in spite of my niggling anger I ravished it desperately, over and over again. She made just passing reference to our final meeting, and her 'silly mistake', choosing instead to bury it beneath a succession of sweet, pretty and honest reflections about her life without me. In a few minutes I was smitten again, embarrassed by my own foolishness and truly homesick for the first and only time.

We continued to learn rapidly, through a succession of unpleasant experiences. To start with you focused on those lessons that kept you alive but eventually you learned the smaller things, the domestic necessities, the procedures and even the strange world of trench manners. I don't remember a great deal of thinking going on, just doing, and for a while we were grateful for that. The local wildlife was quick to introduce itself; black, swollen rats scuttling among us with the confidence of lions. The old lags would tell us frequent, grisly tales of the way the rats would target the dead, emptying still-warm insides in a loud, guttural frenzy. We didn't know how true these stories were but the size of the vermin and the way they moved, with drunken, gluttonous abandon left you in little doubt. Even the most delicate of man, cooing at the occasional, optimistic birdsong, wouldn't think twice about despatching a rat with spade, rifle or bayonet. A man could spend an hour cleaning his bayonet and yet still drive it through a distracted rat without missing a beat. He would consider the further hour of cleaning to be time well spent.

For all that we hated the rats, it was the lice that drove us mad. You were never free of them, not even for a second. Sleeping men would shift and stir, pawing at themselves, searching for a few moments of release. Some of the men suffered terribly, I know Rupert did, and their skin was permanently burned dry with the constant cycle of bite-scratch-bite-scratch. There were endless theories about how they could be overcome. Numerous potions, lotions and powders arrived in parcels from home but it was like trying to flavour an ocean with half an onion. Even those men that were able to halt the invasion knew that by morning they would be riddled once more. Then there were the flies, those fizzing shadows of death, as large as your thumbnail, hundreds for each man, feasting relentlessly.

We dreamed of course of a bath; a hot, stinging bath with soft, perfumed soap. We dreamed of a fresh uniform, straight from the tailor's needle. We dreamed of a trip to the barbers, soft socks, pillows, beds, home-cooked food and proper tea. We dreamed a lot when we had the time, which was why it was so important that we kept each other busy.

In those long summer months of 1915 we sometimes dared to hope for winter, and the deep frosts which would surely tame some of our unwelcome guests but when that first winter caught up with us, during a short spell further north at Lillers, we would have given up every comfort we still retained for just a cup-full of that remembered heat. Female relatives were raised to sainthood with relentless knitting. Gloves, socks and scarves were begged, stolen and borrowed, making each man double his natural size. Had Fritz decided to mount an attack during one particular December snowstorm then he would have fallen upon an army too bound up by wool to present any defence, but of course we knew that however we suffered, so Fritz suffered too. Whilst our esteemed leaders sat in the warmth and safety of their perpetual ignorance, so we shared rats, lice and aching cold with men we had been trained to hate. That winter God perhaps said more than he ever had about the folly and frailty of man.

The war itself appeared to be happening elsewhere and we saw very little in the way of fighting. Some men were careless of course and paid for their abandon with their lives, but on the whole keeping safe was no longer as utterly, crushingly consuming as it had been when we'd first arrived. Small groups of men would sometimes leave the trenches at night and venture into No Man's Land hoping to overhear something vital from the German line. They would edge right up to the German wire before scuttling silently back with whatever they had found. Sometimes these men were lost but more often than not they returned unharmed, occasionally bringing a captured Fritz with them, somehow lifted from a quiet corner of the trench. None of us were ever ordered to go on such a raid and although Sid liked to make out that he was keen, he did it fairly quietly.

For all the hardship we'd experienced since arriving in France and for all the horrendous things we'd learned and seen, there were still opportunities for us to enjoy one thing that we'd brought across the sea – our friendship.

Walter remained sad, small and somewhat resigned; a distant, breathy echo of the man we once knew. Sometimes I felt we carried him along, like an infirm but revered elderly relative. With little real intention, he was blending into army life and his soldiering had become less forced and less clunky but to achieve that improvement he had all but sacrificed his attachment to our shared past. He would treat Hattie's many letters with soft, bewildered veneration, unwrapping them delicately for fear that they would disintegrate in his fingers. He would read them repeatedly and then, later, look beyond the words, staring deep into the paper, hoping perhaps to see into that world he'd left behind. Those letters were many things to Walter – escapism, focus, salvation even, but they were never an obvious source of happiness. I had long since forgotten the last time I had seen my friend happy.

"Leave him be," Rupert whispered to me one day as I watched Walter unhappily hunched over Hattie's latest missive. "He's got to find his own way now."

"It breaks my heart to see him like this Roo."

"I know it does, we all feel it. But I'm not sure how we can help."

"Did he tell you that he *expects* to die? That he's just waiting for it?"

"Not in so many words, but I guessed as much. He's not the only one Harry. Some of the original lads have lost so many pals and you can't blame them for wondering."

"But not Walter, why would he think that?"

"It affects everyone differently. There's no right or wrong way of coping. It's just about getting through. Through today, through tomorrow."

"And how are you coping Rupert?"

"Me?" He scoffed softly. "Fascination and curiosity. It's a remarkable and beautiful thing this war Harry, if you look closely enough. I'm rather keen to see how it all turns out…"

The letters I received from Betty warmed me no end, stoking my confidence, my purpose and my intention to return to them all once the job was done. Sometimes even father would write; short, information-led notes usually about the church, the community or, occasionally, the sad demise of a distant acquaintance. There were never letters from mother. She excused herself in no end of ways but the woman that taught me the layers and glory of language, just couldn't find the words. In many ways I understood that. I'm not sure what I could ever have said in reply.

Whether those small, seemingly insignificant notes were from parents, sisters, brothers or sweethearts they were greedily absorbed and in that thin, fragile moment we all felt normal again. Very occasionally, when we were out of the line, that normality spread wider and further. As that bitter, vile winter curled itself over into 1916, we crammed ourselves into the numerous, modest estaminets to keep warm and drink heartily to our continued existence and the longed-for trip home. Although the prospect of leave hung tantalisingly in the air it never seemed to fall within reach and those long, rowdy nights became our release, our home from home.

We were walking back to our billets one such merry, moonlit night when Johnny suddenly skipped ahead, reappearing moments later with the old bat that he'd carried across his shoulders since leaving Blighty and something that looked very much like a tennis ball. It didn't take long for us to slip back into a familiar routine.

With the alcohol warming our blood, we thought nothing of discarding some clothing to make a rudimentary set of stumps and pacing out an approximate twenty-two yards. What happened next was more concert hall farce than sporting encounter.

Johnny had first use of the bat but he struggled to see the dull ball against a background of bluff and broken buildings. Terry was trying to bowl, with drunken enthusiasm, and time after time his feet sped in opposing directions on invisible films of ice, sending his limbs into a wild, waving frenzy of collapse. When he did finally manage to release the ball, it arrived at Johnny's forehead on the full, slapping against his receding hairline with pleasing resonance. The fielders, dotted absently around the bat, roared with laughter and appreciation at every hapless twist of flailing incompetence. There was childlike screeching whenever a catch was affected and when Charles struck the ball powerfully into the mid-distance he circled the bat around his head like an unbreakable gladiator. Even Walter, who had waited in the wings with Rupert for much of the time, took a turn to bat. For a while he looked as lost as the rest of us until, in a shimmering instant, he stepped forward to drive the ball through our ragged attempts at fielding with the grace and timing of an ice-dancer. Spontaneous applause broke out among us and Walter's face filled with diluted pleasure. The next time Sid bowled, the ball shot along the ground and bumped into the pile of clothes with a thin crump. Sid bellowed in triumph, Walter's shoulders slumped in spite of his face and he disappeared once more into his shell.

Lost as we were in our game, we failed to notice two shapes striding down the street towards us. By the time we realised, it was too late, and the imposing propositions of Major Bradshaw and Lieutenant Huff stood among us, stern looks on serious faces.

"What in the name of Hell is going on here?" the Major barked, bringing us to order and something approaching attention. "Well?"

Johnny took half a pace forward. "Just a game of cricket sir. Just letting off some steam. We certainly didn't intend to cause any harm sir."

You had to admire Johnny. Less than an hour ago he'd been trying to weigh the breasts of a local Madame but, faced with a very different challenge, he had seamlessly become the very air of respectability. I always felt that Johnny had a dash of greatness about him, just a dash, a thin streak, but it was definitely there. I have no doubt that he could sense it as well and was endlessly frustrated by its modesty. Major Bradshaw scanned us with a well-practiced glare.

"This will simply not do," he stated firmly, striding confidently across to where Tommy had allowed the bat to drop softly to the floor. Major Bradshaw nodded towards the bat and held out his hand. Tommy stooped uncomfortably to retrieve the bat, his fit shifting as though he were balanced on the stern of a small boat. The Major poked Tommy out of the way, moved towards the pile of clothes and turned to Lieutenant Huff.

"I shall show you how this is done. Lieutenant, do you bowl?

Lieutenant Huff looked a little startled but he hid it reasonably well, nodding enthusiastically. He handed me his coat, took the ball from Donald and proceeded to pace slowly backwards before turning, running and then finally bounding towards the wicket. Predictably enough, his landing foot just kept moving, slipping onwards towards the Major, throwing the Lieutenant horribly off balance and to the floor in a crumbled, creaking heap of man and well-pressed tunic. He made an unpleasant noise as he landed and an inadvertent squeak of surprise left his mouth. For a moment nobody moved, not even the Major, and then, with a sense of release that cracked through the clear air the new batsman threw his head back and howled in raw, uncultured laughter. We joined in immediately, unable to do anything else, and our attempt to lift Lieutenant Huff took doubly long as we failed beneath infant giggles.

The Major and Lieutenant stayed on for a while, passing time and making ever improving efforts at cricket in the frozen night. When they moved on they made it clear that the game was over and so we reunited men with clothing, bundled ourselves back into our billets and slept as well as we had for many nights. In the morning, many of us stung with half-frozen fingers and knotted toes but we had nothing on Lieutenant Huff who, we later discovered, spent much of the next week on a hospital bed with an unpleasantly twisted back.

*

We had some happy times when we were out of the line. Not happy in the sense we'd come to understand at home perhaps but happy nonetheless. We were also learning about each other. Our friendships were like the weather, shifting, changing and endlessly reminding us of other times and other places. They had the capacity to frustrate, irritate and dismay but also to delight, surprise and fill you with wonder. Without them we had nothing. A couple of years ago I would scarcely have believed that I could become closer to those boys. I would have doubted that there was anything about them I didn't know but each day brought something different and the more we suffered, the more we struggled, the more we did it together.

As the spring of 1916 began to perfume the air, so the frozen tundra of Northern France began to melt into vast pools of filthy, secretive water. The night chills still scraped at your skin but the daytimes were brighter, kinder. Just when you felt this bruised and battered land could not be revived, so it sent its many messengers through the surface to remind and reassure. Tiny, flimsy flowers stood and then flourished, laying beds of colour along the landscape with the impudence of the eternal.

Moving about behind the lines was a slow and laborious process. The landscape dipped and rolled with a thousand shell holes, making every trip a journey and every large scale movement a logistical epic. The largest shell holes, which could be twenty feet across, were actually quite dangerous, particularly when the rains had filled them with water and left their sheer sides slick and unstable. One afternoon, after yet another set of back-breaking drills, we came across one such crater where the lip had collapsed, sending a poor, stray horse down into the water below. The horse was fighting to keep its head above the surface, yelping pathetically, eyes vast and wide, foam rolling from the side of its mouth. Even in a world of frequent pain, suffering and death it was difficult to watch. A handful of us turned away.

"Tommy! For fuck's sake!" Gordon exclaimed suddenly and as we turned back we saw that Tommy had climbed halfway down the side of the hole, trying to grab at the horse's bucking head. In a flurry of arms, and with the help of a broken cart panel, Tommy was hauled back to the surface, with more expletives ringing in his ears.

"What are you doing?" Johnny shouted, "You could drown in there, especially with that thing flailing around."

"So what, we just leave it to die?" Tommy replied, his uniform caked with dragged mud.

"Well…come on Tommy, look around you, look at all the…it's just a horse Tommy."

"I'm not leaving it here to die. You lot can do what you like," and with that he shuffled onto his bottom and began to edge down into the hole once more. Charles dropped a heavy hand on his shoulder and held him still.

"Okay boy," Charles said with surprising softness, "we're going to need a rope."

There was a collective exhale of fatigue from the rest of us but, to a man, we turned and began to help. Rupert and Peter went looking for a rope whilst the rest of us pottered around searching for any general debris that might, in some small way, help the sorry beast.

"As soon as we get it out I'm going to shoot it and eat it," Johnny said under his breath.

After twenty minutes or so it became clear that the horse was tiring and Peter's appearance with many yards of rope was both welcome and timely. Using the pieces of the cart as stepping stones, Tommy and Charles lowered themselves into the hole and, with much fuss, eventually managed to secure the rope around the horse, bringing the other end to the edge of the hole and our many, waiting hands. By this point a small crowd had gathered, offering a mixture of support and ridicule. With rain starting to fall we braced ourselves and began to heave.

Immediately the horse reacted, lurching forward uncomfortably, its long tongue swinging from its mouth like a dry, leather strap. For a few seconds we moved consistently backwards but then our steps shortened and stilled. We regrouped and went again, with the half-mocking encouragement of the crowd spurring us on. We bellowed our efforts into the skies but the weight at the end of the rope didn't move any further. We'd raised the horse just a few feet and, if anything, he looked more uncomfortable, more tired. More men appeared and more rope was found. There were suggestions, arguments, ideas and then more failures. Suddenly it seemed that half the army was there, trying to drag one unhappy looking horse back into the unpleasant world we all shared.

"I hope Fritz doesn't attack now," Johnny called over his shoulder as we tried once more to raise the animal with fraying rope and burning hands, "I don't want to be the one to explain to the Field Marshall how the Germans took Paris whilst we were dragging a fucking nag out of a hole."

Johnny didn't get a response, and I doubt he expected one, but even Tommy and Charles were beginning to wonder if we were all just wasting our time. Eventually, with the horse wrapped in all manner of rope and chains we made one final effort to pull it free. Heels were dug into softening mud and, with a great roar of effort, every soul within 100 yards pulled with all their might. The weight gripped again, holding firm for a few seconds until, with a sudden jerk, it bounced forward. Loud calls of encouragement filled the air and so we drove on, our bodies angled backwards with the effort. Gradually we edged the animal onto the slope and dragged it up the side of the hole. Occasionally it would try to stand and the rope would buck and twist in our hands until the poor animal fell back to the earth, dropping a few feet with gravity. After a few more excruciating minutes the horse's head appeared below the rim and, in just a few more moments, above it. Tommy and Charles split from the rest of us to steady the beast and, very carefully, we eased it back to the surface.

Men responded to the slackening rope with great cheers. They swarmed forward to look at the horse, the hole, the rope; to review their effort and their triumph. Tommy and Charles tended to the horse as well as they could, offering it fresh water and removing the fiercest ropes. With dusk gathering and drizzle everywhere, most of the men slipped away leaving the eleven of us back where we'd started, reluctantly caring for an orphaned horse. We stood there for a moment, watching the animal gasping for air, rain washing the mud from its flank in long, weeping streaks.

"It doesn't look very well does it?" Gordon whispered.

None of us knew where the horse had come from, what it had been doing before the war began and how it came to be here, with us, at the edges of a great man-made hole. None of us knew what it had been doing when war was declared or where it had been when we'd carved our initials into Dead Cat Tree. None of us knew anything like that, but we all knew it was dying. The realisation moved among us slowly, and one by one we cast our eyes to the floor. Tommy was frantically trying to make the beast respond, even to get it to stand, but Charles just stroked its head with large, filthy hands. Tommy was the last to accept what was going to happen. Eventually the horse stopped fighting and its breath rattled out into the evening. Tommy stayed still for a moment before falling gently on to the seat of his pants, his hands clasped over his face.

Rupert stepped forward and hugged Tommy's head, whispering reassuring words into his ear. Broken and embarrassed, we slid away from the scene, leaving Tommy alone with his despair. Not long after he appeared again, with Charles at his side. We patted him with our kindness.

"Thanks for all your help," Tommy said earnestly, "can I ask you for one more favour?"

"Of course," I replied.

It didn't take too long. Having destroyed the lip of the hole during the rescue, we were able quite easily to slide the body back down the slope and into the water. It held above the surface for a few seconds and then, with a shifting of mud and a short show of bubbles, it disappeared and with it went our morale, for a few days at least.

I can no more easily explain what happened that day than I can explain any element of the vast madness of war. Men were dying in scores and humanity was failing before our very eyes and yet, somehow, that horse became everything to us. Maybe it was something we thought we might control, maybe it was boredom, maybe it was compassion or maybe we just saw that horse as one of us. German, British, French; man, woman, beast. All just caught together on the relentless Ferris Wheel of war, climbing to the top to abhor the view, sinking to the bottom with the vain hope of getting off, but always going round. Round and round and round.

Chapter Thirteen

By the May of 1916 we all knew that something was up. Nothing had been said but rumour was running riot and all the signs suggested that the big push was looming. We were finally going over the top.

We had started to spend quite long periods out of the trenches, way behind the lines in fact, where we were given suspiciously comfortable billets and more leisure time than we had known before. When it came to drills though, we were worked incredibly hard. We had started to practice the art of the trench attack, which included the grotty business of hand-to-hand fighting, and the officers were badgering us constantly about the cleanliness and readiness of our equipment. In late May we were marched right back to within a few miles of the coast and there we spent a couple of weeks going over and over the same principles. One morning we woke to find that white tape had been laid out across a freshly ploughed field, apparently replicating a section of the German trench line on the Somme. With the tape cracking and shifting in the breeze, we advanced in groups, climbing from behind one line to attack the next. The sun came and went, and with it we rolled forward and back, taking and defending, defending and taking. This went on day after day until our bodies creaked with painful repetitions and by the end of the fortnight the techniques had been stamped deep into our bones.

And we weren't the only ones being put through our paces. The Lewis gun teams seemed to be endlessly assembling and dismantling their weapons – faster and faster. The artillery boys were being tested and timed, and even the RFC were busy, buzzing overhead every day, watching, counting and recording. When we marched back towards Carnoy after our final training camp we found the roads choked and broken beneath an endless stream of guns and supplies. Everyone it seemed was going to be involved. We were going to be part of something very, very big.

Confidence was high, I have to say that, and even Walter seemed to have a little more electricity flowing through him. We'd barely fired a shot in anger during our time in France but at last it seemed we were going to get our chance. Not that we were blind of course. We realised that the growing swell of guns meant an equivalent reaction was likely from Fritz and everyone swallowed hard when we marched past the Pioneers digging huge pits just behind the support lines. We all saw what they were doing but no-one looked back and no-one mentioned it. Not once.

June slipped away. Fritz could sense the movement on our side of the war and he became twitchy. His artillery started to scratch at us, day and night, and our attempts at distraction and diversion were only moderately effective. Tension started to build and men, packed so tightly together, started to unravel a little. Skirmishes became more frequent, exchanges more blunt, more urgent. It was, as always, the waiting that tried the nerves.

Our final, detailed orders didn't come through until after the start of the bombardment; that tuneless music that would herald our arrival. And what a bombardment it was. It went on for about a week, bringing with it the most astonishing and unyielding sound. It seemed as though everything was shaking, everything we touched, everything we could see, shaking in bewilderment and terror at the power and intensity of our grown-up toys. It was a wonder that the earth didn't just tear in two, splitting down the middle like a beaten conker. I was taken back to Cromer pier. To standing on the very tip of England as the sea thrashed, writhed and punched against the frame, constantly talking, threatening. That feeling returned, that sense of being unnerved and nearly desperate with fear but too fascinated and too impressed to turn away.

The Germans retaliated of course, bringing all manner of death and suffering down upon us. Our casualty figures began to rise again for the first time in months and we felt the scorching heat of Hell at every turn. We seemed to be digging endlessly, like the gardeners Gordon swore we would become. Sometimes we dug to rebuild our shattered accommodation and other times, more frantically, we would dig to lift a comrade from the ground, buried in a screaming shower of earth. But for all that we suffered beneath the thunderous skies, not one of us would have swapped places with the Germans for a second, cowered among the corpses of their countrymen, beneath the industrial indignation of a furious England. It seemed almost unsporting to bring such awesome power to bear, and quietly one pitied poor Fritz but at least he could be reassured that, one way or another, his war was nearly over.

Somehow, beneath that cacophonic violence, time moved on. The week grew, peaked, and then declined towards its inevitable climax until, without fanfare, we began our last full day walking among those now familiar earth-lined streets. Final rations, resources and orders were issued and devoured. Our objectives seemed modest in many ways, but we knew that covering the broken ground would be difficult and until zero hour we couldn't be sure what opposition we would face, if any. There were of course still the formalities to be managed and so we were all instructed to complete the short wills in our pay books. It was a sombre task that we treated as a joke, threatening to leave our meagre possessions to pets and trying to convince Johnny that we could be trusted with his family silver. What was much harder, was penning those last minute letters home.

I wrote to Betty. The pencil, buffeted by cantering shells, shuddered its way across the card in erratic and unfamiliar shapes. I kept the words simple, the information thin and irrelevant. I ended quickly via a few carefully chosen words; a short but heavy embrace. And then I wrote to mother.

I never had any intention of writing to mother, no intention of breaking our unspoken agreement; that after Walter's wedding we had set a barrier between us, a barrier that would only come down when I was safely home again. But to be crammed inside the Earth with hundreds of other men, all braced like rigging against the storm, and not to be writing to your mother seemed somehow perverse, short-sighted. I wasn't obliging her to reply, not at all, but maybe I was obliged as a son to send a bearing home, a beacon of light to guide them until the skies broke.

For all my good intentions though, the words I shared were no more guidance to my true position than those softly wrapped simplicities that I sent to Betty. I gifted to my mother what I rather suppose she had gifted to me since my birth; harmless lies knitted together with the very best of intentions. I referenced the big push, vaguely, in a manner that I hoped would skip passed the censor and gently prepared her for the newspaper tales and the long, frameless wait for information. I sent my respect and affection to father, both truly meant, and wished for her to enjoy the English sunshine on our behalf, until we could be beneath it once again. I contemplated mentioning my concerns for Walter and his sad, fatalistic demeanour, but only for a moment.

Across from me, in an ever-tightening ball, Walter was writing to Hattie, scratching away with the tiniest shard of pencil. A small piece of paper was stretched across his knee and he seemed to be bitterly focused on filling every inch of white space with consideration and affection. His face was a picture of determination and intent, teeth clenched, eyes fixed and firmly forward. How he had changed over the last few months, his youthful features whittled away to hollow cheeks, sharp nose and chin. Even his hairline had become unfamiliar, creeping back along his crown as though it were edging away from a face it no longer recognised. Dark, dirty stubble had developed where soft, blonde down had once climbed and plump, boyish flesh had been gnawed back to the bare necessities for posture and movement. I turned my head away from him and studied my boots with a focus that I hoped would break the spell of sadness welling inside me. A single, insubordinate tear broke free and ran down my face. I closed my eyes to hide the secret and was surprised later when I realised that sleep had slipped in and stolen a little of what it was owed.

Dreams had been rare in France. The more tired I got the less my mind seemed to indulge in such casual, nocturnal fraternisation. Even dreams of home were infrequent, something which gladdened and saddened me in equal measure, but that late afternoon at the end of June I was treated to a nightmare so vivid and determined that I could taste its bitter sting on the back of my tongue long after I woke.

We're playing cricket at Norton Park and the surroundings are sweet and familiar. The sun is hot and bright without being oppressive and the colours of summer are gloriously loud. We're fielding and I'm in close with only the batsman for company, waiting for the bowler to deliver. The grassy thud of approaching feet grows behind me, followed by the swish of an arm and then, instantly, the crushing thud of a cricket ball into my right shoulder. I turn, startled, and there, mid-pitch is Johnny or rather what is left of him. His bowling arm is missing at the shoulder and there is a deep, purple crater where his right eye used to be. His hair is patchy and matted and fresh blood is running down the leg of his cricket whites. He stares at me with his one remaining eye and my insides turn to warm water. It's at this point that I become aware of the other players around me.

Tommy and Rupert are blind, leaning against each other for support. Macabre, dirty bandages are wrapped around their heads. Rupert's fingers are locked in a permanent grasp, like an eagle's claw. Gordon appears from behind the stumps, using one bloodied glove to stop his entrails from falling to the floor. Charles is next to him, his face packed with mud, his breathing short and laboured and Sid is lying on his stomach out towards the boundary, twitching with sickening irregularity.

I notice Peter walking in from deep cover, a single red dot in the middle of his forehead. He carries Donald's broken, black and bloated torso in his arms, staggering on two broken ankles. Terry sits in the near distance, looking with longing towards his legs which lie nearby in a dozen pieces. I spin round and round, trying to break my way out of the horror show, trying to find any sense of recognition or connection with my broken friends. Steadily, they converge in on me and I start to run for the pavilion. Halfway there I see Walter, with his back to me, talking to Hattie. I call his name over and over again but he doesn't respond. Eventually I reach him and desperately grab at his shoulder, spinning him round.

Walter's face has gone. His hairline is there still, and the cut of his chin is unchanged and distinctive. But in-between there is nothing but a shifting and stinking mass of scorched flesh and maggots. A sound emerges from the middle of the maelstrom and slowly it rounds into words.

"You should have left me to die Harry. Why didn't you let me die?"

I open my mouth to scream and a vast explosion of bluebottles emerges from where Walter's eyes once were and slaps into my face like hail. I turn to run but find hands upon me, holding me back. Hattie is there and so is Mother. There's Ruth and her Aunt, Walter's mother, even Tommy's little sister, slamming their hands against me in desperation like they were trapped in a shrinking room. They chant tunelessly.

"Why did you let them die? Why did you let them die?"

Finally I break free, striking one or two of them to the floor with sickening fury. I start to run again. I'm just yards from the edge of the park when the grass in front of me begins to darken, change shape and break into hundreds of huge and vicious rats. They surround me, force me to the floor and, with razor teeth, tear into my flesh…

Rupert told me that I had woken with my hands slapping frantically against my face and neck as though I were being attacked by a swarm of wasps. It is the only instance I can ever remember of being glad to wake up in the trenches but as the disorientating fear of the half-light faded so the heavier, harsher tones of reality began to return.

The sun was a long time setting that momentous night. It was hard to pick its distant light amidst the relentless, kaleidoscope of fire but intermittently I could see it blinking through the clouds, almost too embarrassed to look. I watched its final moments, its last, soft sighs rolling sadly across a poisoned horizon, thinning, spreading and then rinsing away into shadows. I wasn't the only one that mapped its meek goodbye. I think we all knew that when it rose again it would cast its light and faultless warmth on a new generation of heroes. And like those boys we were, searching for the pot of gold at the end of the rainbow, we would chase its echo all the way to Berlin.

There was a lot of movement, coming and going, but we stayed put, busying ourselves with running repairs and preparation for the attack. I lost count of how many times I checked and cleaned my rifle, how many times I fixed the bayonet, removed it, fixed it again. I had a terrible fear that I would be unable to do it in the morning and as the whistles blew I would be left behind, frantically struggling with the blade.

We were all fretting somewhat, as you'd expect, itching for the daylight and the blessed end to the agony of waiting. The tension vibrated through us, driven by the metallic, bone-shaking rhythm of the guns. Sleep was impossible and so I watched the grey shadows of my childhood fidget and ricochet around me in equally ill-fitting patterns. Rupert edged himself next to me and laced a conversation carefully through the din.

"Have you worked out how to fix that bayonet yet?" he asked, nudging me softly and smiling happily beneath the rim of his helmet. I smiled back.

"Let's hope so."

"It's going to be a lovely day tomorrow Harry. The sky is so clear."

I lifted my eyes a little and looked out across the grey sheet, pulled tight around the curve of the earth. I still felt that instinctive twitch of discomfort looking into the endlessness but I can't pretend that the fear was the same, not anymore.

"Not sure I'll be hanging about to get a tan," I replied.

"Ah now, no running Private Parker. Just a lovely morning stroll through Picardie remember. This time tomorrow we'll have Montauban to our backs and a few thousand Germans on the other end of the bayonet. If you remember yours of course..."

*

Daylight comes early in the summer, and by 5 o'clock the business of the day had begun. Breakfast was cooked and eaten. Some men fed with real purpose whilst others forced away a mouthful or two of tea but could tolerate no more through dry, pursed mouths. Ladders were leaned against the side of the trench, cigarettes were consumed with half-conscious obsession, bayonets were checked and checked again. Many men were off in their own little worlds, eyes closed, perhaps taking a last chance to go somewhere else, to see someone else, perhaps to talk to them one final time. The rum ration arrived and was taken by all.

I looked down the length of our trench and could see, just before the traverse, a diminutive Private, his hand already braced upon the ladder. It took me a while before I could place him but eventually I did – Norwich Recruiting Office, August 1914. We had seen him turned away that day but, like Donald, he'd obviously found a way. His face, flushed with emotion when I'd seen him last, was hard, pale and hurting. I wondered if he was thinking of that day, just as I was.

We pulled together our equipment, loading ourselves with everything that a soldier could possibly need. We had no plans to come back for supplies. We would be spending the rest of the war on foot, on the move, on the advance, and so we had to carry our world with us, for all that it dragged at us, held us back. At last I was glad of the training, glad of the long runs in the fields of Essex and the endless bitter drills. I didn't know much about Fritz. I didn't know what remained of his army beneath those mounds of tossed earth but I couldn't believe that he'd be fitter, better trained or more determined than those many lines of men that stood waiting to greet him in the moments after zero hour. I couldn't conceive that at all.

Lieutenant Huff checked his watch once and then again immediately afterwards as though he'd forgotten what it said. His lips were tight and determined. Time was moving on and the mists of dawn were inevitably losing their battle with the blazing sun. The bombardment found a new level, an unmistakable crescendo. Rupert appeared at my side.

"Harry?" In his hand he was brandishing a small, bruised and dusty copy of the New Testament.

I looked at him, and then beyond him to my friends, all lined together. They looked back at me. I turned to Walter, the only one of our number who was on my right. His gaze was to the floor.

"Of course," I replied in a cracked whisper.

With exquisite tenderness, Rupert took my hand and then Tommy's as well. One by one they linked down the line and we held hands to pray. Four fishermen, two farm labourers, a builder's apprentice, a printer's apprentice, a delivery boy, an under-achieving aspirant and a carpenter's son; just boys that dreamed of being soldiers. I looked at Walter, separated from the rest of us by a few physical inches and a thousand emotional miles, but his head didn't move. I swallowed hard and, lowering my eyes, recited some of the first words that I had ever learned.

"And forgive us our trespasses…"

I suddenly became aware of Walter's fingers seeking my right hand and wriggling into my palm. I found the rest of his hand and grasped him tight, feeling the rim of his helmet drop timidly against my arm. I hesitated, losing my way. Walter's voice rasped like a crisp autumnal leaf.

"As we forgive them that trespass against us…"

We finished the prayer together and then stood still for just a moment, drawing out the sense of finality, the sense of a mountain climbed, a life lived. I took the opportunity to add my own private words to God. I prayed for my friends. I prayed for their safe passage, their unwavering courage and their undamaged pride and I prayed to see them all again.

Two huge mines exploded, hurling us out of the moment and nearly off our feet. Vast quantities of France leapt to the clouds and fell again in dark, scalding rain. Then, like a memory from another time, there was silence; like that magical, floating gap between jumping from the pier and landing in the sea. A definite sense of falling, foreboding and screaming excitement but also nothing at all.

Lieutenant Huff moved his whistle to his lips. It shone in the sunshine, briefly but gloriously, and my heart took an extra beat. He looked at his watch, waited, drew in one long, powerful breath and then blew.

It was only then, as that whistle cut into the morning air with a sharper and more pleading noise than any you could ever imagine, that I realised the ultimate genius of it all. Friends joining up together, with their shared history and shared community. Friends that had relied on each other, lived with each other, loved each other. Friends that would stand-up for each other, look out for each other, protect each other, fight for each other. No man could watch his friends climb the ladder, break the wire, walk into history and not feel compelled to follow. Thousands of human magnets, dragging each other forward, unthinking, unquestioning and unbreakable.

I can picture them all at that moment, although there is no way that I could have seen all that I seem to remember. The faces that I had looked upon so many times before; in classrooms, in the streets, playing cricket or just fooling around. I can see them all, clambering out of the ground, my precious friends and, at the last, I can see Walter again. My beloved Walter.

Chapter Fourteen

I can remember the feeling of the ground beneath my feet and the way my legs wobbled and doubted themselves for a few steps. I can remember the heat; it was much warmer out of the trenches, and I can remember the modest shuffling sound as hundreds of men kicked their way politely through sharp, ankle-length grass and fists of drying earth. I can remember the silence, the calm. Just like any other morning walk. Like walking to Ruth's for a summer breakfast.

Then I felt the man on my right blow on my neck. I turned to look but saw no-one. Then it happened again but this time through my hair. I wondered if it may have been a fly or perhaps a bee. Then I realised what was happening and instinctively broke into a jog. So I jogged, my eyes fixed on our first objective, step by step, quicker and quicker. Eyes fixed forward.

I didn't see the shell land, or even if it did land, but a vast, vengeful catastrophe of noise heralded its existence, spraying the air around me with countless fragments of flying steel. I took two blows to the chest, lost my balance and dived into a shell hole.

*

There was a poppy on the rim of the hole, a few feet from my head. Its flower was balanced impossibly upon a thin, wiry stem. It twisted painfully against the breeze, reaching out across the hole and then ducking back. I could see its four petals, quite distinctly, with tiny slithers of light separating the colour. From a distance it would seem as though they moved as one but I could see that each petal had its own way of moving, its own shape, its own dance. I couldn't see anything else from within that hole, just my poppy and the vast, silver sky.

*

I had a four-inch tear in my tunic and two small pieces of metal stuck in my chest. There was a lot of blood coming from one in particular. There was some pain, although not as much as one would expect. I put my finger into the tear to feel the wound and nausea swept up my body. I looked at the bright blood on my finger and, after a few minutes, I saw how it began to dry at the edges. Eventually, the sun turned much of that stain to dust, leaving a purple crescent looping along the bottom of the nail.

Later, I noticed that the poppy had lost one of its petals. It had fallen away from the others and settled onto my shin. It took me a few minutes but eventually I reached it and held it up to the sun. The light burned red around it, through it, highlighting the vast subtleties of life therein. I placed that petal softly into my tunic pocket and patted it paternally.

*

"Have you ever wondered what God looks like?"

My eyes, seemingly closed, snapped open and desperately searched for the voice. A bright and scratchy light flooded in, drowning my vision. I blinked furiously until the shape of a middle-aged man appeared and hardened before me. He was sitting next to my poppy, his legs dangling down into the hole. He was younger than father, but not significantly, and his broad and confident moustache was edged with grey. He wore a sergeant's uniform, pristine and proud. He asked his question again.

"Have you ever wondered what God looks like?"

"I have," my voice was weak, my throat dry and sore, "but not for a while."

The man nodded thoughtfully. He produced a pipe from his pocket, filled it precisely and began to smoke. He removed it from his mouth and looked at it admiringly.

"And what did you imagine?" he asked finally, wisps of smoke creeping from the corners of his mouth, sending that sweet, creamy smell of tobacco into the air.

"Erm," my mouth made a short, harsh sound like a plough striking a large stone.

"Oh, pardon my manners young man, would you like a drink?" I nodded gratefully and he released his water bottle and placed it carefully into my hands. I drew it to my mouth and drank modestly. It was searingly cold, scraping itself against my tired teeth. The man gestured for me to carry on and I took a second and then third gulp, bringing life to the surface like a summer shower. I let a little run across my stinging face before returning the bottle to the stranger's waiting hand.

"You were saying?" he encouraged.

"When I was a young boy, there was an old fisherman I used to see. He'd always be sitting in the same place on the pier, on a small stool, dangling a line into the sea. He seemed impossibly old, crooked with age, and his face was battered and lined like well-worn leather."

"And?"

"And I suppose, at that age, he seemed to fit the image I had of God. I suppose I felt comfortable, content with the idea that he looked like God."

"Or maybe that he *was* God?"

"No, I don't think I believed that. Even as a boy I knew he couldn't be God."

"Why couldn't he be God?"

"Well…I suppose I'd been taught that God was in Heaven and I'd never had any reason to doubt that. I'd never considered that he could be among us. I'm not sure that I would consider that even now."

The sergeant stayed quiet for a while, his head tilted upwards in thought.

"Why does God have to be like an old man?" he asked eventually, almost accusingly.

"Well…we know he is a father and he has such wisdom of course, such wisdom that can surely only come with age...and time. The wisdom of God can't sit with a younger man."

"Or a woman?"

"A woman?"

"God couldn't be a woman?"

"Of course not. We know God is a man. Don't we? I don't see how anyone could see God as a woman. I don't think anyone would be convinced by that."

"Yet we have Mother Nature?"

"But that's different."

"How? How is that different Harry?"

"Mother Nature isn't real. It's just a way of describing things, giving nature a human face, a human, thinking mind. It's a convenient, happy inconsequence. At best Mother Nature is like a character in a book or a play – you can believe in her, for a while, but you know it isn't real. You can't compare Mother Nature to God."

"Can't you?"

"Certainly not, of course not. If anything, He made Mother Nature, through us, through our minds. I think He does that a lot, helps us to decide, helps us to help ourselves. He has shown us the way. Without Him, our lives would be rudderless and tossed to the winds. But with Him we have the freedom of choice, and the knowledge that as long as we follow Him, we will never be lost."

"And so we follow Him to war?"

"No. Man makes war, not God."

"So He doesn't approve? Shouldn't we then all just get up and go home, to our families and our churches?"

"I didn't say he doesn't approve. Only that war is man-made. God would never seek war, but He would also know that sometimes it is necessary, to drive out evil and clear the path to Him."

"And so you believe Fritz to be evil?"

"If I'm honest, I don't know anymore. It was so easy to believe that at the start, so welcome to have that certainty to drive you on but despite all the suffering I have seen them cause, despite all the wrong I know they have done, I do now have doubts. I continue to abhor the German race, but can I run that hatred down to each and every man? I'm not sure I can. Or if I can it reaches each individual Fritz so diluted that I can barely taste it."

"And yet you still fight?"

"I fight to honour my friends, my King and country, my father and mother. I fight for them and their God-given freedom. I fight not for God, but for His people."

This answer seemed to satisfy the old sergeant and he nodded sagely. He stared into the mid-distance, unseeing, and drew on his pipe with purpose and pleasure. I noticed that he had blood on the palms of each hand yet appeared to be in no discomfort. His sergeant's uniform was immaculate and clean in a manner that suggested a first wearing. I looked at my vaguely bloodied finger and tried to imagine how it had looked when it had also been so perfect.

"You're a good man Harry, has anyone ever told you that?" he said suddenly, turning vast blue eyes on me in a flash.

"Once," I replied, my voice breaking down to a whisper. The sergeant offered me his water bottle again but I held my hand up to decline. "I was told that once."

*

The heat became quite something. My poppy was bending towards the ground, trying to become its own shade. It was no surprise when a second petal fell to the soil. It was further away this time and it took many minutes of shifting and wriggling before I could rescue it and tuck it in my pocket with the other one. My water bottle was nearly empty, but I managed to lay a few dribbles at the bottom of the stem. It drank greedily, desperately, and within seconds the earth around it was parched dust once more.

*

I spent a long time contemplating the sky. I think I finally came to terms with it, lying there. Things change, don't they, as you get older? As a child there were secrets and vagaries in the sky that I simply didn't understand. I suppose other children were just able to accept these things and carry on with their games and their lives but I couldn't. I could believe in what I could touch and see and I could believe in God and Heaven, but the notion that there might be something in-between was too much for me.

Growing older, one finds that childhood fears hold less significance and less control. They still grind at you of course, just as anything learned in childhood is difficult to forget, but when all else is on an even keel, the rational, adult mind can much better deal with the uncertain and the unexplained. One thing in particular that I had learned over the previous few months was that there would forever be things in life I didn't know and even the wisest of men would sometimes have to accept, embrace and adore the mysteries of life. In some ways, what happens in the gap between asking the question and finding out the answer is everything. Indeed, it is your life.

I slept for a while, I think, and by the time I woke a small and slightly shrivelled poppy petal was lying on my stomach. I rescued it and tucked it away. My poppy was fading, its remaining petal tugging at the stem like dog pulling at a leash. In my mind I wept for it, but in the shell hole, no tears came.

My feet were the last to be relieved of the burning sun. I watched the light pass over the edge of my toes and move relentlessly on. I could feel my feet running with sweat, choking, the thick socks and winding putties starving them of air and hope. I could feel my new metal appendages shifting and dragging with each breath, pulling at skin that was trying to heal around them, fixing them into place. I could smell the dried blood on my tattered tunic. I closed my eyes again for a second and felt an overwhelming fatigue gather along the length of my body. Sleep drew dangerously near but a small sound nudged my attention awake; a soft, sorry sound like the cough of a kitten. I opened my eyes again and stared upon my naked poppy, its last petal leaning sadly against the base of the stem. It see-sawed this way and that against the thin strip of plant, waiting for a small draft to send it scuttling into someone else's life. I watched it for a moment, hypnotised by its steady rhythm until, with a short, swift movement I grabbed it and brought it to my lips. I kissed it sadly before laying it in my pocket with its brothers.

The naked stem quivered shyly, twisting and writhing with sadness like a bereaved mother. In the end I couldn't bear to watch any longer and so I closed my eyes, lay my head back against the earth and waited.

Chapter Fifteen

One of the stretcher-bearers had a thin silver band on the fourth finger of his left hand. It struck me as remarkably clean and it intermittently spat tiny fragments of light into my eye. Other than that guiding star I was bundled along in almost total darkness, climbing and dropping unsteadily, like riding a bicycle with buckled wheels. Time after time I felt certain that I would fall to the ground but each time, just as my weight threatened to tip, I was jerked back to something approaching horizontal. The pain had changed by this point, spreading and stretching, and each time I bounced my swollen chest sang out into the night like a trapped animal.

The makeshift casualty centre was relatively quiet. Those wounded in the early hours of the attack had been moved on, with some already aboard ships bound for Blighty. The men that remained were cheery, the excitement of the battle outlasting the pain and discomfort. The M.O. looked tired but he worked smoothly, with order, giving each man his undivided attention.

"Sorry son," he said when it was my turn, "this one won't get you home. They'll have them out down the road."

He made a short, illegible note on some paperwork and moved on to the next man. A nurse removed the sad remnants of my shattered tunic and dressed my wounds as best she could. The pain had become more unpleasant, like I was being repeatedly branded. The nurse soothed me as best she could, mainly with her cotton words, but she did pour a little sweet-smelling liquid onto my wound which, after the worst burst of pain I had ever known, eased my suffering slightly.

A short while later I was led to an ambulance and given a bunk alongside three other men. For over an hour we were tossed in all possible directions, taking turns to hit the floor of the vehicle with uncompromising solidity. I cannot describe to you the misery of that time, the desperate sounds emerging from the other men and the shattering agony that swept the length of my body. When we finally arrived I was too tired to even answer my name and the nurse repeatedly had to drag me away from the determination of sleep and dreams.

By the time I was taken to the tented operating theatre the light of morning had arrived, once more brilliant and warm. The stiffness in my neck meant that I could not really see the wounds as I was being undressed, although I was aware of many large, dark, unfamiliar marks on my pale body. I had been given a little something for the pain but its effect was patchy and uncertain, sending me hopping unsteadily between complacency and horror. In the theatre I was asked to breathe slowly on a gas pipe and everything changed, rotated, turned inside out and then disappeared.

When I finally awoke in my surprisingly comfortable hospital bed I could have been convinced that I had been asleep for a week. My head was muffled like I was wearing an oversized hat and my limbs felt new and inexperienced. It was a few minutes before I noticed the pain, itself gagged by a tight, insistent bandage. It chirped away at me rhythmically to the beat of my heart, but I knew that the worst of its sting had been drawn.

"It's Harry isn't it? Harry Parker?"

I turned my head sharply and was chastised by aching muscles. The soldier in the bed next to mine was no more than a boy. I wondered if he were even sixteen, let alone nineteen. His face was a little grubby but otherwise pale and elegant. He looked well, but had his right leg tightly bandaged across the knee.

"Yes, yes it is," I replied, my voice squeaking and spiking.

"You're friends with Walter aren't you – Walter and the others?"

"Walter? Did something happen to him?"

"No, not at all. Well, I don't think so anyway. We reached the first objective together and just before I was hit I watched them bound on towards Montauban. They were leading the way."

"Of course they were," I replied, exhaling deeply. "Just as I thought they would."

"He asked me to look out for you."

"Sorry?"

"Walter. He came back to put the field dressing on for me, very well too, and he told me to look out for his friend Harry. That's how I knew who you were you see. He described you perfectly."

"Really?"

"They'll be delighted to hear you're safe. I know a few lads that have lost pals out here and it's terrible, a really big blow for them. Having your pals around you makes such a big difference, don't you think?"

"Of course. I can't wait to get back out there to be honest."

"Oh I don't know. I could get quite attached to some of these nurses!" He tipped me an amused wink and his face aged considerably. I smirked and dropped my head back onto the pillow. I was shocked at how heavy it felt and how tired I was after just a few moments talking. I allowed my eyes to close again and drifted off, hoping to be back with the Regiment before the war was won.

*

I was five days in the hospital, although after a couple of restful nights I was allowed out of my bed. I spent many hours walking around the makeshift hospital camp, talking to other wounded men and cringing at my new friend's inadequate attempts to court the fiercely efficient nurses. Although I enjoyed the comfort, the cleanliness and the recognisable food, I still felt a short thrill run through me when I was declared fit enough to re-join my boys.

The journey back to the front was long and frustrating but easy to tolerate after the agony of the trip I had made in the opposite direction the previous weekend. As we approached the old front line I began to notice what an immense triumph had been achieved. We took to our feet and marched through the trenches that had been our homes for many months and on beyond the first and second objectives. By the time we began to enter the traffic and bustle of the reserve lines we were in sight of Trones wood.

Not all the wounded men were destined for their original battalions, but I was instructed to slip straight back in with my friends, if I could find them! From what I could tell, the progress had been so dramatic that any sense of order or control had temporarily been lost and some of the new trench lines were little more than scratches in virgin earth. Everywhere men were scuttling around like ants – lifting, shifting and digging. Suddenly one of the ants stopped, peeled away from his duties and bounced towards me. It was Rupert.

"Harry! Harry! Harry! Ah, what a sight for sore eyes you are my boy!" he exclaimed, wrapping me up in an embrace that stung my new scars but warmed my heart.

Discarding the load he was carrying, just as a young girl might drop an out-of-favour doll, Rupert took my arm and introduced me to my new home – a temporary dug-out moulded into the side of a sunken road. Having dumped my pack, Rupert took me through the new lines, finding each of my friends in turn, their warmth and relief evident and endearing. Walter was the last, the dusk gathering behind him as he appeared carrying sacks filled with outstripped rations. He smiled broadly, edged in the pink of a fading summer sun and took my face like a proud father.

"Don't do that again!" he barked with mock anger, wrapping me up in an embrace long enough to push the war into the background. He stepped back from me again and studied my face.

"Where are you hurt?" he asked thoughtfully, brushing his open palms across my chest.

"It's fine," I replied, "not a problem."

"Good to have you back my boy, we missed you." Walter smiled broadly, exposing small, tidy teeth. His tired, pale and scraped face began to flush again and, for the first time in months, I could see him the night he became engaged. The finest of men in his finest hour.

Walter tried to object when I gathered up some of the ration sacks but I persisted proudly, in spite of the tugging pain in my chest. We walked on slowly.

"Look Harry, I just wanted to say how grateful I am for your kindness over the last few months. I've really struggled here but you never abandoned me.

Maybe you should have but you didn't, and I'm grateful. Without your friendship I'm not sure I would be here."

"Nonsense," I replied firmly but with limited conviction.

"You kept me alive Harry. That's the only way I can describe it." I smiled, Walter didn't. I patted his shoulder tenderly and we walked on, through the last memories of another strange, uncomfortable and glorious summer's day.

*

Officers were bustling around with animated but grumpy faces. All their planning and precision had been obliterated by the moment, the opportunity to drive the Germans further and further back. Men had thrust way beyond where they were originally told to stop and evaluating the full extent of the advance was proving a headache. Not that we cared of course. We revelled in the achievement and made merry in the happy tolerance earned by success. There was much to do to make this regained patch of France into a new, hopefully temporary, trench system and we worked tirelessly to build ourselves another shelter, another platform from which to advance. But we rested with just as much vigour, playing and pranking behind the reserve lines like times of old.

The boys told vast and glorious tales of the attack, unrolling them with eloquence and glee. Many had returned with souvenirs of victory and none was more acclaimed than the German helmet Sid had carried all the way from the first captured trench. It was more rounded and elegant than our own dull tin helmets and it was topped by a short, aggressive spike. After we had become bored of its novelty we started to use it for games, thrusting the spike into the ground and using the upturned bowl as a target for finished cigarettes. Our finest game was to convince some unlucky soul to don the helmet whilst the rest of us sought to land something perfectly upon the spike, like one might pick up leaves with a sharp stick. The challenge of course was to find suitable objects to throw. Apples were ideal but they were few and far between so we tended to resort to tightly packed balls of mud, many of which would contain more than a fair handful of stones. Eventually, we all took our turn beneath the helmet, shutting our eyes, gritting our teeth and hoping for mercy from the firing squad in front of us.

How magical and precious it was to see the old Walter again. He had begun to wake as the time for the big push had drawn near and each day since he had been returning, like a frozen pond melting in the spring. He was still thoughtful, quiet sometimes, but the boy that I had grown up with, the man he had then become, was back again and it filled me with joy. He had taken his position at the heart of all the games, just as I had always thought he would, and within just a few days he seemed to regain the strength and youth he'd left in England.

One of our jobs in those happy few days was to return to Montauban on a salvage mission, collecting strewn weapons and supplies. The army insisted that we re-use everything we could and huge mounds of equipment popped up, all destined for the factories of England where it would be revived and returned. Rifles, clothing, helmets, trenching tools, boots, anything that could be made useful again, piled up in the open awaiting their transfer home. Just outside the village, a paddock of sorts had been erected and scores of unhappy looking horses were milling about aimlessly. Occasionally one would be dragged away for a duty and the others would watch sombrely with a mixture of curiosity, relief and regret.

None of us had known Montauban before the war, but it was probably a stranger even to the handful of brave villagers that remained. There were no recognisable buildings. There was the occasional wall, even a couple of walls, and every few hundred yards something resembling a roof would be visible, but there was no longer any history in the village. Nothing had a purpose anymore, nothing had character, nothing had a place. Closing my eyes I tried to imagine what it had once been like but I couldn't, there was too little even for imagination to make whole. I could only wonder at what it was for the fine people of France to have their land so raped and raked. When the war was won, what would the winnings be worth?

The village church was leaning alarmingly to one side, its east transept lost to a large crater. The bell had slipped from its tower, dangling precariously overhead like a huge acorn. The wind rolled lazily around its sad bulk creating a thin, haunting whistle. Large planks of wood had been hammered across the north door and the scars of fire were visible around the windows. Charles and Johnny approached the blocked door and pulled at the planks. They came away easily, exposing the original, shattered door and deep, foreboding void beyond.

"It doesn't look very safe to me," I commented, peering into the gloom.

"We'd better have a look," Johnny replied, "Fritz could have stored all sorts of treasure in there. Just keep clear of the bit that's trying to fall down."

We entered nervously, in single file. Even in this state, there was still something substantial, something weighty about being inside a church, like everything meant a little more beneath the Lord's roof. The air was bitter and heavy. The smell of burned wood was unmistakable yet it was accompanied by other stranger, less wholesome flavours. The windows were all blocked with wood. One by one we tore down the rudimentary shutters, allowing the day to yawn in from all angles. Thick shafts of yellow light, curdling slightly through fragments of stained glass, bore down upon the nave, giving shape and personality to previously anonymous shadows. As is its way, the light exposed the secrets and the nonsense of the dark, only this time the horror of the day was worse than the insecurities of the night.

They were all huddled together, the faces of the children buried in their mother's breasts. There may have been a dozen of them, there may have been two dozen, it was difficult to be sure. They had probably tried to escape but in the end they had nothing left but prayer. There was no way of knowing if they had been alive when the fire had reached them, but when it arrived it had made short work of the air in their lungs, the blood in their veins and the limited fat on their bodies. They had yielded to the fire and it had respected them for it, sparing the small, simple features that had made them who they were. The mother nearest me had her daughter in her arms. Their noses peaked and dipped in unison, running along wide brows and then down behind narrow, deep eyes. They stared together into the far, invisible distance, to a time beyond all this madness, or perhaps before it.

"What happened…?" Tommy breathed into the silence.

"They boarded the women and children into the church...and then they set it alight." Rupert's voice toned softly but firmly.

"Why would they *do* that?" Donald asked.

A sudden commotion outside the church broke the miserable spell. Lieutenant Huff appeared in the doorway, his face flushed.

"Everyone back to the line immediately! Fritz is counter-attacking and we're struggling to hold on. Go, quickly!" His eyes fell upon the bodies in front of him. His face changed and winced sharply.

"Go!" he repeated in spite of himself. "Go!"

It took us a while to draw ourselves away from the scene, to drag ourselves passed a frozen Lieutenant, away from the church and back into the startling sunlight. Officers were hurrying us forward to the transport, but many men were clearly intending to cover the short distance on foot, bounding their way through the shattered remains of the village and back in the direction of the gathering storm.

It was Walter that burst into the paddock first, grabbing an agitated looking grey by the mane and dragging himself aboard. It tried to fight him off but, like that golden day on board Farmer Rumpole's old mare, Walter stuck fast, propelling the shocked animal forward in a flutter of panicked legs. Other men followed Walter's example and before long more than a dozen riders were visible, trotting and then galloping into the distance. I joined them, uncomfortable at first, guiding an underweight beige pony through the outskirts of the village and onto the bustling country roads. In a couple of minutes we were all flying, each horse dutifully chasing the one in front, happy to be momentarily free. They burst great holes in the air as they charged, pushing fresh wind through our hair and blasting summer's forgotten cologne into our sun-stained faces. With the calls of our comrades ahead of us, and the memories of the church behind, we screamed our way through what God had once called France. My chest heaved and tore with pain but beneath the wounds my heart thudded to the rumbling of hooves, drumming its rampant salute to those distant childhood dreams. I may feel more alive than that one day, but frankly I doubt it very much.

The line was leaking. Germans were among us, hands stuffed with bombs, knives and the fiercest, most evil looking clubs you could imagine. Our boys were doing their best, more than holding their own, but they were thin on the ground, caught on the hop by a swift and telling attack. We discarded our horses, many of which turned in an instant, running back from whence they'd come with simple, faithful instinct. Orders were spat across the din and, grabbing weapons of our own, we joined the desperate defence.

Corporal Harvey took me, Walter, Sid and Donald, armed with all the bombs we could carry, through a fading communication trench and towards the shouts and sounds of hand-to-hand fighting. Fear appeared frantically at my side but it quickly realised that I had no time to consider its wares. It was hard to tell how many Germans had originally broken into the sap but about ten of them had reached the trench itself, thrashing and bombing their way along each traverse. The remnants of A Company were holding them back behind a hastily constructed barrier of soil and sandbags but there seemed an inevitability about the situation, like watching a fox chase a tiring rabbit.

Corporal Harvey exclaimed an order. It was completely inaudible but as clear as the incongruous sky. We launched our remaining bombs across the failing sandbags and followed them, vaulting into the lap of the Gods. A strange thought broke at that moment. I thought of a cricket ball stuck beneath a blackberry bush. I thought of it sitting there, snared and unreachable, perfect but useless. I thought of the frustration, the disappointment and the fast-developing realisation of what would come next. I thought of that silly, facile image and then I thought of closing my eyes, biting my lip and stepping into that bush, driving my bare, boyhood legs into those thorns to rescue our ball, our game and ourselves.

I used the bayonet for the first time that day. I killed a man just as he realised he was about to kill me. I didn't watch him go, there wasn't time. Then I killed another man, digging the blade into his side and through his ribs. I felt the rifle jerk twice as it moved into and then through his body. He bent in half and tried to move away from the blow but he knew I'd got him. He looked over his shoulder as he fell, perhaps wanting to see the man that had ended his war and his life.

We all ran with blood. My hands were drenched with the bayonet's tears and Sid had an ugly wound to the knee. Walter had taken a foul scratch to the forehead. Corporal Harvey was dead. He had been first, and the first man never has a chance. He'd been struck more than once and every German, those that fell and those that fled, wore great scarlet streaks of his fading life. Whilst further reinforcements chased Fritz back into the screaming death of No Man's Land, we picked the Corporal's body up and carried him back to the reserve lines.

The sun set in rare silence that night and then rose again the following morning to our collective relief. Word got around, as it does, and soon we were all together again to pay our sad, silent respects. We thought of that night near Colchester. We thought of Snowy's dinner party and the poor Corporal's purple fury. We thought of that, and little else. Perhaps it was better to half-drown in the melancholy of another man's passing than to contemplate just how close we came to our own.

Chapter Sixteen

We spent many weeks on the back foot as Fritz attempted to regain all the ground that he'd lost that scorching day at the start of July. For all the progress we'd made in that advance, it seemed that this defence was more important somehow, like each day was hurting the Germans as much as it was hurting us. Charles and Donald were both lightly wounded during this time, although neither was out of the line for very long.

When in reserve, we spent much of our time in and around Montauban, continuing salvage operations, mending and servicing supply lines and being reminded of the fastidious expectations of the officers. Here we were safe from the sharpest teeth of the German bite but still within range of their fidgety artillery. Occasionally a lucky shot would send a handful of boys home but more typically they crashed into heavy oblivion, further sieving the crumbs of a devastated village.

One damp, sludgy October morning, we returned to the village church. The tragic, huddled bodies had long since been removed and buried in a large, communal grave to the rear of the broken building. Someone had left a scrawny bunch of flowers on the freshly turned earth in way of a tribute. The church was continuing to lose its battle with gravity, curving into the earth at an increasingly alarming angle. It was only a matter of time before the ever declining clock tower reached the horizontal.

It was rare for us all to be together like we were that day, helping the Royal Engineers repair the main route to the front line. Due to the various, shifting demands of army life, we could easily lose touch for days, passing through each other like clouds on a windy autumn evening. Sid had spent a few weeks away acting as a runner to HQ, Terry and Gordon had been training with bombing units and Charles had spent a brief time working with a Lewis gun team, carrying the dismantled weapon and ammunition as easily as another man would carry a water bottle and pocket-knife. Invariably however, I was with Walter. The distant Walter had drifted into distant memory, lost in the history of the war like nineteenth century landmarks. We would talk about it like it was another time, another person. Fear does strange things to people and for a while it made Walter disappear, but he had returned, digging in to me, playing all those tunes we'd learned as boys. I can clearly remember the day that Walter emerged fully from the gloom. It was the day that he asked me, with a fair twinkle in his eye, if I meant to marry Ruth on my return. I think I surprised him with my reply.

"Really?!" he exclaimed, "Why that's wonderful, she'll be overjoyed!"

"Do you think?" I responded.

"Of course! Everyone will be thrilled. It will be perfect. Walter paused for a moment and relaxed his countenance. "I have to say Harry, I'm a little relieved."

"Relieved?"

Walter nodded and made a small sound of confirmation.

"Why relieved?" I asked, checking that none of our friends were obviously in earshot. Walter seemed to need a few seconds to find what he wanted to say next. I stopped any pretence at working and waited for him to speak.

"I suppose I was starting to wonder if you'd ever be truly happy."

I can't remember what I intended to say in response. I can't even remember how I felt but I can remember that I opened my mouth and I can still feel the sensation of the blast as it rolled across the surface of my teeth.

I lay with my face pressed hard against packed earth. It was still vibrating softly. The outline of the church began to appear amidst thick, warm smoke. The clock tower was gone. I peeled myself from the ground and became aware of a sharp heat in my abdomen. I dropped my hands to my belt instinctively but found everything intact. My trousers were torn at the knee, the pinkness of peeled skin just visible through the hole. Laughter emerged into the clearing air. All around me my friends were sitting up, leaning on an elbow or climbing gingerly to their feet.

"Bloody Hell! That was a little too close for comfort!" Donald had a huge beam across his face.

"Everyone okay?" Rupert shouted from the mid-distance. "Anyone hit?"

"Just the church," Gordon replied. All eyes turned to look at the building, still settling.

"It didn't sound that close," said Sid. "It sounded like it was going to land another 100 yards or so away."

"I didn't hear it. Didn't hear it at all," I replied. They scoffed at me.

I caught Tommy's eyes, smirking. I looked at his happy face and slowly watched it change. I watched his eyes drift to my left, stop and then fix. He mouthed something that I struggled at first to make out.

"Walter."

They rushed past me, slowly, as though wading through waist-deep water. I tried to turn but the current denied me, keeping me still, keeping me adrift. I became aware that Donald had fallen to his knees, his head bowed beneath clasped hands. He was saying '*No*' over and over again. I could feel water at my chest, pushing, and within moments it was at my throat, threatening to overwhelm me. Just a few feet behind me, great commotion was playing out to an orchestra of broken strings. Still I didn't turn, my eyes instead fixed on the horizon, watching it warp and distort beneath the low cloud.

"Harry, Walter's hit! He's hit. Harry! Harry?" voices from everywhere and then an arm, dragging me backwards, spinning me around, throwing me to the floor, pulling me from the suffocating sea.

Walter was on his side, tucked neatly into a small elbow of wall. He had one hand clasped fiercely to his stomach. His face was coated in green sweat and his frame had been shortened, reduced. Free from my trance, I crawled over to him, allowing his head to drop limply onto my thigh. From there I could look straight down upon his wound, straight into it. It was emerging from between and around his fingers. His hand was lost to a coat of blood and other colours were exposed, the autumnal colours of viscera and the pale tones of bone. Walter was badly, badly broken. A sweet, metallic smell filled the air, like freshly turned earth.

Johnny was fussing with a field dressing, growling in frustration at its palpable inadequacies. I heard the hard rumbling of feet as men arrived and left. The call for stretcher-bearers rolled into the distance like the thunder of a passing storm. Walter's eyelids flickered as though beneath a bright light. Those petite and perfect eyeballs rocked beneath their lids unnaturally as though at any point they may roll down his face and to the floor. He made a strange, coarse, echoing noise. The sound of a well being drawn dry.

Sid was behind me, talking to Johnny unsteadily. I heard mention of sheep and foxes, but nothing more. Johnny scolded him over my shoulder, spared me a glance and then continued attempting to stem the blood from Walter's middle. Another voice a few feet away pleading angrily for help. I attempted to tuck Walter's hair behind his ear. It was soaking wet and the skin of his face felt cold. My hands were somehow bloodied, and I cut three, thin red tracks across Walter's face.

Then Rupert was there, grabbing my head with two hands and holding it still. His face contorted as he spoke to me, spoiling its usual, elegant shape.

"Talk to him Harry."

Rupert's eyes grew heavy with tears. He blinked them slowly and two symmetrical rivulets of water rolled over his cheek bones and curved towards the corners of his mouth. He cracked his lips open instinctively to allow the drops to disappear.

"Please Harry, talk to Walter."

Rupert stood slowly. He stepped across to Johnny and, hooking a hand beneath his armpit, lifted him to his feet. Johnny protested for a moment and then yielded to Rupert's half embrace. Like a shepherd guiding his flock, Rupert then edged everybody backwards a dozen or so paces, leaving Walter and me alone. Together and alone.

Walter's head was heavy. I shifted to sitting and lay his head on my lap. Walter's eyes wandered between me, the sky and the timeless comfort of their own cocoon.

"I'm sorry Walter, I'm so, so sorry." I cupped his face in my hand. His eyes blinked firmly, possibly in response, possibly instinct. "I didn't hear the shell. I didn't know it was coming. Did you? Did you hear it? Look, it will be okay. The stretcher-bearers will be here soon and they'll get you off to the field hospital. They'll soon sort it out. They give you this gas, it's rather pleasant really, and you won't feel a thing."

One of the many field dressings Johnny had applied slipped from the wound and hit the floor heavily, followed by a fresh trickle of tired blood and a couple of small pieces of something that looked like goose fat. I bent forward to pick it up but I couldn't reach it. Out of the corner of my eye I noticed someone start to walk towards us but then words were exchanged and the figure melted back into the pack.

"I reckon that you might be home with Hattie really soon though. They'll surely send you back to recover. I'm sure they will."

At that point two stretcher-bearers scampered over the bank and appeared beside me. One of them surveyed the scene before him and smiled sadly. He had a silver band on the fourth finger of his left hand. His partner laid the stretcher beside Walter and moved as though to lift Walter's feet. The first man coughed sharply and shook his head. Leaving the stretcher, they backed away into the small crowd.

I watched them go. They reached my group of friends, produced cigarettes and sat on a pile of duckboards to smoke and to wait.

Reality thudded into my chest, shoving the air from my lungs and bringing thick, bitter bile to the back of my throat. Lights grew and burst before my eyes and a heat ran across my face like a passing flame. I looked down upon Walter and tried to picture this fading shape as he had been just a few moments earlier; standing, talking, effusing and caring. I slammed my eyes shut and tried to bring Walter's true face to mind, the image that, at that very point, would be looking out at his mother from her mantelpiece, beneath the crude beauty of her stinging art. I tried to hear the lilt and tone of his voice, feel the warmth of his hands, smell the gentle, familiar musk of his skin but nothing would come and in panic I placed my palms on his frantically heaving chest, desperate to reconnect with him, to find him.

I closed my eyes again and was relieved to see him there, in cricket whites. He's about seventeen, maybe a fraction older and his deep, bronzed arms suggest the summer is nearly done. This is typical Walter. He is playing with me, mocking me even, but those familiar eyes are too easy to read, too warm to fear. And then he's at school, standing at the board and being reprimanded by Mrs Cawser for his casual grammar. I feel bad for him, desperate for him to be right and to be relieved from the moment. My view is side-on and his hair is in one of its longer phases, bouncing out a little above the ears in a manner that acutely irritated many of the teachers. His fingers are bunched at the end of the chalk, pressing too hard and causing heavy flurries of dust to fall to the floor. Suddenly he says something and the class is laughing happily. Mrs Cawser raises a hand to admonish him but without intent. She is also amused, entertained in spite of herself. Walter skips back to the desk in front of me a little more heroic than when he stood.

Walter's body flinched beneath me. I opened my eyes but his are closed, heavily closed, as though he is approaching the very centre of a night's sleep.

I am taken to our first summer away from school. We are playing in a park. Mother is sitting beneath a tree with Betty. Her broad hat casts a smooth, semi-circular shadow across her summer dress. Her eyes are closed, just resting. Walter and I have played every game we can remember or invent. We have picnicked heavily, greedily, and the hottest sun is beating down. We find the shade of another tree and flop to the ground. Mother lifts the brim of her hat, finds us, waves happily and then rests once more. We lie facing each other and we talk about all those things that only interest young boys. We are passionate, convincing and creative with the truth. We spread our immature imaginings out upon the grass and watch them skip, scrap and scramble like a vast family of rabbits. We feel our muscles relax, our necks soften and our heads descend ever closer to the thick, long grass. There is of course never a moment when you fall asleep, only those moments before and those moments after. I wake first, my head heavy and my arm tingling beneath its own weight. Walter sleeps for another ten minutes or so. I lie and watch him, measuring each breath in and each breath out. For some of the time I imagine that he is in a mirror, my pretty reflection. I copy him, his mannerisms and the unconscious ticks of sleep. When I bore of that I just watch his round, brave face, pink from exertion and heat, tiny little hairs holding hands across his top lip. I imagine for a while what it must be like to be him, to have his thoughts and his memories.

Walter's body grew in weight and shrunk in shape, as though he were trying to curl in on himself. Occasionally, a half-grunt would leave him, fading like an unheard scream. The floor around my feet was tacky and treacherous with his blood. It had rolled in thin strips some ten feet or so, gathering in tiny pools like the departing tide. I had dreamed many times of a life without Walter, of losing him, of being lost, but never, even in childhood nightmares, had I dreamed this brutal, unforgiving tale of woe. I looked up to the sky, that fateful and faithful companion and it gave me nothing. No explanation, no apology, no triumph and no regret. It was, just as I was, nothing.

We're toddlers, maybe three at most, running along the beach. Walter's footprints are bold in the wet sand and then, within seconds, they disappear beneath the layers of froth. He falls, I fall. He stands, I stand. I feel the splashing sea running down the insides of my thighs, cool against the breeze. Walter doesn't see me. He knows I am with him but he doesn't see me. We're at that age when your companions are just those people that life leaves behind when it moves on. He knows I am Harry just as I know he is Walter but only later will we learn what that means.

Walter made another sound, more pleading this time, more apologetic. The deep scar on his forehead was no longer pink. I sensed that the important part of Walter had gone, leaving just the barest remnants of the man I knew. Just the shell. Almost impossibly, his eyes unfurled, searched the excruciating light and found my face; they held me, spoke to me. I dropped my face to his, feeling his wet breath go meek against my cheek. His face was carved in china but his lips moved slowly; so slowly that I could hear the skin stretch. He edged his head forward, with agonising effort, and laid his lips against mine, for just a moment. He breathed into me, barely a mouthful. His lips were already cold.

*

We buried Walter at dusk on a patch of sloping ground to the north of Bernafay Wood. We bound a spare tunic over his vast, cooling wound and the chaplain covered Walter's face with a sack. I tried to help carry him but I simply didn't have the strength; my body ached in a way I had never known before. And so they carried him, my friends, tossed and torn like they'd fallen from a tree, eyes edged in the colour of their souls. They were so gentle, and I loved them for it, lowering Walter's echo into its tight resting place. I was locked in a stare, watching the sheen of moisture on the inside of the hole suck Walter in, eating him up. The chaplain read a prayer, committed Walter to God and then stepped back, evaporating through the night to wherever he would be needed next.

The ten of us stood along Walter's flank, arms draped across shoulders for comfort and support. The two hands on my back gripped hard, burying fingers deep into my muscle. One of the burial party stepped forward to fill the grave.

"No," Charles instructed softly.

The man took his hand from the spade and stepped back. Charles broke away and others followed, leaving Tommy and Rupert as my bookends. As gently as it was possible to imagine, they layered soil on Walter's body until all but his head was lost. Johnny looked at me and I nodded. Softly, so softly, earth was laid across that precious sack. In a few moments Walter's shape had gone and inside five minutes the ground in front of us was nearly flat. Peter and Donald pushed the cross into place, taking a few seconds to ensure that it was straight. Walter's details sang out from the crossbar like the sweetest lament.

Their work done, they returned to me, faced Walter's grave and snapped to salute, like the immaculate soldiers they had become. As they held their tribute, Johnny stepped forward and lent his cricket bat against the cross, as if it were resting on the pavilion wall, just waiting to be used. They broke down then, to a man, taking themselves away to pray for time to be undone, for that day's sun to be born again, for a different past and a different future. I sat on the floor, eased Rupert away, and stayed with Walter until well after the darkness had overcome the light.

"This was supposed to be our adventure," I whispered. "It wasn't meant to end like this."

I always remember as a child how much I used to like being sick. It wasn't something I would choose, obviously, but it often came as a blessed relief from the swollen nausea, the headache, the dizziness. Being sick seemed to signal the beginning of the end, the first step in getting better, and so at that moment I vomited forth all that trapped emotion, all that pent-up misery that had threatened to smother my senses. I grasped my earth-lined hands to my face and moaned my way through great, husky gulps of sadness, tears hitting the ground so heavily that they might have fallen from Heaven. I pulled at my fringe, feeling the sweet scratch of hairs breaking free, tumbling to the ground, over and over themselves. For a few moments I was dying myself, collapsing into the earth, digging myself into a trench at Walter's side, to hold his hand amidst the weight of France. My lungs fought for air, fought to be heard, to be served, but they were being drowned out by the memory of guns, the laughter of boys and the earth-carving torrents of dismay.

Eventually I lifted my thumping head up to see all but Walter had been lost to the invading armies of shadow. I crawled to beside his sack-covered head and, with great effort, traced a shaking finger along the angles and curves of his name, his rank, his regiment. I drew that finger up and down the cross, left and right, tracing the shape of the crucifix time and time again. Slowly, like a much older man, I shifted my body around until that cross was at my head as well. My best friend was at my side, just as he always had been, and together we surveyed those bright and peerless stars.

"It frightens you doesn't it?" Walter asked me suddenly. I tried not to look at him but failed.

"What makes you say that?"

Walter didn't reply. Softly, he edged himself a little nearer to me, shrinking the gap between us and making the roof whinge lightly. What it was, I thought at that moment, to be that known, that understood. I felt ready to tell this young man almost every thought that lived in my head but I also knew that I probably didn't need to, as he'd put most of them in there himself.

"The stars are interesting," Walter said softly.

"If you say so."

"You'd be less scared if you looked at them properly."

"Walter, I am not scared of the sky."

Walter didn't respond, he just edged his body nearer to me again and pointed upwards, encouraging my eyes to climb his arm, his hand and his long, thin finger. "That," he began, "is the North Star. That one over there is Hercules and that one is some sort of bear I think, or maybe a dog."

"Right," I replied, feigning disinterest.

"And there's a hunter here somewhere as well, on a horse I think," his finger drifted along the stars, flicking and circling them tenderly, looking for a pattern or shape.

"There's a cross there," I said, spotting a large, six point crucifix directly above us, almost perfect but for a slightly sloped cross-bar.

"So there is," Walter replied, patting me tenderly on the arm. He drew his finger over it slowly and deliberately, up and down, left and right before shifting himself back over to his side of the roof.

"You're not scared anymore are you Harry?" he whispered.

"No Walter," I mouthed, "not anymore…"

Chapter Seventeen

The water was cold by the time I climbed from the bath. The pads of my fingers had gathered into tight, uncomfortable swirls. The smell of my mother's fragrance had gone but my body still hummed happily to her kind, loving touch and my skin still gasped for the cleansing strokes of the cloth.

I stepped out of the bath onto numb, splintered feet. The pink spots of my fingers had no sisters in my toes; they remained deathly white like threatening fungus. I hugged a large, old towel around my shoulders, struck by how big it seemed. From where I stood I could see down into our yard, into the small out-building. If I had moved nearer the window then I would have been able to see across the wall and into Walter's yard, where we had once danced in the freezing moonlight, and to the shed roof where we had spent so many nights dreaming of our futures. My legs felt like paper at the thought and instead I edged away, feeling along the rim of the tub for support.

I had been hidden away behind the front door of our safe little house for a few hours and much of that time had been spent in the bath, failing to wash the war away. In a rare act of kindness and humanity the army had sent me home. I was due leave anyway, we all were of course, and Lieutenant Huff recognised a useless man when he saw one. Initially I refused to go, protesting meekly, before realising that I was utterly empty, utterly broken. I blew home on the prevailing wind like a drying leaf.

The door clicked again and opened modestly. The outline of my father's profile appeared at head height. He had been out in the parish when I had returned and mother had sent Betty to fetch him. A stark and shocking taste appeared in my mouth but I couldn't place it.

"Harry?" he croaked. I made no sound. "Harry, you need to go next door, you need to speak to the Crouchers. Harry?"

I remained still and silent, my poor hands gripping the towel tightly, bunching it in the middle of my chest. The door edged open further and my father's head entered ridiculously, his eyes to the other corner of the room.

"Harry, I know you can hear me." There was just the slightest hint of irritation in his voice.

I saw him take a deep breath. His head disappeared for a moment and then reappeared, attached to his body this time. He stepped with overly-practiced confidence into the room, closing the door behind him politely and purposefully. He turned and looked at me and I was shocked at how small and old he looked. His eyes looked starving and his moustache was limp, as though a determined squall might throw it into the sea.

"Look, Harry," he began, his hands clasped together, "deepest, deepest condolences for your loss. This is indeed a sad, sad time."

"Stop it!" I snapped back. "Stop it at once."

"I beg your pardon?" he responded, his limited patience already so thin that the light of the afternoon was shining through it, illuminating the back wall.

"I am not one of your parishioners. Don't you dare talk to me like some old widow."

"Harry, you are not to talk to me like that. You must remember I am your father."

"And I am your SON!"

It was the first time I had ever shouted at my father. I heard small feet scamper across the landing and down the stairs. Father's eyes flashed with anger, and then tiredness, and then something so, so sad that I almost pitied him. I stared at him with unforgiving, unyielding intent. Two or three times he drew in breath to speak, tightening the air around us and bringing the walls nearer.

"What happened to Walter was a terrible tragedy Harry, but it is at times like this that we must…"

"What? What must we do dear father because frankly I have no idea. I had no idea what to do when I got out of the bath. I have no idea what to do when I leave this room and I as sure as Hell don't know what to do when I step outside that front door."

"Harry, please"

"What?"

My father shook his head slowly. He looked to his hands, rolled his thumbs absently and then re-took my gaze.

"At times like this we must trust in God..."

"No."

"Harry..."

"Now is not the time to trust in God...your God. Now is not the time to talk to him, to consider him or to ask him for guidance. I've just marched away from France leaving my childhood friend, my brother, buried in a dozen inches of French shit. Now is *not* the time."

"But for the grace of God," my father snapped back, "but for his grace that would be you Harry. He has protected you and you *must* be grateful."

"Grateful?!"

"Yes, grateful. He has kept you safe, preserved you. Your faith has been recognised and rewarded and those that have forsaken him have..."

"No!" I shouted again, my voice cracking at unusually high octaves. "Don't you dare say that, don't you dare!"

"We both know he had doubts Harry. At times like this you have got to protect your faith. You protected yours and you have come home. Walter weakened and he has not."

"You bastard!" I spat at him, stepping forwards. He also stepped nearer, pushing his portly, puffed face under my chin and jabbing his finger into my hidden wounds.

“Grateful. You are my son and you will be grateful!” he wrapped his hands tightly around mine and began to pray. I recoiled sharply, thudding the back of my legs against the tub. He followed me and continued. “Pray! Say the words damn you.” He grabbed my jaw with his hand and I shoved it away before driving my fist into his chest, propelling him backwards and to the floor.

He scrambled to his feet and made to come at me again, his face reddening in rage, but my towel had fallen to the floor in the first scuffle and we both grabbed for that instead like it was the truth. We engaged in a brief, surreal tug of war before he let go, his expression opening and closing. My father’s eyes ran along my body like drips of sweat. My battered and twisted shape stood between us; burned, bruised, scarred and starved by two years of soldiering. My ribs were prominent, my muscles writhing impatiently behind thin, grey skin. The rips in my chest had healed into raised and purple screams. I dropped my hands to my sides and turned my palms towards him. He was transfixed, his face still but for a dragging twitch in his left eye.

“Is this what I have to be grateful for father? Is this what a saved man looks like?” I whispered heavily.

After a few seconds he clambered to his full frame and backed out of the room slowly as though retreating from an angry dog. He didn’t look at my face.

I heard him descend the stairs, quickly and with purpose. I then heard him crash through the back of the house and into the yard. I shifted to the window and watched as he edged his way into the dim and cluttered out-house. He pulled the door closed firmly, but it bounced back a few inches to leave his shape just visible to me, half-shadowed beneath the low roof. I watched as he dropped to his knees and clasped his hands together in near frantic prayer. And then I saw his words fail and falter before, in a sudden capitulation, his face crumbled in despair. I stood naked at that window for many minutes, watching my unswervingly stoic father do something I had never known him do before. He cried relentlessly, beating his chest as though to free something stuck in his throat. Occasionally a sound would reach me, a yelping breath cutting through the thin glass, and each time I felt nauseous and almost painfully guilty. I prayed for him to stop, for the madness to pass but by the time it did everything I thought I knew about my father lay shattered and unrecognisable on the floor.

*

The door was open. Mrs Croucher was sitting in the front room in near darkness, her heavy frame filling a small armchair. The fire had not been lit and the room hung with the damp chill of a grey autumnal day. I guided myself by memory to the far wall and brought life to the two old oil lamps. Light curved up the wall, along the ceiling and dived into previously hidden nooks and crannies. Mrs Croucher's demeanour changed little, the musty light highlighting the shadows and failures in her large face.

Feeling sick and weak, I sat down opposite her, perched anxiously on the very edge of the seat.

"I'm so, so sorry," I whispered. Mrs Croucher didn't react at first but slowly her eyes searched for the sound and found me.

"Everybody's sorry Harry," she replied hoarsely, as though she had a mouthful of broken glass. "Everybody wants to say sorry but no-one wants to take the blame."

My heart punched away against my ribs, bashing from side to side like the pendulum on a falling grandfather clock; my guilt was large and odious in that small room. As I searched my dim surroundings for rescue, so I noticed all Mrs Croucher's new paintings. Some were leaning down haphazardly from the walls, others were propped against furniture, and one was on the window-sill obscuring the view of the street. They were not happy pictures, not at all. Many of them were vast, swirling pieces, thick with paint laid over paint over paint, but it was the one on the window-sill that caught my eye. At first glance it was obviously Walter's father, a handsome portrait of a middle-aged man. The lines on his face cut and curved pleasantly and the arc of his chin was as familiar as the sound of his voice. But then there was something about the shape of the mouth and the specks of light she'd dabbed into the eyes. There was a warmth coming from the canvas that didn't make me think of Mr Croucher; it made me think of someone else. This wasn't Walter's father, this was Walter. This was Walter as the man he would now never become.

"He should never have gone. He should have stayed at home with Hattie. You know that Harry, don't you?" she was looking at me more distinctly, more definitely. I nodded quickly and earnestly. "So why did he go Harry? What made him go?"

My mouth ran dry. My eyes searched instinctively for the door but the lamps faded for a moment, obscuring my options.

"I did Mrs Croucher. I did."

The words left me before I even knew I was going to say them. The hairs on the back of my neck snapped to attention, cold air striding down my back. My guilt smashed out through the window, expanded down the street and soaked-up the ocean. Mrs Croucher shrunk a little before propelling herself to her feet with a small sound of exertion. I tried to swallow. She stepped nearer to me, laid a large, masculine hand on the crook of my neck and kissed me hard on the cheek.

"No Harry," she whispered as she drew away, "not you Harry. Not you."

She left the room and went to the kitchen, returning after a short time with a pot of tea and a slice of fruit cake.

"Please," she gestured and I poured us tea. I bit into the cake with as little enthusiasm as was possible but my frantic appetite betrayed me, gushing in delight at the flavour, the texture and the love. The sad lady in front of me warmed a shade as I ate and so, for just those few seconds, we shared a thin pocket of pleasure amidst it all.

"Walter's favourite," she stated when I had finished. I nodded again. With a small motion of her hand she directed me to the mantelpiece and that last photograph of her son. How glorious he was then. I can remember the picture being taken as though it were yesterday. I had been standing to his side and had I chosen that moment to stretch my arms out in front of me then my fingers would have been in the picture too. I glanced at him quickly as I passed him to his mother. She held him in her lap, angled so that only she could see him smiling back. Tears queued impatiently behind my eyes; an old, familiar door holding them back.

"Thank you for coming round," she said thoughtfully, "I know it must have been hard." That bowing door creaked ajar but I caught the tear before it broke down my cheek. "You'll never know what it means to be a mother Harry and right now I envy you that, really I do." I looked at my hands, studied them, too afraid to meet her eyes. I nodded my head and then realised I should be shaking it.

Mrs Croucher lent forward in her chair, causing the back legs to leave the ground for a moment. She took my hands in hers and stroked my thin fingers with her fat, calloused thumbs.

"Harry?" I could smell the faintest hint of alcohol on her breath. "Harry, I need to know. You understand that don't you? A mother needs to know."

"Needs to know what?"

I lifted my eyes to meet hers. She was soft and doughy, like an ancient bear. She didn't need to say anything else. Understanding soaked into me like butter into freshly baked bread.

"I'm not sure I can," I replied, my words fading away.

"You must."

So I told her about the shell. I told her that I'd been with him and that it had been quick. I told her as much as she would ever need to know and not a single word more. I said nothing of his pain, the way he looked, the shape his body made or the rich slick of blood that even then I could see running across the carpet, over her feet, into the fireplace and up the walls. I told her all about the burial, where he lies and the way the sun sets across the small, quiet slope. I told her about the trees at his feet and how each spring they would be swollen with blossom and the sweet sound of unrepentant birdsong. I did everything I could and then, to my deep disappointment, I melted into her arms and wept for her, for myself and for that wonderful, haunting picture on the window sill. Mrs Croucher held me for a long time in a spell that was only broken by the back door being opened. Walter's father appeared in the room.

"Oh hello Harry," he said effortlessly, "have you seen Walter? I've got something to show him."

“Not now dear. Go and get washed-up for your tea.” Mrs Croucher’s voice was suddenly soothing and light.

“Very well, see you soon Harry.” Mr Croucher left the room, whistling, and mounted the stairs two at a time. I tried to remain calm but my face was clearly dancing with panic.

“It’s all right, he’ll be okay.” Walter’s mother said to no-one in particular.

“Doesn’t he *know*?” I asked as quietly as I could.

“Come with me.” she instructed, leading me through to the back of the house. Three large oil lamps had been lit, throwing light all the way across the yard. Where the strongest arcs of light mixed, there was a tall, imposing trestle and on it there sat a vast oak coffin.

“Oh God,” escaped from me. I clapped a hand to my mouth and held it in place with the other.

“He knows,” Mrs Croucher whispered. “He just doesn’t understand yet.”

Tears ran from me again. That retaining door had long since been swept out to sea. Mrs Croucher held me until I calmed.

“Have you been to see Hattie?” she asked me eventually, sending yet more heavy jabs crashing against my tired and bewildered heart.

“Tomorrow,” I whispered into her bosom.

Chapter Eighteen

At the front, men dream of leave.

They dream of being back with their families among the alien comforts of home. When they go, their faces are broad vistas of contentment and hope and how we envied their freedom and their fortnight. Yet when they returned to us, kit bulging with the bounty of home, they often told us of sad exchanges, sorry incidents and a misplaced sense of belonging. Some even claimed that, for all their horrors, they have no home left but the trenches of bleeding Europe. We would mock them, disbelieving, happy in the knowledge that our homes, our real lives, were happier and warmer than theirs. When we got our leave we would have the time our lives.

I walked to Hattie's family home through sheet upon sheet of late October rain, marvelling at the solid ground beneath my feet and the burning colours of an English autumn. A member of staff opened the door and I was politely ushered into a large, expensively decorated room with views over a rich, green lawn. To start with I assumed that I was waiting for Hattie but eventually I realised she was already there, looking out across the view from a high-backed chair. Another chair had been positioned as a mirror opposite to where Hattie was sitting. I lowered myself into it with trepidation.

For all the trauma of the last few days, Hattie was immaculate. Her dress was neat and delicate and her hair had been sculpted ambitiously. On her hands she wore fine, lace gloves and expensive perfume effused the air from the folds of her gown. Her eyes were in the mid-distance, glazed and lost. We sat for ten minutes in ever-tightening silence until I finally spoke.

"How are you?" I asked her. Hattie broke from her stare quickly as though my voice had been shockingly loud.

"I am a widow Harry, how are you?" She looked at me with something approaching contempt.

"I'm so sorry," I replied.

“You know Harry,” she continued, disregarding what I had said, “you’ve never been a great deal of use to me. You’ve always been so very…so very *there*.” Her teeth were gritted, forcing out her jaw unpleasantly. “But I thought if anything, you were at least reliable. You could be relied on to always be there, protecting him. But I rather suppose I was wrong.”

My face creased with a combination of anger and upset.

“Ah, I am sorry my dear Harry. Does it hurt to hear someone tell you the truth? Did you not realise? Did you not realise that was your job, your purpose my dear Harry, your whole raison d’être? Oh I’m sorry…it means ‘reason to be’. It’s French.”

“Stop it Hattie. Please stop this.”

“I am bereaved Harry! Your failure has left me bereaved and I shall do as I please.” Hattie pouted in my direction like a truculent schoolgirl before turning her eyes to the lawns once more. I watched her pupils suck in the scene and her face return to stone. I stood, waited a moment for her to speak again and then, gathering my hat and coat from the housemaid in the hall, swept back out into the rain.

*

I arrived at Ruth’s front gate running with water. The desperate sadness of my trip to see the Crouchers had become great fury at Hattie’s rudeness and by the time I arrived at Ruth’s home I was near desperate for the sounds and smells of the Regiment. I leaned over the gate to unfasten the bolt and heard the front door shudder as though hit by a gust of wind. A second later, Ruth appeared in the doorway and, without a care, she sprung down the path and leapt into my arms, fixing her mouth onto mine with sheer desperation. I cannot be sure how long we stood there, thick with embrace, but by the time we entered the house Ruth’s blonde hair was two shades deeper, raindrops sitting on her forehead and cheeks.

“It’s so good to see you Harry,” she breathed excitedly. I chose to ignore the deliberate way she spoke my name and I was pleased at how willingly that bitter memory yielded. She led me through the kitchen and into the back room, standing me in front of a raging fire. "My Aunt is upstairs, asleep. I will wake her so she can see you as well, but not yet..."

Ruth disappeared out of the room for a while and then returned with a towel and a steaming cup of tea. She kissed me on the cheek again, the first happy smile I had seen since landing in England.

"Try and warm up, and get those shoes and socks off," she said maternally, taking my hat, coat and jacket, "I just need to go and..." she gestured at her wet hair and clothes.

"Of course," I replied, following her invitation.

My hands were still shaking in fury from my one-sided exchange with Hattie but the tea was sweet, kind and calming. The heat from the fire battered against my shins and thighs. I dropped to my knees and let the warmth run across my chest and face. I closed my eyes and felt it hammer against my eyelids, feeling steam lift off my hair and evaporate in the orange glow. At some point it seems that I fell asleep, just for a few seconds, and only woke when hot tea ran over my fingers and onto the hearth. I drained the cup, placed it back on its saucer and dropped it gently onto the mantelpiece with a pleasant, high-pitched tone. I ran my hands through my hair, removing the final few drops of rain, and dried them quickly in front of the flames.

To my left, the door at the back of the room creaked open, and a bare-footed Ruth tiptoed in through a large pile of cushions, her hair roughly dried and her body draped in a soft, ivory nightdress. The nightdress breathed in the orange light, reflecting it back in tones of peach. I struggled to avert my eyes. Ruth walked across to me and, wrapping her arms around my waist, she laid her head on my shoulder.

"I'm so sorry about Walter, poor Walter. Poor Harry." I could feel the heat of her face against my neck and the faintest brush of her breasts against my chest. The smell of her hair and skin drifted upwards, bringing with it the kindness of happier times. After a moment or two she stepped back and looked at me, her pure, blue eyes alive and questioning.

"Your wounds," she said tenderly, reaching to my face.

"They're fine, all healed now," I replied quickly, "all forgotten."

"Show me."

"You don't want to see them Ruth. They're just a couple of ugly scars, nothing to see really."

"Show me," she insisted, lowering her hands to my shirt buttons and beginning to undo them.

"Ruth, really," I stopped her, grabbing at her hands and dropping them to her sides. Her mouth pouted sadly. "There's nothing to see, really there isn't."

"I don't want to see them Harry…I want to touch them." This time, when she raised her hands, I let her remove my tie and undo the buttons of my shirt. She peeled the shirt from my back and laid it on a chair. With her eyes locked to mine, she then lifted my undershirt up my chest and, with my help, took the clammy garment over my head.

"Your Aunt," I whispered.

"I told you Harry, she's asleep. She won't be disturbing us."

Ruth picked up the towel and dabbed it lightly over my chest. Her eyes were directly in line with those ugly bursts, but she made no sound. Laying the towel down Ruth stepped inside me again, beneath my eye line, and ran small, pale fingers across the scars. I winced at the cold and she drew back, startled.

"Do they still hurt?" she asked, concern on her pretty features. But I was already shaking my head.

"Just cold hands," I replied.

Ruth smiled softly and moved closer still. This time, she placed her cool hands on the back of my trousers and laid her warm lips against the scars. She kissed the pitiful upturned knots of skin lovingly, moving her mouth across my chest, backwards and forwards, planting light, absorbing kisses every few inches. After a few moments, she tipped her head up towards me, took my chin in her fingers, and pulled me into a long, deep kiss. I felt her tongue bump gently against the inside of my teeth, her lips open wide, covering my mouth.

We kissed for a few seconds, one of Ruth's legs dropping outside of mine as though to hold me in place. It may have been the heat of the fire, or the sad bewilderment of the time, but there was something reckless in the air that afternoon, as though all the rules of the world were but playground rhymes.

Ruth drew away from me, leaving my chest feeling cold and exposed. She stepped to the back of the room and, for a moment, I thought she was leaving. But she wasn't. With the slow elegance of a ballerina, she turned, crossed her arms over her stomach and began to gather up her nightdress in her fists, sucking the hem up from the floor inch-by-inch to expose more and more of her flame-tanned legs. Her feet were slightly apart, and, as the nightdress drew high, I could see the soft swells of her upper thighs resting lightly together. The hair there was pale and exquisitely fine. Ruth lifted the remainder of the nightdress from her body in one movement, the neckline catching puckishly on one of her ears. She dropped it to the floor absently, her face colouring with a dusting of rose. For a minute or so she just stood, a dreamy, honest expression on her face, her skin glowing a warm, unbroken white but for the tight, dark symmetry of her nipples.

Then she stepped towards me again, her narrowing eyes hooked onto mine impatiently. Barely blinking, she undid my trousers, loosened them, and pushed them to my knees. Drunk in the happy warmth of the moment I shifted my feet inelegantly until the trousers fell to my ankles and then to the floor. Ruth's eyes were still following mine, mirroring the way they flicked and fixed. I felt her reach for the waistband of my underwear. Her hands brushed hard against me as she did so, her fingers warm and adventurous. I turned my hips slightly as her head dropped out of sight, my underwear pushed to the floor and away. I could feel her breath against my thighs. She kissed me hard.

Ruth climbed back up my body, drawing her lips and breasts up my chest until I could kiss her again. If ever a moment was timeless then it was this one, drawing out the distance between home and the trenches like an unbreakable thread of elastic. We held each other there, the fire at its hottest, spreading dampness on our skin where it met. We danced just as we had before, Ruth moving against me, with me, rocking and pushing against my frame like a building breeze. Every few moments we would kiss and I would feel Ruth bend further towards me, as though she wished to pass right through my body.

By the time she broke away, the fire was down to the embers, blisteringly hot but calm and measured. Ruth moved to the back of the room once more, gathered together a mound of cushions and lay down.

I looked at her there and I loved her; a sweet, pretty lady in her early twenties. She placed her hands behind her neck, gathering up all but a few strands of her light hair. Her pale skin fell down over her body as though it were running milk, over her breasts, her hips, down her thighs, knees, shins to her toes. Slim and womanly, her eyes locked in place, holding my gaze. I walked towards her and dropped to my knees. With fine and frightened care I drew my fingers over her shoulder and down the front of her chest. The skin beneath my fingers drew up into a million tiny bullets, fine hair reaching out to me. My fingers continued to move downwards, heat playing at their tips. I glanced up to see Ruth looking at me, her mouth slightly open and her eyes tearing into me like starving dogs.

"Don't let me stop you Harry," she whispered firmly. She beckoned me onwards and I obeyed, lowering myself carefully down by her side.

*

"Thank you for your letter."

Mother and I were tidying the kitchen after a thick, perfunctory family meal. My last formal meal indeed before I had to board the train back to the south coast. As always, she had turned the wheels of my stay with simple efficiency, but we had barely spoken. Indeed very few words had been exchanged in the house at all since my altercation with father.

"It was very important to me," she continued, fussing her way around the kitchen, her heavy eyes casting slowly around the room. I desperately wanted to reply, to cultivate the conversation, to talk about Walter, but none of the endless words at my disposal seemed remotely useful.

Mother snapped the creases from the tea towels, hanging them over the handles of the range to dry in the fading heat. She pulled a long, kinked thread of metal from the back of her head, allowing a few errant strands of hair to break free. She rubbed her fingers hard into the space it had left behind, as though to satisfy a deep, deep itch. I moved near to her and grabbed her shoulders. At first she was stiff and reluctant but in a moment or two I felt some of the tension melt away down her back. I placed my fingers either side of her slim neck and pushed my thumbs tentatively into the globes at the back of her head, ruffling her hair and causing her head to shift gently from side to side. She hunched her shoulders up before relaxing and tipping her head back towards me. Half a moan escaped from her. I continued for a few minutes, changing the strength and position of my grip, watching the top of her head dance in the silence. Eventually she let out a small exasperation and allowed her head to drop back completely onto my chest.

"What was it like next door?" she whispered.

She hadn't been round. I knew father had, more in a professional than personal capacity of course, but in all the time I had been home I had never known mother even go into the yard for fear of being overwhelmed by the sadness seeping through the wall.

"Like the inside of a cave," I replied through a swallow. Mother exhaled deeply through her nose.

"I will go and see her, I will…just not yet."

"I know you will mother," I wrapped my arms around her neck and she hugged them like a thick, warming scarf.

"I just feel so…" her voice trailed off, our attention momentarily taken by a short, loud noise from the Croucher's side of the building. Mother flinched.

"I know, so do I," I replied, dropping my forehead onto her hair and smelling the dusty, sweaty odour of a domestic life.

"Harry…I'm glad you came home. Even if it meant…I'm just glad you came home." There was some flavour of shame in her words and a soft, childlike sense of bewilderment. Mother began to cry, in that much-practiced secret way of hers.

"But what about Walter?" I asked.

“I cannot grieve for Walter,” mother replied quickly, “at a time like this I can’t afford to grieve for another woman’s child. I don’t have the energy.”

“But it’s Walter. This isn’t just another picture in the paper mother. We’re talking about Walter.”

“Look Harry,” she began fiercely, turning to face me, her eyes unable to hide, “maybe I’m not like other women. Maybe other mothers are different, better. I’m sorry, but all I think about when I wake in the morning is getting through to the night again without someone knocking on that door. I live in the silence Harry, the utter, blissful silence. Because if there is silence then there is no-one telling me that my son is dead. I heard them knock on next door Harry, I heard that knock and I ran upstairs to the back room. I hid under the bed Harry, searching for that silence. I was still there when your father came home. I am sorry that Walter is dead, really I am, but I only have one son.”

Mother walked out of the kitchen and padded softly up the stairs. I knew better than to follow her. Later, I asked her if she had ever wished that I had been more like Walter.

“It is only you that has ever thought that. You’re the only one that wanted Harry to be more like Walter, only you.” And with that the conversation was over.

*

Father shook my hand on the morning of my departure, making a point of seeking me out before he left on his morning rounds.

“Your mother would like you to come home for Christmas this year,” he said, closing the door as he did so. I watched him walk down the road, hat pulled tight over his ears against the wind and I wondered if he wished he too were bound for France rather than the ever-decreasing circles of parish life.

Mother held me for a long time, intermittently breaking free to stuff some other keepsake of home into my pack.

“I don’t want you living in silence,” I told her, my finger a crook underneath her chin.

"I like the silence," she replied.

"Then at least promise me you will read. Read all the books you can find and then when I come home you can tell me all about them. Story after story after story."

"I will, I promise." Mother turned away quickly, causing one insubordinate tear to flick from her cheek and mark the wall.

Betty stepped into the rain with me and walked to the end of the road. I was struck by the woman she had become. Taller than most, striking and nearly beautiful, she had something of an air of the regal about her and a grace that mocked the child I remembered. We hugged at the end of the street.

"We all hope you come back soon," she told me that afternoon, "but only when the job is done. You have to finish it Harry." There was something hard in her eyes, an anger, a wound. I nodded and kissed her cheek.

"We know what we have to do," I told her, slipping into the cloud and marching away to the tune in my head; the tune of my friends, the tune of the regiment and the fast-gathering pace of the victory charge.

Chapter Nineteen

A couple of days after saying my goodbyes to Betty, I was back with my friends at the foot of Trones Wood. The trenches had taken a battering in the autumn rain and an air of damp discomfort sat limply on thousands of hunched shoulders. They were quiet in my company, too polite, too restrained and most of them looked light on sleep. In spite of themselves though, they were thirsty for trinkets of home. I dished out my bounty like a fading grandfather, bringing grateful smiles to faces bereft of happiness.

After a few hours Rupert came to see me.

"How was it?" He asked. "How was it really?"

"Dreadful," I replied, "Unspeakably dreadful."

Rupert left me for a few moments, pressed some ill-fitting iron sheets back into service against the shifting trench wall and then crumpled down by my side. He let silence do the rest.

"I fought with father," I began, "and Hattie was simply spiteful, but it was Walter's parents…that was awful. I don't know how you're ever supposed to cope with that."

"What did you say?"

"I can't really remember. I remember she was very nice to me, Mrs Croucher, very kind. And then there was…" I trailed off, unsure as to whether I wanted to finish the sentence.

"There was what?"

"A coffin."

"A coffin?!" Rupert repeated, his left eyebrow jagged and high. I nodded quickly.

"He'd spent three days on it apparently, joining it, planing it, varnishing it. And when he came in he asked me if I'd seen Walter. I think I just sat there with my mouth open. It was horrendous, just awful."

Rupert rubbed his face, pushing fingers into his eyes as though he was trying to scrape them clean. A long, frameless sigh rolled out of his crooked body.

"I never thought I'd say this," he husked, "but I wonder now if I'll ever go back."

"Don't talk like that Roo, you know not to talk like that."

"No…no that's not what I'm saying. I'm just not sure that Cromer can be my home again. Too much has happened, too much has changed. I'm not sure we'd recognise each other anymore."

I knew what he meant; a home without Walter felt like no home at all, but then there was mother and Betty and Ruth. It seemed to me that, whatever happened, I would have to go back and face what remained of my life.

It didn't take me long to get back into the routines of trench life. My friends emerged from their sadness slowly, tentatively, like baby birds chipping their way out of their eggs. Over time, they helped me to find my own stability and comfort, such that it was, and within a few weeks we had managed to layer thin muslins of time over the loss of Walter, masking it slightly. There would be days when I would think of him constantly but then there would be others when life would assume different characteristics. There were never days without Walter, or even hours, but there were snaps of life in spite of what had happened and, in these tiny fragments of fresh air, I found enough strength to carry on.

*

As the second winter of 1916 gathered ominously at the edges of a rusted France, so familiar noises began to be heard among our vast, sprawling ranks.

"Surely it's too late now," Johnny said one day, balloons of white air puffing from his mouth as he spoke.

"Maybe that's exactly why it's the right time, when Fritz isn't expecting it?" Peter replied, to general murmurs of approval.

"It's not much of a choice is it?" Tommy asked. "Back over the top or another winter here? I think I'd rather go over."

"Me too," Gordon agreed.

"I don't know," Donald joined in, "it might be bloody uncomfortable but no-one's going to shoot me down here."

"Don't be so sure!" Sid quipped and a modest ripple of laughter rolled through us.

"Maybe we will be home for Christmas after all," I added, thinking of what father had said. I felt the air in our small dugout change as everyone swallowed that thought away.

All around us, the great machinery of war was being oiled, tested and calibrated once more. Sights were being set, measurements taken and contingencies embraced. We didn't know it, not at that point, but within the week we would be taking to those short but significant ladders again, lifting ourselves out into the open and baring our teeth to the Germans once more. And this time our final objective would not be the blood-slapped tree stumps in the foreground, or the broken village on the horizon. Indeed it wouldn't even be the mythical towns that supposedly existed a short bicycle ride away. Our objective this time would be to blast a hole in the German ranks so wide, so vast and so substantial that they would have no alternative but to fold up their picnic blanket and scamper home; home for Christmas.

A lifetime had passed since we'd first gone over the top, amidst the hot knives of summer. We were unrecognisable from those boys, our distant sons, and my heart ached for the innocence and nostalgia of it all. It was too much to think of Walter that bright morning, to think of his surrender, his fatalistic focus, and so I forced those memories deep into the shadowy crevices of my mind. Our anxieties were changing. On one hand we were exposed to the realities that our naivety had previously kept from us but on the other we had become toughened by the intervening months, brutalised even, and our focus was not on what might happen to us, but rather on how we might happen upon others. For all that my scars itched and stretched beneath layers of filthy clothing, I thought little of being wounded again. I had learned that fortune pays no attention to fear.

The hardest thing for me, as we thinned out the paraphernalia of soldiering into portable pieces, was not what faced me above the ground, but what I would be leaving behind beneath it.

In all the time I had spent as a soldier I had never once disobeyed a direct order, or even considered it if I'm honest, but twenty-four hours before we launched ourselves into the unshakable shadows of Trones Wood I was in the shadows of an entirely different set of trees. I had asked the Lieutenant for permission to pay my last respects at Walter's grave and my request had, in no uncertain terms, been denied. But, nonetheless, I had seized an opportunity of moderate chaos to melt through our reserve lines and, under the anonymity of darkness, cover the short distance back to where Walter lay, at the foot of Bernafay Wood. I rather suppose a court martial could have awaited my return but, fortunately, my absence was never noticed, or never recorded at least.

I ended my journey beneath the earliest flirtations of dawn, a thin line of light spreading itself out behind the farthest silhouettes of the distance. The closer I got to Walter's grave, the harder it was to place myself in the sea of undulating mud. A world without landmarks is a shocking and disorientating place, particularly when the very shape of the earth is being changed daily by the grinding battery of munitions. A stretcher party passed me, with intent of some sort, so I stopped them and asked for guidance. They were a group of Australian soldiers.

"Were you looking for something in particular?" one of the men asked me, the greying stub of a cigarette in his lips.

"Well yes, one particular grave if that's what you mean." The man pulled a face like he'd just bitten through his lip.

"The top line of graves starts just over that brow, past that clump of tree stumps over there, but it's probably not how you remember it…it's taken a bit of a battering in the last few weeks."

I nodded a terse 'thank you' and the men moved away. They exchanged words and then shared a cackle of laughter that slapped me across the face. I clambered unsteadily up a small rise, slipping a couple of times on the damp dirt. When I reached the crest I could easily make out the top line of graves, many dating back to the summer, but beyond these graves, as the land leaned downwards to where we had buried Walter a few short weeks earlier, there was no such order. Here, destruction had fallen upon death with guiltless abandon. Giant shell holes dotted the slope, scarring the sacred earth and mixing the broken crosses back into a pile of forgotten wood. Every few yards, a grave would sit pristine, untouched by the rape of the land and as quiet and settled as the day it had been filled. These corners of peace were rare however and as far as the straining eye could see, the horrors of war were dancing again, to a new tune. I clambered my way through the wreckage, stopping occasionally to kick dirt over those shadowy half-shapes that had once been at rest.

Eventually, with the help of the ever-lifting light, I came to a familiar corner where trees were at my feet and the sun would linger longest in the evening. I knelt down and felt the strange warmth of the earth. Right in front of me, where my precious friends had lowered Walter, there sat a beautifully smooth bowl, carved with precision and emotion. It curved from my toes, down deep into the earth before climbing again with remarkable symmetry some twelve feet beyond my reach. I could smell the heat of the kiln.

There was nothing left of Walter's grave. No cross bearing his name, no earth mounded to his height. The shell blast had been so accurate, so telling, that for a while I wondered whether Walter had ever existed at all. War makes strangers of our long-held emotions and idiots of the people we think we are. I sat by that huge hole for many minutes, unable to conjure anything from the life I had lived to help me tie down the way I felt. Desolation I suspect is the only sufficient word; how else does one describe the pain and relief of utter emptiness? In the end, all I could think of was Mr Croucher's sad, obsessive project, its futility and its poignancy. Whether we would make it home or not, we would never be able to inflate ourselves enough to fill the gaps this war would leave behind.

On the far side of the shell hole, I could see a few pale inches pushing outwards, creating an ugly bump in the otherwise smooth lines. Lowering myself into the bowl I edged slowly towards it, unable to determine what, or who, it might be. Even as I lowered my hand onto it, I was unsure as to whether or not it would yield beneath my fingers. Happily it didn't, it was just another faceless fist of wood, and I tugged at it with limited enthusiasm. As it worked free however it began to take a more recognisable shape. After a few inches the wood narrowed into the neck of a dark handle, a good dozen inches in length. I worked it free and lifted it to the light.

It had belonged to Johnny's grandfather originally, no mean cricketer himself, and Johnny crowed and glowed about the runs that it had made. Obviously we responded by reminding him how few of them had been made by his fair hands but we all envied the history that had been preserved beneath decades of dirt and oil. Johnny had brought it with him across the channel the way the rest of us had brought our optimism. In all the upheaval and drama, trauma and mystery, that cricket bat had stayed with him, and with us. It had become a mascot of sorts I suppose and for as long as I live I will never forget the sight of Johnny laying it on Walter's grave. Like Walter, like so many others, like our optimism, it had become a casualty of the thundering farce. The blade was torn across the middle, making it little more than a bitter looking club. Its days of summer glory were gone and its future, if it were to have one at all, would have to be different. I wiped it on my tunic, cleaning it as best I could. I thought for a moment that I could see blood on the handle, but at the next glance, it was gone.

As I walked away from that ploughed graveyard, the broken piece of wood held tightly in my hand, I began to feel sharp spikes of anger poking away inside; anger at myself, at the war, even at Walter and, for just about the first time, at the Germans. Without them there would still be Walter, there would still be cricketing summers and partying winters. There would still be marriages, children even, and the opportunity to become something valuable. Without them there would still be the sweet, invisible glory of normality and maybe one day there could be again, but not until we had ended this war, even if it meant throttling the life out of the Germans with our own bare hands.

I didn't need to explain to the others what had happened. One look at my face and the shattered bat was all that was necessary to convey the scene. I still roared with fury, my jaw locked tight and my neck pulsing heavily. It was a feeling that barely left me all day; a raw, grinding headache the inevitable result, and when Lieutenant Huff came seeking volunteers for an advance party, that feeling spoke through me as though I was no longer there.

There was the Lieutenant, and then four other men that I knew by sight rather than name. We huddled into a small dug-out as darkness fell.

"Listen chaps, we've got a troublesome bugger just on the edge of Trones wood – machine gun post – and it has to be taken out before we go over at first light, or we're done for. No artillery this time, so it's all about us."

Lieutenant Huff spoke like the man he was, private school educated, a career soldier who accepted war as simply the fulfilment of life's expectations. His demeanour was constantly one of mild irritation and a fidgeting sense of self-doubt. He looked at us each in turn.

"I'll lead," he continued, "we need to get right under Fritz's nose on this one, bombs at the ready, and then finish the job by hand. Once we're done I'll signal back for the first wave. Get this right boys and there'll probably be commendations all round. Fuck it up and we're not going to survive to see the mess."

For the first time I understood that fatalistic shrug Walter had carried with him for so long, but rather than allowing it to weigh me down, I tried to use it to make me bigger, stronger. As we gathered in the sap awaiting the Lieutenant's order, I imagined Walter at my side, watching me. In my left hand I carried a Mills bomb, with three others strapped to my body, and in my right I grasped the handle of a broken cricket bat. I grasped it so tightly that much of the blood and most of the feeling had run back down to my wrist. In that intangible gap between the end of the night and the start of day, we entered No Man's Land.

As instructed, we followed the Lieutenant, shifting in behind him as he snaked along the ground. Occasionally, he would gesture with his hands, holding us still, keeping us down or perhaps guiding us passed a stray thatch of wire. Our progress was painfully slow and I felt sure that dawn would arrive suddenly and spectacularly, exposing us to the German fire. After a few minutes we began to hear the unfamiliar intonations of the oblivious enemy. I could just make out the machine gun post away to our left, a dark raised bulk above the parapet. With unexpected grace and efficiency the Lieutenant slid on further, in barely disturbed silence. As we closed in, I had to summon all my control to stop myself from jumping to my feet and storming the post alone. We settled into our final positions, just feet from the machine gunners. They were whispering to each other urgently; four, possibly five of them. There was the unmistakable creaking of a gun being swivelled from side to side. My heart rattled in my throat like a trapped bee.

The Lieutenant held us for a few moments until silence and the element of surprise returned. He then leapt to his feet and, with an ancient exclamation of intent, hurled himself and his bombs upon the target. We followed, bounding towards the noise and commotion, explosions rippling through our hair and clothes. Pistol fire followed, and then a scramble of activity to our right as the Germans realised what was afoot. Raised voices followed and then a horrendous cry, two more blasts and then the deep, bitter smell of heat and metal. I found the entrance to the post and burst into a scene of murder and counter-murder. Two of our men were down, whilst a couple of theirs had splattered their way out of the canvas sides. Lieutenant Huff was driving a knife into a third. Out of the darkness I noticed another German climbing to his feet, with bayonet drawn. Just as he moved to the Lieutenant's side, I stepped forward and brought the remnants of Johnny's bat down onto the side of his unprotected head. There was a noise like a vast stone being dropped onto a frozen pond and he went down, instantly still.

One of our corporals had exchanged fire with their officer and both were down, seemingly in a bad way. Lieutenant Huff emerged from the tangled bodies on the floor and swung the machine gun round sharply, opening fire back down the German trench. Shouts and grunts were audible above the chattering death.

"For God's sake get this in the air Parker!" he bawled at me, slapping a flare into my hand. I scampered to the door, waited for the Lieutenant to open fire again and then scrambled back into No Man's Land. I lit the flare with shaking hands and watched in awe as it curled into the sky, screaming brightly back at our trenches. Within moments there was a response, and small scruffy shapes began to emerge above ground, just a handful at first and then many, many more. They seemed to cover the ground quickly and soon I was part of an army again. The machine gun had fallen silent and I returned to the captured post to find the Lieutenant trying to put the gun out of use once and for all.

"Here," I said, handing him the bat, "use this."

Chapter Twenty

Trones Wood fell quickly. By the time the shortening day narrowed to a point, the only Germans left among those bloody trees were dead ones.

Our new front line had been the German reserve line when the sun had risen and how we revelled in our luxurious and novel surroundings. The dugouts were deep and sound and the food stores were far less modest than those we had outpaced. All around us there lay the ashes of a quick escape – strewn clothes, abandoned weapons and dozens of helpless wounded. They looked at us mutely, with the grateful eyes of the liberated.

Word of our raid on the machine gun post spread quickly. Only the Lieutenant and I had survived the assault and for a short while we were the focus of much attention.

"There'll be a medal in that for you, no question," Johnny said, clapping gloved hands across my back.

"Damn right too," Sid echoed, "Well done Harry!"

I smiled at their kindness and their vigour but felt only sadness, regret and a pervading, hopeless sense of disgust.

As the night folded-in upon the evening, so many men were sent back to rest, to gather themselves again. We however remained braced against the front line in case Fritz mounted a last desperate attempt to gain some sort of foothold in the war; a war that was threatening to burn itself out quickly, into a deep, scorched and weeping scar. The night had a purple quality to it, a richness of light that spun a little magic into the chilled air. Behind us, we could sense the surviving trees trying to breathe, to take something from the night, something that would nourish them until the spring when, surely, they would be allowed to grow again. In front of us there were vast acres of nothingness. Dream upon dream, nightmare upon nightmare; teasing and provoking our tiredness. It was hard not to feel that the end of the war lay just out of sight, just beyond perception, but at that moment we knew a hundred feet no better than we knew a hundred miles.

"Can you feel him watching?" Tommy whispered into my ear.

"Walter?" I replied at once. Tommy's pause left me cold.

"No…Snowy."

I smiled broadly at the thought, only to feel the loss of Corporal Harvey jab me in the ribs. Johnny appeared to my other side.

"Fritz better not be setting up a fucking dinner party out there," he added.

Just at that moment a short, sharp sound leapt into the air, like a marble being dropped onto a tin can. We all started, lowering ourselves along the sights of our rifles, fingers red-hot on the triggers.

"Shit, that got me!" Johnny laughed after a few moments, raising himself back to his full height.

Everyone allowed themselves to breathe again. I tried to move my finger back from the trigger but for some reason I couldn't straighten it, couldn't relax my hand. I thought little of it at first, such cramps were common in the damp and cold, but after a few seconds I began to get alarmed. There was no pain as such, but my finger was tightening on the trigger, the hand closing into some sort of claw. I began to panic. My other hand tightened itself against the underside of the barrel, carved into it like a knot in wood. Even my shoulders were frozen. The only part of my upper body I seemed able to move was the finger on the trigger. I opened my mouth to ask for help but by then it was too late.

My single gunshot burst into our lives like a bottle breaking in the middle of the night. It's hard to put what happened next into a confident order. My paralysis snapped clear, sending me flying backwards onto the floor of the trench, curse words and gasps emanating from those around me and, an indeterminable distance into the future, a German soldier cried out in pain. Later, I would receive two commendations; one for my cricket-bat wielding exploits at the machine gun post and the other for that single shot, a shot which identified and foiled a clandestine counter-attack and brought all manner of screaming hot metal down upon what remained of German hope. A shot which, one senior officer would tell me later, was the starting pistol for the final stage of the war.

In the end it was easier to ride the acclaim than to explain. I pretended to have seen my target. I pretended that I had seen him about to launch a trench mortar. I pretended all manner of things just so I didn't have to talk about what had really happened. In truth I don't know who or what fired that rifle. I just know that I didn't.

*

Not since we had been cooped up in Colchester had we been so impatient to get going. With the temperature dropping daily and the Germans reeling, we were straining at our leashes like hounds, desperate to be allowed to complete the kill. To the rear, vast and famous regiments were being mustered, their uniforms starting once more to fill, their heritage looming large in their eyes and their cap badges glinting in the new winter sun. Like a great choir they mustered behind us ready for the chorus but we would be going first. Those boys of 1914, those fully-qualified amateurs, those strong-willed, strong-boned yet hopelessly untrained wisps of English pride would lead the way. We had earned their respect and we had earned the right to take this great army back to glory, back to the pages of storybooks and back into the hearts of a nation.

In the end we waited two more days and, throughout that time, the artillery slung giant rocks at our invisible, departing enemy. The deep puddles of rainwater shuddered with every shell, breaking up the thickening scabs of ice into a thousand triangles of misted glass. We cleaned our equipment, an endless task in the throttling autumnal filth, wrote short and optimistic letters home and distracted each other as best we could. We were soldiers by this point of course, as much as any man around us, and we were no longer burdened by the weight of our own fertile imaginations. But there was still fear, our peerless and loyal companion, rubbing away like a tree branch at a window pane. We busied ourselves in its presence, shrugging off its grip and rejecting its pleading gaze. The night boxed us in, deep and tight, threatening to blank out the dawn, a thousand dawns. There were chances to sleep, but few were taken, men choosing instead to bounce from one foot to the other, reminding the blood to move, encouraging the toes to feel the shells' rhythm drumming through the earth.

The dawn did come, but it was excruciatingly modest, lifting the light just a couple of shades. Deep, white clouds sat across our heads, moving slowly and sombrely like vast, heavily-laden ships, pushed along by an invisible breeze. The cracking cold of the night broke a little but not enough to wake tired limbs, soothe swollen toes or hide quickening breath. Time ticked on and we gathered again to pray, linked together just as we had been that summer's day a couple of lifetimes ago. The fingers of my right hand reached out for Walter and through closed eyes I could feel his skin against my gloves – warm, soft and alive. I kept my eyes closed long after the end of the prayer, until, eventually, I felt Walter leave me once again.

The bombardment climaxed and then stopped abruptly. Bayonets were fixed and watches checked. Way above our heads small, translucent scrapings of snow began their vast and meandering journey to earth, landing around us with violent poignancy. The first snowfall of winter; another winter. Lieutenant Huff blew his whistle. It choked a little in the cold, before shrieking through to our bones like finger nails down a blackboard.

"Home by Christmas boys!" he shouted.

We scrambled out of the trenches and jogged forwards, dragged on by the officers, their faces pink from bawling into the cold air. I waited for that familiar, sinister chattering of the machine gun, or the air-slicing heavy death of the shells. I waited for sight or sound of the mighty German armies, gathered just beyond vision, preparing for a final, glorious defence. I waited for death to dance with us again – teasing, flirting and then choosing. I waited for long enough to have all these thoughts time and time again. We had travelled some five hundred yards before arms waved ahead and we dropped to the ground. More time passed. I watched snowflakes gather on the barrel of my rifle, melt slightly, slip to the underside and then, as freezing drops, hit the earth. The commotion on the horizon passed and then we were ordered to advance again, slower this time, closing in on the ominous shape of Delville Wood.

We had moved to within two hundred yards of the first, splintered trees when the German guns finally opened up from deep within the wood. Quick bursts of rifle fire, that stomach loosening machine gun rattle and a handful of mortars cut through the thickening snow, searching targets among our rapidly advancing numbers. We fell to the floor again, scrambling this time for shell holes and cover. I saw the Lieutenant signal wildly to the rear, pleading for artillery support. He then jerked sharply and fell out of sight with a short, curtailed yelp of pain. I scrambled from beneath the cover of a broken cart and dragged myself forward, intermittently burying my head in my helmet as machine gun fire skimmed the ground. I had got within a short sprint of the fallen Lieutenant when the machine gunner spotted me again, swinging bullets along the length of my body, missing me by inches. Realising I had only a few seconds until the gun swung back, I leapt to my feet and dived full length into the shell hole. I crashed my face into the ground, shuddering my jaw. Blood ran quickly and heavily into my mouth, filling it uncomfortably. I spat the blood clear and clambered across to where the Lieutenant was lying, his head nestled beneath the lip of the hole.

He was hit through the shoulder, a big, open wound. I released his field dressing and applied it as best I could but the blood still came hard, soaking through the gauze before I had finished tying it. The Lieutenant was the colour of melted candle wax. His mouth was open and there was blood on his lips. His eyes were closed tight against the pain. I called repeatedly for stretcher bearers but my cries were lost in the blizzard, helpless against the elements and the growing confidence of the Germans guns. With no other option, I crouched in front of the Lieutenant, dragged at his uninjured arm and pulled his substantial weight across my shoulder. Getting to my feet took an almighty effort but I managed it, my back arched and my knees braced. With bullets whistling passed me, I carried the Lieutenant back towards our lines, breaking into uncontrolled running as the terrain rose and fell. I can't say how long it took, or how many times we fell, but eventually I broke back through our wire and dropped the Lieutenant's weight into the trench with a guttural roar of effort. A handful of men appeared with a stretcher to take him to the makeshift field hospital. As they lifted him on to the stretcher I noticed he'd been hit twice more in our retreat, glancing blows to the arm and leg, and the blood from his shoulder had soaked down his back and into his trousers. He had a dusting of snow on the brim of his helmet.

The artillery bombardment the Lieutenant had requested came moments later, as I scuttled back to join the attack. The vast, telling sound guided me through the snow until I found myself crammed into a large shell hole with a dozen or so other men, including Tommy.

"We're about to go in!" he shouted above the din, "As soon as the bombardment moves further into the wood."

A small, wiry corporal was crouched at the head of the group, loading a pistol and talking incessantly to the man at his shoulder. His head was bare and vulnerable, the snow in his hair ageing him dramatically. We braced ourselves, pleading that the artillery would be accurate and our attack would find nobody at home. So many prayers rose to Heaven from such a small corner of the world, I wonder how many of them were heard. The artillery paused for a beat or two, nothing more, and as it did so we flew into the trees, stumbling our way over twisted roots, broken tree stumps and half-concealed bodies. Other men joined us, many of them screaming their intent, their bayonets offered. The Germans remained, barely, their resistance drawn together into one small network of trenches, just a few yards across. They scrambled back into position just as we descended upon them, two huge swords crashing down on top of each other, braced in attack and in defence.

Tommy and I burrowed our way into a hole behind a giant tree stump and unleashed rifle rounds as quickly as we could. Men were falling around us, in front of us, behind us. Some men had entered the German trenches, bombs and bayonets making their mark, whilst others had fallen at the final step, slumped, bullet-riddled across the wire. Clambering above ground, Tommy and I bombed our own way passed the wire and into German territory. There were men everywhere, a sprawling ant's nest of activity. The wind was certainly with us, closing in on the Germans from all sides, like the returning sea pulling down a child's sandcastle. Sid and Donald were right in the thick of things as well, their bayonets reddened with combat and their faces marked with endeavour. It was a frantic and crazed time, full of the worst and hardest human realities, but the skirmish itself lasted barely an hour before the remaining German forces were killed, quelled or captured. Delville Wood had stood as a symbol of the horrendous journey to victory for so long and, before those at home had contemplated lunch, it was well and truly in our hands. The artillery began to speak again, seeking the retreating German tail, and our orders came to push further into the belly of France. Occasionally we exchanged fire with Fritz but on the whole we moved steadily on towards Bapaume, passing through gathering crowds and growing optimism.

The snow stopped early that afternoon and the clouds cut to reveal fingers of blue sky and the occasional blast of nourishing sunlight. We were warned to expect some sort of Hell when we reached Bapaume but at that point nobody realised what was happening to our North at Thiepval and across the Belgian border at Ypres. It seemed that this day was to be the day we had been waiting for, the day we had been promised by our history lessons, our storybooks and our long, happy days at play. Suddenly we were ordered to shelter in a sunken road; hundreds of men smoking and chattering away with confusion and excitement. Then there came the noise, like the drumming of fingers on table-tops, the hammering of hail on tin roofs, conkers falling in an autumn storm. Defying orders, we raised our heads above the banks of the road and watched in awe as thousands of men on horseback stormed through the open curtains of war to launch the finale. How remarkable they looked, how impressive, upright, determined and utterly at ease. Rigid colours flew back as they charged forwards, minute after minute of thundering hooves and grasping breath. Oh how we cheered and roared them on. What a sight it was, and what a sound it all made.

"They're through at Thiepval as well! The Ridge has fallen!" Johnny called above the excitement. "This is it gentleman, this is it!"

*

We reached Bapaume the following day to find it swarming with battalions from all over the country – Liverpool, Glasgow, Hull, Sheffield. There were even a few familiar faces we recognised from playing cricket in Lowestoft. The Germans were in disarray, retreating at Ypres and all across The Somme. There was even word that they were close to defeat at Verdun, where the French had sent so many of their sons to die.

We were given some time to rest and the ten of us passed it quietly, huddled around a boastful fire. We were elated, of course, but no-one wanted to talk about the end of the war, no-one wanted to tempt the fates. We just sat there, warm and tired, allowing the fire to draw moisture from our eyes and toast the battered edges of our skin. We spoke only occasionally; thin, happy memories, jokes we had shared before, days we had passed together. We shifted our positions, sharing the heat along our bodies and ate what modest rations we had been given. A couple of people closed their eyes for a while and we left them to dream. It was a heavy, poignant time. We all knew that this great, terrible and irreplaceable adventure was drawing to a close and for all that we yearned for victory, for all that we were desperate to survive, it was a little too much to contemplate the move back home. We'd had a life without war, and then a life of war, but none of us really knew what our next life would be like, only that it would be different again. I thought of Walter of course, and I know I wasn't the only one. I also thought of Ruth, of mother and of Betty but mainly, I thought of Walter.

That afternoon we were split into pairs and sent through the streets of Bapaume to salvage what we could and to rinse out any remaining Germans. Rupert and I were very careful, nervous even, taking turns to cross gaps and pass corners. There were hundreds of abandoned properties in the town, most repeatedly ransacked, and signs of life were few and far between. We approached a burned out charcuterie with some trepidation. The meat hooks still hung in the window but the wooden counter and shelving had gone. A curved piece of glass was clinging on to the top of the frame with illegible half-figures peaking up from its broken edge. There was a small fire still burning to the rear of the front room. I entered first, pushing the door open with the end of my bayonet. The smell was deep and suffocating and the air dry. I inched towards the fire, my eyes desperately fighting the shadows. And then I heard the unmistakeable sound of snoring.

He was so tightly squashed into the corner that he was barely visible. Lying there asleep, his head on his shoulder, his lips slightly apart, he looked no more than a child, a young teenager at the most. I motioned to Rupert and he drew alongside me. We stood there for a few seconds, bayonets fixed just a few inches from the youngster's ribs.

"German?" Rupert whispered.

"Got to be."

Rupert shifted his feet, making a sharp scratching noise on crushed glass. The boy jerked awake, his eyes wide and fearful. He saw us standing in front of him and mouthed a silent scream, trying to squeeze yet further into the corner of the room.

"What are you doing here?" I asked him, my rifle firmly focused but my finger back from the trigger. He stared at me pitifully, desperation and hunger slapped across his pale face. He shook his head slowly, climbing up the wall. His eyes flicked between our weapons and our faces. I jabbed at his hands with the bayonet and he revealed them to be empty, filthy and tiny.

"Out," I demanded, prising him away from the wall and shoving him towards the middle of the room. He made a short noise of fear but then responded, stumbling across the floor and through the doorway.

When we got outside we were able to take a better look at the poor lad. He wore an oversized British tunic but his uniform was unmistakably German. He was painfully underweight, his cheekbones drawn and his skin grey and stained. His hair was trying to be blonde and his blue eyes were too prominent. His breath came in sharp, painful gasps, like a child trying to fight away tears. He showed no inclination to speak.

Rupert searched the young German's pockets and found a handful of breadcrumbs, a single bullet and two small cigarette butts – a pathetic bounty by any standards. The only other thing that he had on his person had been tucked deep into the heel of his unlaced left boot. Folded once down the middle, the photograph was thin, faded and lifeless. It crackled nervously as Rupert opened it up, like a dried flower. Rupert stared deep into the picture, his eyes lighting briefly with some sort of acknowledgement. The young German was in the picture, but it took a few minutes to recognise the fit, pretty boy he used to be. He was crouched down in the bottom right, his face a warm ball of happiness and enthusiasm. Above his shoulder there were others, gathered together in a casual, scruffy pose. They leaned across each other, into each other. Arms were lazing across shoulders, smiling faces just inches apart.

The lad watched me nervously as I eyed the picture. After a few seconds he became impatient and thrust his hand forward. I held back for a moment, struck by his insolence in the circumstances, before re-folding it and allowing him to nip it from my fingers. He crouched quickly, stuffing it back into the heel of his boot.

"Your friends?" I asked him gently.

He looked up at me, his hand still on the picture. Initially I assumed that he hadn't understood but then he slowly stood, bringing the picture back with him. He opened it tenderly, his bleached-white fingers vibrating softly.

"Friends," he repeated in a deep accent, his voice soft and sore. He then snapped the picture closed, dropped to his haunches again and buried it quickly beneath the frail leather of his left boot. When he returned to his modest height there were tears in his eyes, eyes that looked unimaginably tired. He held my gaze stoically, trying too hard to show that he wasn't scared.

"Where are your friends now?" I asked him, the hairs on the back of my neck dancing in a sudden draft.

His eyes glazed over, seemingly unable to understand. He then made a strange sound in his throat and spat fiercely into my eyes. I yelped in disgust and spun away, wiping my face firmly on the arm of my tunic. Turning back I saw Rupert standing over the boy, bayonet inches from his nose. Rupert was shouting furiously. The boy kicked out petulantly, undeterred by the smell of steel, his legs flailing sadly, both boots flying into the air to expose feet that were black almost to the ankle. I stepped forward to calm Rupert. The boy shrugged himself clear, hobbling onto rotten feet, before losing his balance and thudding down on his backside. That final indignity seemed to break him and he stilled, dropping his tired forehead onto his lifted knees. Rupert's anger fast dissipated into pity.

I walked over to his boots and picked them up. They were both almost through to the sole and they smelled of blood, heat and rotting flesh. The folded photograph sat limply at the bottom of the left boot. I approached the boy and crouched in front of him. Tentatively, I lifted his right foot by the ankle. He flinched at first but then relaxed as I slipped the foot back into the boot. I did the same with the left foot, taking care to remove the photograph first, lacing it through his fingers. He lifted his head, crying steadily, and looked at me, through me, and then at me again.

"They're dead aren't they, your friends? Dead…tot?" I whispered, my face just a few inches from his.

His reply was a tiny nod.

"Alle von ihnen?"

That nod again.

Rupert swore under his breath and took a couple of steps away. My muscles creaked as I lifted myself back to my full height, stepping softly to Rupert. We stood together for a while, looking across to the small, ragged adolescent.

"We need to get someone to look at his feet," I said eventually, "and then we need to get him home."

We draped his arms across our shoulders and carried him back to the field hospital where the M.O. soothed and bandaged his feet as best he could. With the light falling from the day, I walked with the German boy to the edge of Bapaume, where all his fellow prisoners of war were being held in a vast pen. We knew that for all the indignity, he would be safe there. As I handed him over, he reached out a small hand. I shook it warmly.

"Erich," he said simply.

"Harry," I replied.

"Good luck, Harry," he replied in perfect English. I smiled at him paternally.

"Go home Erich. They'll be waiting for you."

Chapter Twenty-One

The M.O. came to find me at dusk, the light of the camp fire dancing in two of the widest eyes of the war.

"I've seen a few young soldiers, particularly German, but I don't believe that lad was even fifteen."

He shook his head as he spoke, so tired, his thin spectacles held together above his right eye by a badly twisted thread of wire.

"Have you heard about the Lieutenant?" I asked him.

"He was in a bad way Harry, a really bad way. But they tell me that they got him on a ship home. I just hope that he made it back. You know Harry, I've heard the Major is going to recommend you for a VC, and well-deserved it is too."

He slapped me vigorously on the shoulder and then melted back into the yawning darkness. We had three M.O.s during my time at the front – the other two were killed – and never had I known men so utterly focused on their vocation. They never flinched, cowered or hid. They simply stood where they could and did what they could, hour after hour, day after day, reinventing medicine. It may be a hundred years before we learn as much again as they learned in those raw, sorrowful months, slowly being hammered into the weeping earth.

For all the success of recent days, our billets remained cold, uncomfortable and dangerous. Sleep came from necessity rather than choice, men making new and mysterious shapes with their bodies, morphing to their surroundings. We huddled together in a frozen barn, much as we had on our first trip to the front. Bales of straw had been hastily piled-up to try and create the illusion of shelter but they were no better off than we were – cold, wet, failing and riddled with unwanted life.

Sleep abandoned me that night, just as it did every now and then. I didn't take it personally; each man took his turn on the unpaid patrol, eyes broad and bored, staring pointlessly into the distance like a broken telescope. I could feel every discomfort; the gathered creases in my tunic, my boots raw against my heels and the hard, uncompromising pressing of the barn floor against the back of my head. All around me the air hummed with slow, deep breathing and the thick, familiar odour of unwashed men.

Just as the lightest trickle of loneliness threatened to become a flood, my attention was drawn to the distant crackle of gun fire and the rolling, rumbling rowdiness of an emptying party. The noises came and went, to and fro, like the feeling returning to squashed fingers, but there was little doubt that they were drawing near; thunder claps sharpening their claws ahead of the storm. After a few moments the noises became voices, excited and demanding, their pitch and tone bending and changing through the air. I sat up, tilting my head to the noise as it built. Seconds later I was on my feet, sniffing my way towards the voices.

I walked tentatively, as though the ground were rich with risk. The voices came from all directions, building to a giant, invisible crescendo and then from the blackness came a figure, head down, sprinting towards us, his fists tight and his arms pumping at his sides. In his right hand there flapped a strip of paper. He almost ran into me, gasping for breath. I held his shoulders to steady him.

"It's over!" he rasped, waving the paper like bunting at a summer fete and stumbling passed me towards the barn. "They've given up…"

Within seconds the barn melted into rapture and noise. I was swept into the air by Charlie and spun round and round until my head fizzed and my stomach lolled. We embraced madly, slapped backs and shook hands. Officers appeared and we cheered them as Kings on horseback.

As the dawn arrived the following day it found many hundreds of men dancing, singing and swaying to the rhythm of stolen rum. The handful of locals that remained in Bapaume emerged from their hiding and joined the party, toasting their liberators and their forever friends. It was a moment that no words will ever justifiably or sufficiently describe. It was every emotion, every human sense and feeling. It was the joy and relief of having our futures returned and the solemn, stabbing sense of futility and loss. And somewhere, deep in the background, it was the terrifying prospect of facing life without war.

We were given orders and we ignored them. For the rest of the day our insubordination was similarly treated. So long as we looked busy, we were let be. I sat on the remains of a garden wall and fussed at my broken webbing. Rupert hopped over, trying to revive one of his boots with a tired old pen knife. For a long time we didn't speak, concentrating intently on the nothingness of our tasks.

"I think Sid might be drunk until New Year," Rupert said eventually. I pushed a small laugh through my nose.

"It's a strange, strange day," I replied, "good, but strange."

"What do you think it's like at home?" Rupert asked, staring into the distance as though he might get a glimpse of Cromer's grand pier, glistening on the horizon.

"I'm sure they're dancing in the streets," I replied and Rupert nodded enthusiastically.

"What are you going to do…I mean, when you get back?" he asked me thoughtfully.

"I don't know Roo, really I don't. I'm sure they'd take me back at Harvey's but I rather think I might stay on in the army and see a bit more of the world, India maybe. Yes, maybe Ruth and I will be married and will go to India."

"Really? You'd do that? I never had you down as much of a traveller."

"Things are different now though aren't they?"

"It's…it's never going to be exactly like it was, is it Harry? We can't go back to that now can we?"

I shook my head sadly, a deep swell of something uncomfortable growing in my chest. I focused intently on my task, ignoring the way the stitches disappeared out of focus for a while.

“There can still be cricket Rupert; whatever we do I am sure we can still summer together. From time to time at least.”

“What, you’d come back from India?”

“Some years, I’m sure. And whenever we’re all back in Cromer we’ll play cricket together. That is what we will do dear fellow. There will always be the summer and there will always be cricket.”

“But it won’t be the same will it? Not really, not…not without Walter.”

“No, it won’t be the same, but the game will go on.”

*

For a week we worked like dogs. Whilst our great leaders signed the all-conquering documents of peace so we laboured our way through the pitiful residue of war. In our small, insignificant way we started the rebuilding of France, a job that they will be completing for generations. Then an army of tired and dirty men began the long, freezing march back to the coast. We stomped through snow, bitter horizontal rain, screaming winds and knee-deep mud but we did it in glad heart, for every painful step was one nearer Blighty. We sang songs of victory, of home and deep, sweet laments for those that we left behind. We laughed together and cried alone, happy for the long nights to hide our tears, our truths and our fears. Earlier that year we had marched into a new and impossible world and as we marched away from it those early December days many of us were as bewildered as ever we had been. We knew we were bound for home, but did we really know where home was anymore?

The crossing was long, slow and grey with many men choosing the freezing blast of the Channel, and that long-awaited first glimpse of home, over the tight airless warmth of the cabins. Occasionally, something would be tossed overboard; some foolish, ambitious memento or a small, heavy tribute to a fallen friend. Pieces of us fell away in the wind, blown clear and clean from our bodies. My face stung in protest at the intermittent hail, but I never turned away from the wind. Alone for a while, I thought of those final hours before we began the march to England, those strange, perverse moments walking up and down empty trenches, drinking in the silence and the absurdity of it all. It wasn't that we felt we would miss the trenches, or even the war, but perhaps we realised how important it would be for us to remember how it felt and how it ended. Those final hours carried a resonance not unlike wandering around an empty school. Every corner screeched loud with memories and, perversely, a form of nostalgia. It was a welcome and much prayed for end but it was an end nonetheless.

I stood alone in what was once No Man's Land and talked to Walter. I told him that we were going home, and that he should follow us if he could. I told him that there would be cricket in the summer and that I would expect him to watch. I told him that Ruth and I would be married and he would need to wear a suit. I promised to look after his parents, and Hattie, and that for as long as I lived I would strive to make him proud. I thanked him for the privilege and joy of our friendship and the magic he brought to my life. I knelt on the ground and wept for him and then vowed never to cry for him again.

As I walked back to the trenches I took the time to look around me, to take a broad and considered view of my surroundings. The near ground was dominated by man-made constructions, mostly temporary, all recent. The majority betrayed their fabric in their colour; the deep, filthy tones of drenched soil, once more resigned to a winter without life. As we withdrew we would no doubt dismantle much of it, leaving behind just the barely healed scars of a harrowing time, like the flank of a badly treated horse. But in many ways it was the distant view which was most shocking. There were no significant landmarks on the horizon, no points of note, no hooks for the compass-carrying traveller. I had no doubt that something incredible had happened over the last couple of years, something that would change the world, redefine it in a way we couldn't yet imagine, but I wasn't sure the French people would ever be able to see beyond the pitiful sorrow of a broken country. The French would bounce back no doubt, but I couldn't help wondering then how fully they would recover, with one of man's greatest failings scratched forever into their palms.

We docked in Southampton amidst cheering crowds and raced through the damp December dawn to the trains that would take us to London, then Norwich, and then, finally, on to Cromer. Hours later, when the train began to approach Norwich station, it slowed to walking pace. There were people all along the final stretch, beside the river, waving frantically and happily as we passed. Young women jumped up to kiss men as they lent from the carriages and small children tossed flowers and sweets through the windows. The train lent to one side as we clambered to the glass and when it finally stopped we poured onto the platform like hot milk. The station was thick with people and the broad, familiar faces of our dreams. I was tossed in the crowd, happy to be moved by the sheer weight of relief. The swell dropped me beneath the station clock, right at the feet of my father.

"Harry," he stated softly, his palms open in a gesture of peaceful welcome. I stepped towards him, dropped my pack at his feet and felt him gather me up in an efficient embrace – tight and safe. He held me for a long time, my body relaxing in his arms as the seconds ticked on above our heads. Eventually I stood my full height again, father's hands clamped onto my elbows and his face tied to mine.

"So proud," he said with warm ambiguity, "your mother and Betty are waiting in Cromer...and Ruth of course." His eyes glinted for a second, in a manner that I feared could irritate very quickly. "Come," he said, guiding me by the elbow, "there is someone who wants to speak to you."

I picked up my belongings and followed him into the station. We bent away from the packed ticket hall and went instead through a heavy, green door marked 'Private' and then another, before entering a small room crowded with important looking men.

"Welcome home Private Parker," said a large man with a fussy moustache, drawing the population of the room to some sort of attention. I nodded politely, albeit with a look of confusion doubtless spread across my face. My eyes were invited towards a chair in the corner where a large man sat, an officer's coat draped across his broad shoulders and a glaring white bandage slicing diagonally across his torso like a sash. His face looked pained and pale but far healthier and happier than when I last saw it. He was very much alive.

"Lieutenant!" I exclaimed, stepping towards him in excitement before remembering myself and delivering a firm salute. Lieutenant Huff dismissed my formalities with a waft of his good hand and shifted his weight forward to welcome my affectionate handshake. “How good it is to see you,” I continued, “truly wonderful…”

“And I owe it all to you Harry.”

“No sir, I was just doing what anyone would have done.”

“No Harry, I shall not have that. What you did was remarkable - for a soldier and for a man. Reverend Parker,” he continued, turning to my father, “your son is a war hero.” My father flushed to the point of passing out and my eyes found my boots.

“Our good King rewards his war heroes Harry,” the Lieutenant continued, “and shortly he will be pinning a Victoria Cross on your chest. Very shortly indeed.”

The room rattled in applause and echoed to the sound of my knotted back being slapped by a dozen rich, swollen hands.

*

They marched us through the town to the Cathedral, where we stood, dripping thick winter rain onto the stone floor, to share a service with those hundreds of people that had come to salute our safe, victorious return. We sang with light hearts and heavy impatience, drumming our fingers and toes to the ringing calls of home. We smiled gratefully and kindly, shuffled respectfully back out into the fading light and then, on the last breath of being dismissed, we raced, screamed and bounced our way to the station and the train that would take us back. Back to the world we had left behind. To the homes of our past, the bewilderment of our present and the first moments of what was left of our lives.

The ten of us were the size of twenty with all our belongings but we squeezed into a single carriage nonetheless and sat sprawled in tall, untidy heaps like potatoes on the back of a cart. There were moments of jollity and glee and then periods of silence as we scuttled through the Broads and back into the scrapbooks of childhood memories. We all carried the weight of the short journey ahead of us like a paunch.

Peter and Donald were preening each other, checking uniforms and cleaning faces as though they were trying to pretend none of this had ever happened. My, how close they had become. How truly they were brothers. Charles and Terry sat back-to-back, using their comparable sizes for reassurance and balance. On the face of it they seemed the least affected by the war, more able than any of us just to live life as it was no doubt intended, one day at a time, and I had little doubt that for every hour that passed they would put sixty minutes of life between them and what they'd been through. Gordon was different – poor, blessed Gordon. The frantic normality of his life had been crushed by the savagery of war and his eyes sat deep with suspicion and caution. He would still leap, I had little doubt of that, but in the future he would look once, maybe even twice, before he did so.

Sid was the biggest character in the carriage that day. In truth, it had only ever been Walter that could live with him. Sid was one of those men who you could sometimes strangle for their selfishness, their untethered self-confidence and the way they never let you forget they were there. But for every minute I would spend angry at Sid I would spend ten laughing in his company. Come what may, come rain or shine, war or peace, Sid would be Sid and how could we not love him for it? Johnny had gone to war as a similar beast, his boiler of belief always well stoked, but he had marched home a bigger man, more than ready for the privileged future that was his destiny, more than ready to do his long illustrious family history very proud indeed.

I felt for Rupert. I mourned with him the passing of his innocence and his wilful naivety. I mourned that he had to see what he saw, had to feel what he felt. I am so grateful that he came to war with us, but we took more from him than he took from us and the war took the rest. No-one lost as much in the war as Rupert, apart from Walter. Rupert sat on one side of me on that final train ride, and Tommy was on the other. Tommy was quiet, but he was full of happiness. Since the day he left for France Tommy had been planning for this moment and under his arm, beneath a long blanket of brown paper he had something very special. Something that he would tell his beloved sister was the finest dress in France.

The first coughs of dusk sat over Cromer's familiar skyline as we came to the end of our five-day journey home. I chose to hang back, allowing my friends the first chance to return to the embraces they had left many months before. By the time I reached the door, Betty was almost on board the train, wrapping me up in her arms the moment my foot touched the platform. She held and kissed my face repeatedly, seemingly oblivious to the layers of grime clinging to my skin like a pauper's suntan and then she stepped aside to reveal mother, immaculate and elegant in her Sunday best.

"Hello mother," I managed meekly, "they're going to give me the Victoria Cross."

A vast, youthful smile spread across her face, cracking open the years and spilling us back to a different time, a time when we were younger, better. We held each other for a long time, the smell of her filling my lungs and tearing with precious generosity at the remnants of cordite, mud and rotting humanity.

"All those books," she whispered to me eventually, "all those stories. Oh Harry I have so many stories to tell you, so many stories." I nodded appreciatively, wiping a single tear from her cheekbone with the pad of my thumb.

"So many stories," I agreed.

Until this point, Ruth had been withdrawn, typically choosing the back of the stage rather than the front, but as I broke free from mother I noticed her step forward, stunning, cold and nearly blue in the early evening light. I reached for her face. Her skin looked so soft and pale that I wondered if my fingers might pass through it as though it were packed flour. Ruth leant her head on the palm of my hand, softly kissing each of my fingers in turn. A lost part of my life returned to me then, like I had come home to myself. In a moment of instinct I dropped to one knee on the platform and took her hands in mine. Someone made a sound, probably Betty. Ruth's features opened wide but gave nothing more away. Everything shook.

"Oh Ruth…please say you will be my wife," I pleaded.

And she did.

That night, with our parents back at home, we all became the younger generation again, paying our way through those old familiar streets of Cromer with our uniforms and our stories. We drank more than we should, said more than we should, promised more than we should and left our regrets for another day. It was a wonderful time, a magical time, right up to the moment I lost my footing on the old sea wall and fell heavily into this hospital bed.

All that time with Fritz trying to get me and I end up here because of a badly tied bootlace and some small glasses of ale. But I guess that about sums me up doesn't it Lily? Lily…?

*

Lily started to feel herself emerge from her trance. The sweeping light of dawn was at her feet, where her tears had left fat, drying stars on the floor.

"Thank-you," she breathed, before leaning forward and kissing Harry on the forehead. Lily's patient didn't react. "Can I get you some breakfast?" she asked him.

"Toast would be nice," came the four word reply, just as it did every single day. It was their game of sorts, but only one of them was playing.

Lily's back and legs ached but the levity she always felt after Harry's story would see her through another day. She absently straightened Harry's bedclothes and slipped to the door.

"Today," Harry said under his breath, "maybe they will come today."

"Maybe they will," Lily allowed herself to think, yet again.

Chapter Twenty-Two

Lily rolled the calendar nearer July with a shiver, happy to hear Florence's increasingly heavy tread approach her door.

"Morning," Lily said brightly, throwing a smile at her podgy-faced friend. Florence made the sound of a disgruntled farm animal and dolloped herself heavily into a chair.

Lily and Florence could barely have been more different. In spite of her modest upbringing, Lily had something of the lady about her, a china doll demeanour born out of the adoration of her father and brother. Florence on the other hand had been shaped by necessity. A ruddy-cheeked and crude Fen girl, Florence was emotionally and intellectually brittle, fighting the natural instinct which was dragging her inevitably back to a life of moderate contentment as an undervalued wife and mother. It wasn't hard for Lily to blink Florence out of her ill-fitting nurse's uniform and strap her instead into the sleeves-rolled-up and flour-dusted world of a country kitchen. Lily knew that this young lady, her life companion for many difficult months, was already better prepared for the role of a wife than she ever would be, and the role of a woman maybe even more so.

When they were first introduced, they cowered back from each other. Lily instantly shrunk before the large, bust-led lady, somehow infinitely older, more womanly and more knowing then she ever felt capable of being and yet Florence ducked her head as well, affronted by the simple beauty of the small, sweet young girl and expecting, as she was right so to do, a smarter brain than her own was tucked behind those God-gifted eyes. For the first few weeks they worked independently of each other, like the windmill and the rain, passing through each other at every turn but adding nothing. But as the grip of their work bore harder into their wrists, so they found comfort in the things they shared. Eventually, as their service threatened to become their careers, they developed a bond so complete that they lent into each other, waited for each other, worked best together. Like the windmill and its wind.

Not that they could see the transformation themselves. They still looked like children from different eras. They still looked as though they had been plucked from the farthest corners of childhood, and brought together to test how their upbringings shaped their endurance. They shared little in the way of beliefs, understanding or expectations but like all those young men they would now never have a chance to marry, they were sharing something far more powerful, far more important. They were sharing a lifetime.

"Good night?" Lily asked optimistically. Florence's body made another bovine exclamation.

"I think some of them are doing it on purpose now," she replied eventually, "I'm sure a lot of them could be discharged. A lot of them seem…well, you know."

"Seem what?"

"Normal. They seem normal."

"We'll let the doctors decide that one shall we?" Lily replied, very properly, the slightest hint of a smile playing across her eyes. Florence replied in kind, her lips parting to expose a wild cluster of large, clumsy teeth.

"I don't think your Harry slept very well," Florence stated, pulling herself to her feet with the effort of a woman three times her age. Lily blushed.

"He is not *my* Harry…"

"No, no of course not. So you say."

"He's not."

"I think he's got a bit of a head cold coming on, can't get comfortable and so on. I gave him a few more pillows but I don't think you'll get any stories from him today." She offered her teeth again, more of them this time and Lily allowed herself to reciprocate.

"Go to bed Florence, I'll see you tonight."

Florence flicked her wrist in a theatrical wave and disappeared out of the door, leaving behind a large drag in the patchwork throw and the familiar, unpleasant odour of continuous mild exertion.

Lily's bright mood continued, egged on by a prize-winning English summer's day. At lunchtime she snuck into the copious grounds for a few moments and allowed the warm sea breeze to bounce into her, pushing her playfully from one foot to the other. In-between the gusts the heat laid itself across her shoulders like a gentleman's arm. In spite of everything, in all its vast, incalculable and unrelenting guises, there were some days when it was possible to see a future that held a little more hope.

Although Lily felt for Harry as his summer cold pulled tight across his nose and throat, she was guiltily relieved not to have him at his most demanding. She was well aware that she would need her strength for the days to come.

"Can I get you anything for the night?" she asked him at the end of her shift. Harry lolled his head to one side to look at her. His sweating eyes followed a little slower, focusing after a few seconds.

"Lily," he said eventually, his voice gruff and pathetic, "I shall be just fine."

*

The following morning Lily was awoken by a polite but insistent knocking on her door. The dawn's light had risen but wasn't fully grown and Lily's clock would have afforded her another hour in bed.

"Just a minute," she said too quietly to be heard, feeling a need to go to the toilet swell as she got to her feet. Her head felt like it needed to be drained. Lily opened the door to find Florence looking even more flustered than usual, a state she somehow managed to combine with an underlying sense of boredom.

"Sorry to wake you early," she whispered, "but Harry's really not well. I thought you'd like to know." Lily tried to make a face of mild irritation but failed.

"What's wrong?" she asked quickly.

"He's got a terrible fever and claims to be aching all over. And..."

“And what?” Lily felt a little unsteady.

“He’s bleeding Lily, just a little, when he coughs...”

Lily closed her eyes and prayed to slip back five minutes into her dreamless sleep. She felt a sweaty hand against her arm, trying to comfort.

“Influenza?” Lily asked eventually, and although she never opened her eyes she knew Florence was nodding.

All things considered, Stapleton Hall had side-stepped much of the recent epidemic. They’d lost two patients since the end of the war, both perfectly fit and healthy men, drowning from the insides out. Lily could still see their faces, the lavender hue of their dying skin and the noises they made as their lungs failed beneath their own mutinous defences. But they still had to consider themselves lucky. They knew of other places, particularly in Northern France, where within a week the nurses had been made redundant by simple colds that became pneumonia or septicaemia and emptied the wards. The stories they had heard made their own sad tales seem like hunger in a famine and it had been nearly a year since the second of those men had died.

“But who did he get it from?” Lily asked, opening her eyes slowly to see, with great sadness, Florence and the daylight were still there, growing ever more real in front of her.

“It seems one of the orderlies has been very poorly with it,” Florence replied, now holding Lily’s fingers in her own. “He would have gone in to Harry’s room a fair few times the week before he was off.”

“What did the doctor say?”

“You know the answer to that,” Florence began, her Norfolk tones rubbing uncomfortably against her attempts to console. “He’s very poorly but we just have to wait and see. It’s out of our hands now.”

“He has protected you and you *must* be grateful,” Lily whispered softly, her eyes dreaming.

“Pardon my dear?”

Lily ducked back inside her room and dressed swiftly, her emotions spilling over the small floor space. She took herself to the toilet and sat with a small tissue pressed firmly across her mouth. She felt nausea rise and present itself in her mouth and then into the bowl. She retched dry for a few moments and then sat on the toilet again, feeling beads of cold sweat gathering along her hairline.

"Are you okay?" Florence's voice crept in from the other side of the door. The words were spoken again, with more urgency, before Lily could reply. Lily's first attempt to stand was unsuccessful but, in spite of a wobble, her second effort allowed her to unhook the door and afford Florence a sight of her colourless expression. Her friend smiled pitifully, making Lily feel like a chicken bound for the pot.

"I want to nurse him," Lily managed, tasting the discomfort on her breath.

"I don't know if Matron will allow that."

"I shall speak to Matron," Lily stated firmly and Florence, no seeker of confrontation, nodded solidly.

With Florence standing in the doorway, Lily dipped her face in freezing water, pinned back her sweat-soaked hair and slapped herself on the cheeks until blood brewed to the surface of her skin. Giving the mirror a look that may have cracked thinner glass, Lily stood her full height, breathed hard, and went to find Matron.

Lily watched the way the shadows changed across the floor. Even at this hour she could track the first salutations of dawn, the start of July, and her longest day. She'd stopped trying to make sense of the pattern of day and night. Without sleep they became no more of a rudder than the twisting discomforts of hunger and sadness. A tiny scratching sound broke her concentration. Lily turned to see a piece of paper had been pushed under the door. Lifting herself from the sharp chair Lily retrieved the message and read the inevitable – Harry's mother would be with them first thing in the morning. Lily knew how these things worked of course. After the parents were summoned there was only ever the Priest.

Harry was peaceful for the moment. For the last couple of days his breathing had rasped and fallen, cried and forgotten, struggled and survived. Sometimes he had coughed so hard that Lily had been showered with blood as his insides tore away at themselves. Harry's colour had fallen from that of a man struggling to live to a man preparing to die. The doctor had tried to explain each stage but Lily had barely listened. She had simply nursed and prayed, nursed and prayed. And when Matron conceded that all they had left was hope Lily hadn't batted an eyelid. Hope was all she'd ever had.

The rising sun began to bring light to the sky and as soon as it dropped into the room Lily rose from her seat at Harry's bedside, unhooked her facemask and moved to the small chest of drawers by the large window. The bottom drawer of the chest had haunted her for a long time and she had decided that she would open it again. The wood squeaked with surprise as she pulled, but Harry showed no signs of stirring. A familiar, unwelcome smell climbed up her chest and into her face. She removed the letters first.

There were four bundles of ever-increasing sizes, like something from a nursery rhyme. Each bundle was written in a different, distinctive hand, as familiar to Lily as her own. The first bundle had just three letters, the next maybe ten. The other two were bigger though. Lily weighed them in her hands sadly before pulling free the only letter that had ever been opened, at the top of the biggest pile, just as she used to do. She didn't read the letter itself, she never had, and instead she felt in the envelope until she found the picture that she knew was there. She tilted it to the optimistic light.

The eleven men, boys really, grinned back at her with rich relish. The personalities of Harry's story melted from the paper and curled into the air, bringing together the sweetness of their shared history. Harry and Walter bookended their friends, Walter particularly handsome, Harry a little more surly-looking than the man she had come to know. There was no doubt that the uniforms added a little something, making them look older and more impressive. As Harry had always suggested, their chests looked fuller, broader and personal though it was, you couldn't help feeling that it was an image fit to grace the history books of generations to come.

Lily laid the picture on the deep window sill in the best of the light before returning to the drawer and reaching inside. Her fingers found the fabric at once and, ever-so carefully, she pulled it to the front. For a few moments she stayed as she was, knelt uncomfortably on the floor with her fingers moving across the half-hidden garment like it was Braille. Eventually however she picked it up at the sides, stood and moved across to the window-sill. Here, she laid the garment carefully down next to the picture. It had been four years, but the tunic had changed very little. The blood stains were a little darker perhaps, like scorch marks, but otherwise the image Lily carried in her mind remained true and consistent. Two bitter rips separated the breasts and tiny colonies of dry mud sat crowded together in the folds.

Lily took a few deep breaths before sliding her fingers softly into one of the tunic's pockets. With a surgeon's touch she gathered up the contents and brought it into the light. Even though she had known what she was going to see, Lily still let a small gasp escape when she saw the petals again. Four perfect slices of life, so delicate that they could vanish yet so strong they could crush a heart. Lily felt a great darkness descend around her, an immense sadness for that poor little man, trapped beneath a horizontal hail of metal, gathering together the shattered memory of a fallen flower. At once she felt sure that she should put them back, put everything back and slam the drawer closed again but for a while she resisted her instinct, kneeling in front of the window, turning the petals over and over again as though she were looking for a secret. She kept doing this, absent from the world, until the dawn brought the merest glimmer of red to their veins once more, flesh to broken bones.

After tidying carefully, Lily dragged her weary body and heavy heart back to the chair beside Harry. He had shifted slightly so his face was away from her but the various sounds of his breathing had returned, moving inwards and outwards with pain and suffering, like the shifting elements eating up a lost and broken fleet.

*

In time the morning broke more assertively, throwing warm cubes of light through the room in well-practiced formations. Harry drifted, bobbing on the top of life precariously, the rope tethering him to the shore fading steadily. He coughed occasionally in his sleep, fiercely, as though he was trying to rid himself of something deep inside. Lily felt burdened by futility again, drying the stretched and shining skin of his forehead, only to watch the dampness return at once. She was reminded of a childhood story of a dry and parched land that could only be saved when one young girl, one child, had knitted all the clouds.

The sunlight suddenly blew harder, drenching the room in its kindness. Lily had to bring her hands to her face to shield her eyes from the scorching intent. Slowly they adjusted and allowed her to make out the broad bedroom window, shimmering and humming, magnifying the sun's efforts into a rich carnival of glory. Before Lily had time to question the phenomena, it changed again, curving at the top into soft ridges like a crown. Lily stood tentatively, still half-blind, and edged herself around Harry's bed, her head being pulled towards the window as though a grandfatherly finger were hooked beneath her chin. As she did so she noticed the crown come nearer, entering the room itself, coming to her. Those ridges separated softly into many fingers of light, reaching towards her kindly, in peace. Lily felt warm contentment soaking through her, wrapping her up and lifting her feet from the floor. She felt her toes kick-out in half-hearted protest, pedalling pointlessly.

The light became richer, rose coloured, and the fingers grew again, entering the room and taking the happy shapes Lily dare not believe they would, like the hills of home emerging from thinning fog. She spotted Tommy first, of course, his silhouette as recognisable now as it had been in those long days of childhood, chasing her around their yard, splashing her in the sea, watching her when he thought she slept. Then the others, just as Harry had said and finally, to one side, Walter. It was their faces that emerged last, beaming like the light that carried them. Lily closed her eyes as tight as she could, holding her breath and feeling her small nose wrinkle like a nervous rabbit. When she opened them again Tommy was laughing, mimicking her face and holding out his arms. For the first time in years Lily burst into a run, hurling herself at her brother until she felt his chest thud back against her face, the harsh fabric of his uniform scratching her, a button pressing into her cheek. Tears came alive and she screamed them out, banishing them into his unbreakable and immortal embrace. Tommy held her tight, his large hands circling on her back as though he were polishing a large, much-loved piece of furniture. The smell of him returned to her, the weight of him, the heat of him and the love for him.

After a few moments, he eased her away and disappeared into the glare, making Lily's heart exclaim with sadness. But before she had time to follow him he was back holding a broad bundle, wrapped in dull paper. He smiled again and passed it through to her. Lily's mouth fell open softly.

"Ahh," she breathed dreamily. "The finest dress in France? Really?"

Tommy nodded, the edges of his face blurring as he moved. Lily hugged him again and knelt before the package, tearing at the string excitedly, pulling it into ever-tightening knots. Behind her, the bed springs pleaded pathetically. A pillow hit the floor with an earth-shifting thud.

Lily's fingers didn't move, they stayed lost in a vast mystery of well-travelled twine, but her head snapped round independently like a threatened owl. It took a few seconds for Lily's eyes to tell her brain the story. Harry stood behind her, his pyjamas limp and oversized, his eyes vast saucers. One hand was braced on the mattress for support and his face was contorted into a smile of such happiness and relief. Lily's attention fell away from the parcel. She dropped to her backside and shuffled back to the wall like a child fearing the belt. Harry's first step forward was onto broken glass but thereafter he gained confidence and stability, his naked toes pointed sharply forward.

He went to the right of the line first, to Gordon and Charles, to Sid and Terry, to Donald and Peter. Each young man embraced him, and each time their heat and light grew, throbbing around the room. Johnny was next, complete with cricket bat across his shoulders. When he reached Tommy, Harry looked across to Lily heavily. The two men fell serious for a while and then laughed in unison at a joke she could enjoy but couldn't hear. Then Rupert, more beautiful than Harry had perhaps described, elegant in the manner of a woman but powerful in the manner of gladiatorial man. Rupert held Harry's head in his hands as though he were inspecting a fine vase. Rupert kissed Harry's cheek as he moved on.

Finally Harry came face-to-face with Walter. A cocoon of white light hid them for a few moments, but the faces of their friends told the story.

Eventually, after a few moments Harry stepped away, turned to Lily and blew her a kiss. Lily watched it dive and swoop across the room until it fell on her forehead and melted through her body like sand through an hour-glass, water through soil, love through time. Harry turned back to his friends and in an instant they snapped to attention and saluted. Harry returned their gesture before, arm-in-arm with Walter, he trod slowly into the light. In turn each man followed leaving just Tommy there, stepping slowly backwards, disappearing back from the world. Lily leapt to him again and grasped his fingers to her mouth. She held them there for a few seconds before she felt them twitch and shift, following him backwards. Lily took one last look at her brother's face. He was smiling at her, adoring her, and there were thin, petal fingers laced through his hair, like tiny memories of home.

For a few moments she could still see them, just as they had been, just as they were in the photograph, just as they were at the pavilion the night it had all started, just as they had been as they'd marched ahead of her, out of her reach down the streets of Norwich, one sad posy of flowers bouncing in her hands as she ran panting after them. But then they were gone, leaving burned against her retinas nothing but the relentless light, the shape of the window and a breathless azure blue sky over a swaying field of golden corn.

Chapter Twenty-Three

Lily had chosen her chair very carefully.

She could easily have spent these long, edgeless hours in one of the two more comfortable old armchairs in Harry's room but instead she had chosen the office chair – hard, miserable and poorly constructed. Lily knew that sleep would surround her like soft, comforting sheepdogs, yapping kindly at her heels, and she had no intention of yielding to its demands. But sleep had waited and waited; patient in a different way, on a different plain, always knowing, always confident and at some stage it had lifted her away.

Lily popped awake and up from the chair as though it had bitten her. She whipped around the bed on a sprinkling of toes, dropping to her knees in front of Harry, her cheek to his lips. Lily expected the worst but he was still there, just, in the distance. She thought back to the evenings she had spent with her mother watching the men go out to sea and how, even after the colours of the hulls had long been lost you could still see their lights, blinking away, blowing kisses back to shore.

Behind her, the morning's work was well underway through the window, grass ticking to the breeze, warmth climbing the long ladder to discomfort. Lily turned to take in the view, the edges of reality melting warmly. She felt a sadness as she reached the glass, feeling its solid reflection, the tough wood of the window sill pressing heavily into narrow hip bones. But there was something else now, a gauze over the wound. Lily took a moment to try to sharpen the pain, reopen the loss, but for now the long-walked avenues to such suffering were blocked, lost to her among the bewildering hours, the kinder memories, the shifting sands.

She leaned heavily into the window, feeling her skin threaten to bruise where it pressed, her damp breath painting and cleaning the window. On the periphery of her fixed stare movement caught her eye. Two figures were walking up the back path, briskly but timidly, heads near-buried in jackets in spite of the weather. Lily's eyes picked them up, watched them for a few seconds and then drew them into focus.

"Oh my God…"

Mrs Parker's first thought was how poorly Lily looked, how wretched. Her second thought was that Lily was running, but she had expected that. The young nurse's mouth was making shapes before Mrs Parker could hear the words.

"He can't come in, you know that," she stammered, pointing to Mrs Parker's companion, walking sheepishly a few feet behind.

"Now, now dear," Mrs Parker began, choosing kindness as her first weapon.

"But the doctors said…" Lily resumed.

"Do you *really* think I care for your doctors now Nurse Parnell? Really?" Mrs Parker interjected, changing gear quickly and smoothly.

"But…"

"Lily, my dear, what's the worst that can happen, really?"

Lily felt the wind change in her sails, bringing colour to her cheeks and self-loathing to her heart. Silence wrapped her up and pointed long, fat fingers into her face. Mrs Parker's companion gathered himself at her shoulder, his soft, apologetic smile familiar in spite of everything, like a much-loved song being played on an out-of-tune piano.

"Hello Lily," he said simply, solemnly.

"Hello Walter," she replied, blushing.

"I'm sorry about Tommy," he whispered into the healing emptiness of Lily's heart, "especially today…"

Each time Walter spoke, Lily saw more and more of him emerge from behind the face of a middle-aged man. In the near-six years since Lily had last seen him, Walter had been through things she could never have imagined. But of course she didn't have to imagine them; someone else had imagined them for her.

"And I'm sorry about, well, everything," Lily's voice almost failed her.

"I would have come every day Lily, if they'd have let me but they said it would kill him, they assured me it would. I would have come every day. You saw my letters…" Walter was beginning to get upset, and Lily felt a little frightened.

"She's knows that Walter, we all know that," Mrs Parker took Walter's hand and patted it maternally. Lily nodded as completely as she could.

Mrs Parker always impressed Lily. From the way she spoke, to the way she walked. From the things she said to the things she didn't. Lily knew that she would never call Mrs Parker a friend but she silently revelled in the small periods of time they had spent together at Harry's bedside, the secrets they had shared, the small, modest games they had played. Harry had described his mother almost mystically, as though she were something more than other people, other women, and Lily felt it as well. Mrs Parker, Lily believed, was how a woman should be.

"We should go in," Harry's mother said firmly and so they did.

Initially, Mrs Parker refused to wear a mask but after a handful of soft words from Walter she took the fabric and held it over her mouth. Lily hung back, just inside the door, to allow Harry's guests time to acclimatise. Seeing Walter in the room made Lily's heart quicken. Damp electricity ran along her nerves. Mrs Parker lifted the office chair from where it had been for three days and placed it by Harry's head. Walter stood behind her with his hand to his mouth. He softly began to weep.

"We weep for the dead Walter," she said suddenly without turning around, "We pray for the living and weep for the dead."

Walter filled his lungs and puffed them empty. He moved one of the armchairs, Lily's favourite, up to the edge of the bed and joined Mrs Parker. Harry's mother dropped one hand on Walter's knee and ran the other through Harry's lank hair without effort, affectation or doubt. For the thousandth time Lily broke down and collapsed in her head without her face, eyes or body showing one single sign.

"Walter, talk to Harry," Mrs Parker instructed with a steady voice.

Walter sniffed, huffed and then crackled into life, first with confused pleasantries and then, with more comfort, memories. For a while Lily forgot her nursing duties and leaned against the door frame, allowing Walter's words to flutter softly around her face. His tales were just like Harry's really, ringing with sunshine, sea salt and the endless summers that only ever seem to exist in the flawless world of reminiscence. Some of his recollections were the mirror image of Harry's story, like two soft hands clapping together to a well-practiced beat, but others were new and different; surprise presents hidden beneath the tree. Walter talked to Harry about the first time they had swum in the sea, the small crab that had appeared between them as the tide drew breath and the speed at which they had run back up the beach, screaming of monsters and nursing what could have been wounds. Mrs Parker's face shared the memory, a bittersweet visage of spreading lips and opening eyes. There were other stories too, other little treats too rich to be swallowed whole. Lily prayed with all her heart to hear Harry's story again.

During the day, doctors came and went. One of them, not a favourite of the nurses, made little attempt to hide his surprise at Harry's continued survival. Matron fussed about Walter's presence but the doctor dismissed her with a shrug of the shoulders and nothing further was said. In his own world, Harry teetered.

"Is Mr Parker coming at all?" Lily asked at one point. Mrs Parker didn't look-up.

"Possibly," she replied, "when he has quite finished talking to his God."

For a few hours Harry's visitors politely declined what meagre food and drink they were offered but eventually they succumbed to human need and prepared themselves for the duration. Mrs Parker frequently lifted herself from the chair and moved backwards and forwards through the room, not flustered, not distressed, just moving life along. Walter had passed from childhood recollections to reading county cricket reports from the paper, or any other snippets that drew his attention. Harry, for his part, had long since stopped struggling for life and instead he simply existed – meek, unobtrusive and small.

In the evening Mrs Parker produced a battered copy of Wuthering Heights from her bag. Pressing back the cover she began reading aloud in the tone and pace of someone intending to read all the way through to the end. Lily watched as Walter closed his eyes and so she followed suit, hoping that perhaps the three children could drift off somewhere together. Somewhere where the biggest drama in life would be the sting of a bee or the smell of burning bread. Lily didn't know Wuthering Heights that well, she had never liked it as a child, and so when she woke she had little way of marking time. Walter's eyes were still closed and heavy and he looked uncomfortable, hunched, as though he could still feel the world's hard edges pushing down upon him. Eventually the room fell dark, lit by just a single flickering lamp, but Mrs Parker continued regardless, without a break, bringing great swathes of gothic sadness into the room, laced together by tireless promises of everlasting love.

*

Mrs Parker may have read all night, Lily wasn't sure. All that she did know was that each time she bowed out of her own shallow slumber the words were still there, ticking away, telling the story. Walter had moved a few times, possibly to stay awake, and by morning he was sat on the end of the bed, a fair distance away from Harry, who remained hunched in a ball beneath his pillows. Instead of breakfast, Harry got doctors. Two of them arrived, with Matron, and tried to prompt a response from the body beneath the covers. After a few minutes they stepped back, exchanged a quizzical glance and then addressed Mrs Parker.

"I would say he was a little better," the elder doctor said gently. "Not at all well, but possibly a little better."

"Will he live?" Walter asked quickly.

"Let's just say this young man. Yesterday morning I would have told you, without any fear of contradiction, that your friend would be dead by tea-time. Today, I am not so sure."

With that the two doctors nodded their heads and shuffled out of the room with Matron following behind like a youngest child.

“Well that’s good isn’t it?” Walter’s words started as a statement but became a question.

Mrs Parker didn’t reply, she just retook her seat beside Harry’s bed, reopened the book and began reading again.

“Lily, may I have a cup of tea? And perhaps something to eat. Tea Walter?” she asked at the end of the chapter. Walter nodded and so Lily allowed normality to sweep her onto her feet once more and back to the kitchens where, in the bustle and scuffle of morning life, Lily afforded herself a little extra hope.

The next couple of days continued in the same vein. Harry’s improvement remained steady but slow and so Walter and Mrs Parker sat beside him, reading, talking and reconnecting him with the conscious world. With the other side rooms empty they were now able to take proper rest breaks, although it wasn’t until the end of the second day that they finally left Harry alone in his room once more. None of them slept that night, they just tossed and turned their way through until dawn, well aware that saving Harry’s life went beyond curing his lungs and strengthening his body. Lily scampered down the stairs the next morning, long before her shift was due to start, almost running into Florence outside the main hall. Florence greeted her with an unusually fresh smile.

“What?” Lily asked suspiciously.

“You’ll see,” Florence replied.

Lily skipped on to Harry’s room, where the door was open and sweet fresh air was billowing in through an open window.

“Morning Lily,” croaked Harry.

He still looked painfully gaunt, but he was sitting up atop a pile of pillows and even from the doorway Lily could see the smooth rise and fall of his chest. Mrs Parker was sat in an armchair, a tea cup shielded between her hands and the early morning breeze playful in her hair. Matron was writing copious notes in her stubby book.

"Morning Harry," Lily replied, a warmth spreading to the tips of her fingers. Lily stepped forward to Harry's bedside and went through the motions of checking his pillows.

"That should all be fine," Mrs Parker whispered playfully.

At that point there were further footsteps in the corridor and Walter appeared at the door, still dabbing a towel at his freshly-shaved neck. Mrs Parker stood instinctively but silently.

"Harry!" He exclaimed, bouncing towards the bed and scooping up one of Harry's tiny-looking hands as though charging a glass. Harry smiled politely but his eyes jerked from side to side as though his head had been hit.

"Stop!" Matron ordered, edging herself between Walter and the bed and ushering him back out of the room.

"Oh…"

"Wait," Mrs Parker instructed and everyone stood still.

"Harry," she said, turning to her son, "do you recognise this man?"

"Really Mrs Parker, I'm not sure…" Matron was stopped in her tracks by the sharpness of Mrs Parker's glare.

"Harry," she repeated, "do you recognise this man?"

The room held still. Everyone looked at Harry. Harry looked at Walter.

"I'm sorry," he said eventually, "but I do not."

"It's me, Walter," his friend replied, slowly deflating into Matron's arms. For a second something flashed behind Harry's eyes and then it was gone again.

"I had a friend called Walter once," Harry whispered dreamily "a dear friend."

Matron ushered a broken Walter from the room. She turned sharply in the doorway and surveyed the unhappy scene.

"Give him time," she stated kindly, "give him time."

Lily looked across at Mrs Parker, whose smooth veneer was starting to crack. For just a moment the floor rocked and shifted beneath their feet.

"Lily, can you get Harry some breakfast?" Mrs Parker asked into the scorching discomfort, her voice strengthening with every word.

"Toast would be nice," came Harry's four word reply and Lily started to cry.

*

Walter returned to Hattie later that day and by tea-time Mr Parker had come to collect his wife and visit his son. As time moved on so Lily's daily routine swept back in to break up the fear and emotion of the previous week. Harry slowly returned to the man he had been since 1916, physically and emotionally, but now he had a new companion; Walter came every day.

They talked of ordinary things, often the weather, and played board games. To Harry, this was just Walter, a man that somehow knew his mother and now wished to know him. To Walter, this was just Harry, a man that looked and sounded like *his* Harry but clearly wasn't. At no time did they dance near the elephants. They never mentioned the war, they never re-visited the past, they never reopened the wounds.

"I don't know how you can be so patient," Lily said to Walter in the gardens one day whilst Harry rested.

"Patient?"

"How long will you wait for him to remember?" Lily asked, spinning an imaginary thread between her fingers.

"How long would you have waited?" Walter replied, holding her steadily with his gaze. They sat silently for a while, not uncomfortably.

"How's Hattie?" Lily asked after a few minutes.

"She's well, thank you, very well," Walter paused for a few seconds, weighing-up the moment. "Did I tell you she was with child?"

"I don't believe you did," Lily replied, feeling the heat glowing in her face. "That's wonderful news." Walter smiled his gratitude shyly. "And what of Ruth?" Walter noticed the change in Lily's tone.

"You mustn't be too hard on Ruth; it's been four very long years. She had to move on, we should understand that." Lily nodded her head but didn't agree. Ruth's marriage had been in the local paper before the blood was dry on Harry's tunic, or at least that is how it felt to her.

"I think Harry really fell for her you know, in the end," Lily said softly but Walter was no longer listening. Instead he was looking at her sadly, like a disappointed father.

"Lily, why didn't you ever come to see me?" he asked sadly, "you knew I couldn't come here but why didn't you come to see me, to talk about Tommy? I could have talked to you, helped maybe. I've always wondered that, why didn't you come to me?"

Walter reached across to take Lily's hand. He squeezed it gently, forcing tears into her eyes. Lily felt herself falling towards him so she bounced up, stumbled and collapsed at his feet.

"Oh Lily," Walter said softly, dropping to his haunches and wrapping her up in his arms. Lily resisted for a few seconds, even trying to fight him off before eventually she yielded, like the last gurgles of water leaving the sink, and disintegrated in his embrace. There had never been such sobbing, such desperate sadness, pouring out of Lily and soaking into Walter's shirt, down his chest and into the waistband of his trousers. Even Walter allowed a little of the past to emerge, pressing his damp eyes against the top of Lily's head and accepting a small defeat at the hands of time. Every so often Lily would feel her composure returning but each time it would fracture again, allowing a little bit more of its marrow to be spilt on the lush, green grass.

"I'm sorry," Lily said eventually, her head thudding and the skin of her face stinging in the sunshine, "but I couldn't bear it, I couldn't hear it. I could say that I didn't want to know but I did. I just couldn't bear the idea of finding out."

Walter's grip tightened on her slightly. Lily felt ready to stand but Walter's embrace was fixed and safe.

"It was just like today really," Walter began, his voice slow and restrained, much like Mrs Parker reading Wuthering Heights. Lily pulled herself into a ball. "But more still, very still. I'd been really low, homesick I suppose, and Harry had been just wonderful, keeping all our spirits up. When we found out we were going over the top it was a bit of a relief, it was the waiting that was the hardest bit. They told us to walk, they said it would be for the best but then I don't think anyone thought the Germans would still be alive. We'd been shelling them for days; such a noise.

"We all got out, hundreds of us...Harry, Tommy, all the boys, and for a while nothing happened, but then the machine guns opened up and shells started to drop all around us. We were trying to dodge but we were moving after the bullets had passed. People started to fall. I didn't see Tommy go down but I know that he did. I know that they all did. The rest of us just tightened our bodies and waited our turn. I scampered on as best I could and I know that I reached the first German line but I can't really remember much after that. We tried to go on but kept getting pushed back and eventually we were relieved, those of us that were left. When we got back they just looked at us like we were the last sheep at the market. No-one spoke, not for hours.

"The next day we wanted to go back with the stretchers-bearers but we were told to rest. They didn't return with much. I heard that they'd picked up Harry, which was such a joy but I couldn't find much out about his condition. I knew he'd been hit when one of the shells had landed but I didn't know anything about the other issue. Not until his mother wrote to me many weeks later. Even then she didn't say very much, just that he was confused. At the time I was so relieved that he was alive that none of that seemed to matter.

"Every time you saw one of the lads from your battalion you'd go through the same routine. You'd ask if they'd seen your friends and they'd ask if you'd seen theirs. Sometimes I'd hear half a story and I'd chase it down but each time it ran into a dead end. I never found out Lily, I never really learned what happened. I just know that they never came back. I'd like to be able to tell you that Tommy felt no pain, and maybe he didn't, but like you I'm haunted by the thought of them lying out there for all that time, praying that someone would come and make it better, or make it end. I'm always haunted by that. The daft thing is that we were so close, so near to them but there was nothing we could do. I'm always haunted by that."

"How did you cope?" Lily asked, her voice muffled by Walter's chest.

"I'm not sure really. The first few weeks after the attack were horrific. I think we were all just waiting to die. We contented ourselves in the belief that it would soon be over. And then I suppose, as time ticked on, we sought solace in each other. We started to find tiny little reasons to laugh and we made this unspoken pledge to look out for each other, to ensure that at least a few of us got home to tell the story…this story I suppose. And then that grew into something more powerful I think, the realisation that we *had* to carry on, or else all our pals lay dead for nothing. We did it for them, we carried on for them. It got to a stage where the harder it was, the more it hurt, the more we felt we were giving back to them, paying our penance, doing our bit.

"And of course Harry was here, so I wrote endlessly to him, even though I knew he might never read the words. And then there was Hattie, dear Hattie. Oh, how her letters kept my spirits up. Every time I weakened it appeared that she would strengthen, like she knew that I needed her help. When the post came through it would always be brimming with letters, parcels, postcards from home. I suppose it allowed me to think of the future."

Lily unblended herself from Walter's clothing and sat up on the grass. Her eyes were punched and her face shone red amidst new freckles, the blessed tiptoes of summer. She lifted a tissue from her pocket and patted her eyes unconvincingly. Every few seconds her breath caught, lifting her shoulders sharply.

"I'm sorry," Walter continued, "I didn't want to upset you."

"No…it's good. You're right though, I should have come sooner."

“Lily, how have *you* coped? I’m not sure I could ever have done what you did. How did you get by?”

“It’s just like you said. We have to cope, that’s our bit. That’s what we do. And then there was Harry’s story of course. Harry’s story got me through.” Walter smiled sweetly.

“You know something Lily, I think it’s about time I heard Harry’s story. You see, it’s been mentioned to me so often yet I’ve never heard it. I think I would like to, I think I’d like to hear his story.”

“But….really, are you sure? Do you think that’s such a good idea?”

“Why not?”

“You know why not.”

“Look, let me worry about that. I’d really like to hear his story.”

Lily carried her doubt back indoors, washed her face and joined Walter in Harry’s room. Walter looked across at Lily and she nodded reluctantly.

“Harry?”

“Yes Walter?

“Could I ask you a favour?”

“Of course.”

“Would you mind telling me about you and the boys?”

Harry’s face changed in a small but tangible way like he was trying to hear a faraway sound. Lily took a step forward, ready to change the subject.

“About how we were heroes?” Harry replied, his face starting to beam.

“Yes, about how you were heroes…”

*

One weekend afternoon in August, Lily entered Harry's room to find him sitting on the edge of the bed with Walter at his elbow.

"What are you doing?" Lily asked, trying to keep her voice light.

"We thought we might go out for a walk," Harry replied, smiling broadly. Lily shot a look at Walter who looked away guiltily.

"Walter, can I have word, outside. Harry, don't move!" Lily stomped out of the room with Walter following meekly behind.

"Look, before you get upset…"

"Upset?! Walter, he's not been out of that bed for four years. Four years! Do you know what will happen if he tries to walk? Have you even seen his legs?!"

"Calm down Lily," Walter replied, lifting his hands up in defence.

"Don't tell me to calm down," she replied sharply, slapping his hands away. "Have you even considered what this might do to him? He won't be able to walk!"

"Erm…hello?" Harry's voice rang out from the room. They both skipped back inside to find him standing, slightly hunched, one hand tentatively floating above the bed. "I appear to be a little bit stiff."

Matron was livid and for a couple of days Walter was unwelcome, but she fairly quickly relented and before long Harry was working every day, learning to walk again. At first the few steps to the window almost broke him, but after a few weeks he was doing laps of the room with improving confidence and posture. Everyone was lifted to see him up and about again.

"I have something I would like to propose," Walter told Lily at the end of one blisteringly hot weekend, "I will be speaking to Matron and the doctors, but I wanted to talk to you first."

"Okay…"

“I would like Harry to come and live with Hattie and me. The house Hattie inherited from her grandfather is far too large for us so we have plenty of room. I have spoken to Mrs Parker and she has agreed that it would be in Harry’s best interests if he left Perryman Hall and continued his recovery somewhere more like home.”

“But...but…what will *I* do?” Lily exclaimed, forgetting herself. “I mean, he still needs care, just because he can now walk a little, it doesn’t mean he can look after himself.”

“You’re right Lily, which is why I want you to come as well. Come and be Harry’s live-in nurse. We’ll pay you well, there’s plenty of accommodation and you could come and go as you please.”

“I don’t know…”

“I think it would be wonderful for Harry, but for you as well. You’d be part of the family Lily, and when the baby is born you can help Hattie there as well, if you’d like.”

“And what does Hattie think of this vast plan?” Lily asked, trying to give her words a slightly haughty, scoffing tone.

“My dear Lily, it was Hattie’s idea, she’s insistent.” Lily stood for a moment, unable to recognise the unfamiliar sense of happiness stroking her face.

“How long?” she asked. “How long would you do all this for?”

“For as long as it takes.”

“For as long as *what* takes?”

“I’m not entirely sure,” Walter admitted.

“I would need to think about it. There’s a lot to think about.” Lily offered eventually, walking away.

“I know,” Walter replied, “of course.”

“Oh, one more thing,” Lily said suddenly, stopping and turning on her heels. “I never asked you what you thought of Harry’s story did I? I never asked you what it was like to hear that.”

“No you did not”

“Well?”

“It was very emotional.”

“And what about…you know…”

“What about him inventing my death you mean?” Walter shrugged his shoulders. “Who knows? Maybe one day he will tell me, maybe not. Maybe he’ll never know himself.”

“But doesn’t it bother you? Of all the things he could have chosen to do…”

Walter pressed his finger to his lips and Lily fell quiet. Harry’s best friend smiled broadly and warmly before replacing his hat and disappearing into the soft, warm sunshine bleeding away at the end of the day.

*

Walter and Harry finally walked together in the grounds in early September, in-between the showers. Lily watched them from the window, unaware of the fixed grin on her face.

“Are you looking forward to coming to live with me and Hattie?” Walter asked.

“I am,” Harry replied, “it will be splendid.”

They walked in silence for a while, allowing the wildlife to busy itself at the dawn of autumn.

“Walter, do you play cricket?” Harry said after a few strides.

“Yes I do, or rather I used to.” Walter replied carefully.

"Good, good. When my friends come we can play, if you'd like. They should be here soon."

"Absolutely. Although I have some friends we could play with whilst we're waiting, if you'd like that?"

"Definitely, definitely. Because the game has to go on doesn't it Walter? It has to go on and on and on."

Epilogue

Lily stepped out of Walter and Hattie's fine home, leaving Harry deep in a book. It had been two days since he had asked about his friends. In her hands was a small bunch of very familiar, sad smelling flowers. Lily walked the short distance to Adcock Farm, stepping tentatively through the field until she found what she was looking for. She found it remarkable that this tree, this small copse, had played such a part in her brother's life yet she'd never even stood in its shade. Remarkable and sad.

Lily ran her fingers over the deep, ragged cuts on the tree, paying particular attention to her brother's initials. She said a short prayer, laid the flowers at the base of the tree and went on her way.

Lily didn't stay at Walter and Hattie's for long. Harry needed her less and less over time and for all their kindness, staying with the Croucher's and their expanding family seemed in some way to be a betrayal of her own slowly recovering parents. By the start of 1922 Lily was in London working at The Hospital for Sick Children on Great Ormond Street, enjoying nursing in a way she had never believed possible. She still heard from the place she called home regularly enough and Hattie kept her updated on Harry's gradual improvement.

In the autumn of 1923 she married Reg Wheeler, a survivor of Ypres, and by the time she made her annual pilgrimage to Dead Cat Tree on 1st July 1925 she was heavy with child. Reg sat on the grass a few yards from the copse and allowed his wife to complete the final leg of her journey alone.

As she ducked into the shadows she was surprised to see another bunch of flowers beneath the tree. Edging nearer, she saw a fading photograph poking from the petals, with eleven smart, young, smiling faces saluting at her from a different decade and a different world. Instinctively she turned the picture over and saw inscribed on the back a single word in an unfamiliar hand.

'Always'

Printed in Great Britain
by Amazon.co.uk, Ltd.,
Marston Gate.